The Caged Heart

Book Two of The Claiming Games

By

Beverly Rae

www.BeverlyRae.com

Edited by Riane Holt & Kasi Alexander
Cover by P & N Graphics
Published by Rae Publishing

Acknowledgments

I am one lucky lady. Not only do I have a wonderful husband and daughter, but I get to wake up every day and do what I love. My office is my both my sanctuary and my torture chamber—depending on how the writing is going—but I wouldn't want to be anywhere else. Okay, maybe sitting on the deck of a mountain cabin overlooking a green valley while I write would be nice, but you know what I mean. Without you, dear reader, it wouldn't be possible. Thank you with all of my heart.

Yours,
Beverly Rae

Chapter One

Mia

If only I could have made my body as tiny as a bug, then maybe, just maybe I could have squeezed under the closet door and escape unnoticed. My eyes had adjusted to the darkness but my gaze always came back to fix on the sliver of light that slashed across the floor. If I concentrated on the light, then I wouldn't go insane.

Hang on. It'll open any minute now. He always comes back and he'll let me out. After he's finished with the others. And then it'll be my turn.

I hugged my knees tighter to my chest. The blistering Mississippi heat outside had turned the house into a sweat box. Worse, I was stuck in a sweat box within a sweat box. Beads of perspiration ran down my back and plastered my shirt to my skin. My hair stuck to my face and streaks of sweat snaked their way down my cheeks. I was soaked under my arms, under my breasts, and between my legs.

A shudder, like many that had come before it, wracked through me. Little by little, they grew stronger until I was sure I'd fracture apart. The walls were closing in, not because of the many items in the closet, but because...

Because walls always closed in on me. I hated confined places. Hated staying indoors for any length of time. I'd never been diagnosed by a real doctor—doctors were for rich people and those who took handouts—but I'd read enough to know I was claustrophobic.

It made sense. After years of my father locking me inside the hall closet, I'd developed a hatred and fear of small places. Small, dark places were the worst, but almost anywhere with four walls would get to me sooner or later. Even a building with windows made me a little antsy if I stayed within its walls too long. Still, out of all the other crazy-ass shit people came down with, I figured my problem wasn't so bad. I could handle it without meds or getting locked up.

The real problem was that my father used my phobia to his advantage.

I wouldn't cry out. I refused to give him the satisfaction. Besides, it wouldn't do any good. The cries of my four brothers and three sisters would drown me out.

No one cared except Mom. Not even the neighbors. Mom would try and cajole him into leaving us alone. She'd even get down on her knees and beg him if she had to. But he wouldn't listen. He never did. Still, she kept trying. She figured if she could get him to take out his anger on her instead of us kids, then it was the lesser of two fucked-up evils.

I'd tried to get her to leave him. Begged her to think of us kids, to get us away from him. But he'd put the fear of the devil himself into her. The one time she'd dared to stand up to him, he'd gone crazy, beating her until she'd finally begged him to forgive her, taking the blame for getting him upset. Worse than the bruises on her body were the bruises he'd left on the inside.

He held all the strings and she was his puppet. He had the job with the insurance to help pay for Johnny's asthma medications. He made the money that put food on the table and clothes on our backs. But that wasn't all. Maybe she could've tried to break away for good if her past hadn't already enslaved her, tying her to him with invisible chains.

She'd been broken by her father and now her asshole of a husband kept reopening those wounds, keeping them from ever healing, every time he hit her. Just as her father had. All she'd done was exchange one captor for another.

Cries escalated, along with the bellowing of my father. He was picking up steam.

Should I try breaking the door down? I'd tried before. Yet, no matter how hard I'd hit it, the door had remained solidly closed. Instead, my pounding only made my father angrier. Then, instead of taking it out on me, he'd get even more furious at my brothers and sisters. I couldn't risk him hurting anyone. Staying as quiet as I could was better for both them and me.

I couldn't leave. I'd tried once and hadn't been able to stay away. As I'd feared, he'd taken his anger at my disappearance out on my mother and siblings. When I'd snuck back to the house to check on them, I'd realized what he'd done. Sure, I'd caught hell the minute I'd walked through the door, but being there, trying to help them in any way I could, was better than the guilt wracking me for leaving them behind.

I still dreamed about escaping every night, but in the morning I'd realize I could only go if my mom would finally get fed up and take my brothers and sisters with her. Would she ever find the nerve to try and leave again? I doubted it. And yet, every once in a while, I'd see her anger rise to the surface. I'd see a glint in her eye that made me think he might've finally pushed her too far. I had to hope that one day her anger would overcome her fear.

Was today my turn? Which would it be this time? A

beating? Or what he called "teaching the girl how a man's hands feel"? A few times I'd gotten lucky when he'd passed out drunk as a skunk and my mom had unlocked the door.

Please, let him pass out this time.

A shadow blocked the light for a moment and I held my breath. My mouth dried up and another shudder shook me. Strange as it was, sometimes I preferred to stay in the dark, trapped in a physical and mental cage, instead of having him open the door and pull me out. Even with the threat of the walls moving toward me, it sometimes felt safer to stay in the closet. At least, for a while. Yet sooner or later, the walls would start closing in and I'd be forced out, like a rabbit out of its hole running straight into the jaws of a coyote. I wanted out, just not out with him.

The shadow moved on. I exhaled, but I felt no lasting relief. The light no longer gave me much hope. Instead, I closed my eyes and sought escape in a different way.

I called it my Happy Place. It was a lame name, but I'd heard it on a television talk show and I'd liked it. It fit. No way would I ever say the name out loud where someone might hear. That would be way too embarrassing.

The Happy Place was a secret spot in my mind where there were no walls and no asshole father. If anyone ever found out about it, I might lose it forever. And, if I was foolish enough to let that happen, then I'd have no chance at getting out of the shithole that was my life. Out of the closet where my father had put me. Out of the small two-bedroom house where the ten of us lived, crammed together like senseless chickens in a slaughterhouse cage.

One of these days, I promised I'd get out of the city and into the country. I dreamed of living in a wide open place where

I could do anything I wanted.

Until then, I did the next best thing. I let the Happy Place take me there. I could see rolling hills, mountains filled with green trees, blue skies, and fluffy white clouds. Animals scurried out of sight before I could get a good look at them, but I knew they were there. The sound of running water gave me a sense of peace I couldn't remember having in a long time. Very few people were around, but the best thing about my Happy Place was that it wasn't anything like the house I lived in now. My new home would have lots of windows and maybe even a skylight. And rooms with no locks on the doors. And absolutely, positively, no tiny, dark closet.

If my mom would take the rest of the kids and go, and I could leave, I'd grab the backpack I'd hidden under a couple of floorboards and get the hell out. I'd stashed it away, filling it with a shirt here, a pair of jeans there, along with any money I could scrounge up, babysitting whenever I could. Whenever he found out that I'd earned some money, I'd give him a little to satisfy him, then hide the rest in the backpack. The last time I'd taken off I hadn't had any place to run to.

Now I did.

A scream jolted me back to the reality of the closet. I opened my eyes to the darkness again. Was that Julie? I hoped not. She was only twelve. But she looked a lot like me with long, black hair and green eyes. Just like our mom, too. Most of us had our mother's coloring, which was a good thing as far as I was concerned. The less we saw of our father in ourselves, the better.

So far, I'd kept my father from playing his awful games with the other girls by either tricking him, or if push came to shove, by sacrificing myself. Like my mom, I'd do anything to keep them safe.

It was hard on my mom. She knew what he did to me. How he'd visit me at night, pushing the other girls out from under the covers and sending them running to her. And she'd tried to stop him. Had threatened to call the cops. But she'd never go through with it. Not after he swore that some way, somehow, he'd take out his revenge on us instead of her. That the cops would find corpses scattered throughout the house. He promised that, if she did leave, he'd track us down. Just like me, she believed him.

She'd begged my forgiveness more than once. For not leaving, for not standing up to him. But in my mind, there was nothing to forgive. How could I blame her when I was doing the same thing?

It made sense for me to get out. I wasn't really helping them by staying. Sometimes I could give them a short reprieve, but the horror always came back. If not that night, then the next. I often wondered if letting it happen would be better. The pain, the abuse was better than the nerve-wracking anticipation of what was coming. But I couldn't leave them behind again.

So far, he'd kept the horror confined to groping and fondling me, but only because he usually passed out before he could do anything more. As drunk as he got, I doubted he could get his ugly, flaccid dick up.

Had they really ever loved each other? Or had she married him because of me? Had she thought he'd be less abusive than her father?

The walls rumbled around me like a monster beginning to wake up. Daring to do the impossible, I reached out and put my hand on the doorknob. But why? I knew it wouldn't turn. Another shout from outside had me jerking my hand away.

Coward.

If only my mom had the money to get out. Maybe then she'd get up the courage. She took in laundry from other women, women whose husbands allowed them to leave the house, to have friends, and to live a decent life. But then he'd come home and demand she give him the meager amount she'd earned. If she was lucky, he'd leave, then spend the rest of the night pouring her hard work down his throat.

I wished he'd keep drinking until he never came home.

Instead of my wishes coming true, he'd started growing bolder whenever he fell into my bed. The last time, he'd slicked his tongue along my cheek and promised he'd soon "fuck me like the little cunt I was."

I had no doubt he'd try.

Yet even his promise wasn't the worst of it. Julie was getting older and starting to fill out with all the "curvy bits" my father liked. If that happened while I was still at home, I wasn't sure I could stand it. I'd rather he fucked me instead. But could I survive it? All I could do was hope that time would never come.

I squeezed my eyes shut and went back to dreaming about what the world would be like outside the house I'd never really called home. One day, some way, I'd make my life what I wanted it to be. But how?

I didn't believe in fate or luck or any of that shit. Especially not for me.

Until the invitation.

It beat the hell out of me why anyone would mail me such a thing, but it was a lifeline I was willing to grab.

Once I was ready to leave, I'd go to the town listed on the invitation. Who knew what it would be like in Cripple Creek, North Carolina? Yet, I didn't care. Anywhere was better than where I was.

The day I'd received the fancy invitation was one of most exciting days of my life. As usual, I was the one who'd checked the mailbox. I lived for the promotional advertisements offering free nights on a cruise or, better yet, in the mountains at a luxurious resort. Just staring at the beautiful scenes on the postcards made me believe in a life outside our shabby Biloxi home. Maybe I'd never live in a beach house or in a mountainside villa, but I was determined to find a better home than the one I'd grown up in. How I'd make it happen was the question.

"You fuckin' cunt!"

I jerked out of my Happy Place and back to the harsh reality of my life. My mom shouted, fear mangling her words. But I understood them anyway. She was begging again, putting herself in front of her children.

I had no doubt the sick fuck was enjoying the hell out of it.

Where were my brothers and sisters? Cowering in corners or gathered together on top of our bed? Was Nate home? Or would Clovis and Ben try to protect Johnny and their sisters?

Fighting the terror, I once more reached for the doorknob. This time I even twisted it.

Locked. Had I really expected anything else?

My breath hitched in my throat. I wanted out. Even out to the awful sounds tearing at me. The walls were getting closer. They had to be. I didn't need to touch them to know they were.

Please, help me. Help us.

But who did I expect to help? No one gave a shit about us.

Even now as the terror worked its ugly arms around me, I could still remember the pretty stationery and the feel of the embossed lettering under my fingertips. I could still recall how surprised I was to see my name in script-style writing.

Obviously, the company sending the invitations didn't bother checking to see if the recipient could afford to make the trip. There was no way my family could take a vacation. Hell, a vacation was getting out of the house to pick up groceries at the food bank. Nathan Travers, my asshole of a father, didn't consider free food a hand-out like he did going to see a doctor at the community free clinic. Getting our food as charity gave him more money to buy cigarettes and booze. As long as Mom's bruises weren't too noticeable. But then dear old Dad knew just where to land his punches so the bruises would be hidden under her clothing.

I'd read and re-read the invitation until I had it memorized word for word. And the plane ticket that had been included with it? Even though I would've loved to take my first plane ride, I'd already hitched a ride to the airport and cashed it in. I'd given most of the money to my mom. If and when I got the chance, I'd hitch my way to Cripple Creek and, hopefully, freedom.

As long as my father didn't find it, that kind of money would keep food on the table for at least a month. She kept the cash I'd given her and what little she could squirrel away stuffed in an envelope and taped to the back of the counter under the kitchen sink. No way would my father ever dig around in all the cleaning products. The man barely kept himself bathed, much less helped to wash the dishes.

Was the invitation on the up and up? I would've bet it wasn't until I'd cashed in the plane ticket. Good things just didn't come my way. And yet, there I'd stood, gaping as the lady behind the counter of Blue Skies Airlines forked over a refund for the ticket. No questions asked. I didn't know much about airline policies, but I'd never heard of anyone getting a full refund. Yet whoever had paid for it had made sure it was fully refundable. Almost like they'd guessed what I'd do.

Now I was even more determined to find out if the rest of it was just as real. But time was running out. If I was ever going to leave, it had to be soon. But how could I leave my mother and family behind?

I moved my mouth to the words scrolling across my mind.

To Miss Mia Travers,

No one had ever called me Miss before. How cool was that?

This is your opportunity to fulfill all your dreams.

Do you yearn to capture a man's heart and have him capture yours? Do you dare to find a man who will treat you to your deepest desires, awaken your heart, and claim you for his own? Are you strong enough to find an extraordinary man?

If so, read on.

Congratulations, you are a semi-finalist in The Claiming Games. If selected, and if you make it through to the end of the games, you will be rewarded with your choice of two prizes. Will you choose an extraordinary man as your prize? Or will you choose $250,000 in cash? Survive the games and decide your future.

The Claiming Games are not for the weak. Your bravery, your stamina, and your courage will be tested. Danger is everywhere. Yet, in the end, you will have won everything your heart desires.

To accept this invitation, arrive at Fang's Bar and Grill in Cripple Creek, North Carolina on July 10th at 2:00 pm. An airplane ticket is enclosed.

Come and risk it all to gain the future of your dreams.

K.O.B. Corporation
Cripple Creek, NC

Find the man of my dreams? Even while still locked inside the closet, I giggled at the absurd idea. A man of my dreams? That was pure bullshit. How could I believe in true love after growing up with my parents? Even if there was love at the start, it wouldn't last. True love only happened in the movies, not in real life.

I didn't care about finding a man. All I wanted was the money. My entire world would change if I had enough money to get my mom and siblings away from my father and into a decent, larger place to live. A place where he couldn't touch them.

If there was anything left over, I'd use it to go to cosmetology college and become a hair stylist. I loved cutting and styling my siblings' hair, but I needed to learn how to do it the correct way. Instead of fantasizing about being one of the beautiful women in a magazine, I wanted to be the one who made their hair look so amazing. If I worked really hard, I'd even open my own salon one day.

Yeah, right. It was just a dream. Saving money and packing clothes was a lot different than actually leaving. If I didn't get up the nerve to go soon, I'd be shit out of luck. The games would start in a few days.

Even as I tried to keep my mind centered on good thoughts, fear kept digging its way in, trying to get into my head and heart. If I allowed it to take over, I'd go a little crazy. My heart would pound, my throat would close up until I knew I was about to drag in my final breath. Then my stomach would rebel and I'd feel like I was going to puke. The high school nurse had seen me lose it once after a shithead bully shoved me into the janitor's closet and locked the door. She'd called it a panic attack. That sounded right. Fear, panic, losing it. They were all the same in the end, no matter what label got stuck to it.

"Hang on," she'd said. "You can learn how to handle these attacks."

Yeah. Sure. No problem.

But that was easier said than done.

I couldn't help but jump when I heard my father bellow. I swallowed back the bile and barely managed to keep from freaking out. Clutching my knees to my chest, I tried to make myself as small as possible. It was everything I could do to keep from going out of my mind.

My little world inside the closet spun out of control. My heart raced, skittering inside my chest like a roach trying to scurry out of sight. I trembled, harder than ever, as nausea swept over me again. Sucking in one tortured breath after another, I tried to block out my mother's pleas along with the whimpers and cries of my brothers and sisters.

"Please, Daddy, please."

No. Not April.

"Daddy, no. Leave her alone."

Stay back, Johnny. You can't help her.

The last time Johnny had gotten in the way, he'd ended up with a split lip. But I should've known he'd stick up for April. Being twins, they had a unique bond, often knowing what the other was thinking without hearing a word. None of the other kids would try to help April, but no one blamed them.

Ten-year-old Ben did everything fourteen-year-old Clovis did, including huddling in a corner and hoping to become invisible. While Ben was long and lean like our mother, Clovis was stocky and pudgy like our dad. He hated that about himself and it wasn't hard to understand why.

But Clovis hadn't been "right in the head" after my brother

Nate Jr. and he had tried to get between our father and mother. Clovis had ended up in the emergency room with a concussion and, after that, a badly beaten Nate Jr. no longer had the guts to try and stop our father. All of which the child protective services lady had totally ignored. Nate Jr. had started staying out all night and showing up only when he was sure our dad wasn't home. Again, no one blamed him. In fact, I envied his independence. But I couldn't do the same. Someone had to stay home to help the others.

Yeah, like I was doing a great job of doing that.

Some say anger is a result of fear. Maybe they're right. The terror gripping me was still there, but anger swirled faster and faster inside me. Why did we have to go through this? What had we done so wrong to make God, fate, or whatever the hell was looking down on us put us in this hell on earth?

I couldn't let my father get away with it again. If I had to die trying to stop him, I would. But the anguish inside me wouldn't let go. The more I thought about moving around, of trying to force my way out, the closer the walls got. Had the walls moved? Rationally, I knew they couldn't. And yet, my twisted gut told me they had.

I hate you. I wish you would die.

Whether I was thinking of my father or the demons that ruled the walls, I wasn't sure. What did it matter? They were both my enemies.

Moaning, I covered my ears again and tried to block out the sounds of my father terrorizing my family. Glass shattered in the kitchen and a door slammed. At least one person had sought safety in one of the bedrooms. My father shouted something I couldn't understand. Then the worst happened.

Silence.

Silence in the Travers' household meant one of three things. Either my father had gone out—which I knew wasn't the case—or he'd passed out. There was no chance he'd finally given in to the alcohol-induced sleep we all prayed would take him sooner than later. Whenever that happened, it came after a gradual slow-down of the yelling. Not with an abrupt end.

That left the third option.

He was so angry he'd lost the ability to yell. When he could no longer shout, when his voice had gone too raw to speak, he started using other methods to abuse us. His hands. His belt. Hell, anything he could pick up and swing.

Oh, shit.

If I reached out, I'd touch the walls. In a moment, they'd pin my arms to my side and squeeze my breath out until I had nothing left to live on. I wouldn't have to worry about what my father would do. I'd be crushed to death first.

Please. Someone help me.

I could no longer think about my siblings or my mother. I was too terrified. I could hear his footsteps. He was headed my way, ready to use my body to get his own kind of sick joy.

I prayed he'd beat me. The other way of releasing his anger was so much worse.

The footsteps got louder, closer.

I clasped my hand over my mouth, trying to silence the wheezing sound as I sucked in air. The walls had just touched me. I'd felt the hard wood press against my flesh. Closing my eyes, I waited for whichever would happen first. Either my father would drag me out of the closet or I'd die squashed between two walls.

The light hitting my eyes ripped the thought from me. I only had time to blink before he clutched my shirt and dragged me out of the closet and into the living room. Somehow, I kept from crying out when he threw me down. I lay on the floor and looked around, yet tried to stay as still as I could. Maybe, just maybe, he was drunk enough to think he'd knocked me out.

My mother crouched against the far wall. Blood seeped from the corner of her mouth and she held one arm as though it hurt too much to let it hang on its own. Her eyes pleaded for my understanding and forgiveness. I wanted to smile at her, to let her know I knew she'd tried, but to do so would risk my dad seeing, too.

And then there it was. The strange new glint I'd seen before.

"Get up, you little slut."

A tear inched its way down my cheek. When he called me a slut, it meant only one thing. He'd use my body for his fun, his hands all over me, his fingers sneaking in between my legs.

Would this be the night he'd finally shove his cock inside me?

I curled into a ball, determined to disappear. It was stupid to think I could, but my mind wasn't working right. Closing my eyes, I prepared myself for a long, bad night.

I'd go to my Happy Place, to the only place where I could survive with both body and mind intact. Even he couldn't get me there.

But I couldn't. My imagination had shut down.

He snagged me by my T-shirt again and threw me onto my back. I yelped, then stared up at him, knowing he wouldn't let me close my eyes. Oh, no. He liked me to watch what he did to me.

He towered over me even though he wasn't a tall man. But he had bulk. His fat belly hung over his dirty jeans and his double chin was covered in the black-gray stubble he thought made him look sexy.

"Get ready, slut." He undid his belt and yanked it out of the loops. "Tonight's the night, bitch. You're finally going to become a real woman."

Would he even notice that I wasn't a virgin? I'd given my virginity to Bobby Hanlen in the back seat of his pickup over a year earlier. I liked Bobby, but I'd fucked him more because I'd needed someone to hold me. Someone who wouldn't call me names while he felt me up.

After that, I'd found other boys. Having sex, sex *I* wanted, gave me back the control my father stole from me. I hadn't done it often. Only when the rage inside me threatened to split me apart. And I'd only done it with guys I really liked.

"I'm going to fuck you so hard you won't be able to run away from me."

I remembered when seeing him pull his belt off meant he was going to beat me. If only I could think the same thing now.

"First, I'm gonna to teach you a lesson for doing wrong." His wicked grin spread wider. "Then you're going to spread your legs and let your daddy get a taste of what's between them."

"No, Nate." My mother's voice cracked. "Leave her alone."

He spat at my mother then wiped his mouth with the back of his hand. "Shut up. It's time she learned how to fuck a man, Lucille."

I hadn't done anything wrong. Unless standing up to him, trying to protect my mother when he'd stumbled home drunk was doing wrong. I guess, in his eyes, it was.

"Nate, I swear I'll call the cops."

But my mother's ploy didn't work. "Go ahead. You do and I promise this bitch and all the rest of them brats won't live another day. You'll watch them die and then I'll send you to hell right behind them."

He meant it. He'd make good on his threat.

In a desperate move, I tried to scramble away. But for a fat man, he was quick on his feet. He got hold of my jeans and tossed me on to my back with a grunt. I tried again to get away, but before I could do much more than cry out, he had his zipper down. Panic, even more than when I was in the closet, took hold and wouldn't let go. I couldn't take another minute with him, his hands groping me, squeezing my breasts. Screaming for him to turn me loose, I decided right then that I'd die before I'd suffer his touch again. I twisted my body, then searched for anything I could use as a weapon. My mother jumped up and ran out of the room. I cried, begging her to help me. For anyone to help me.

His hands gripped my ankles as he dragged me, on my belly, toward him. I grabbed hold of the cheap rug under the coffee table, grasping for anything to keep me away. "No, Dad. Stop!"

"Aw, hell, slut. What's all the fuss about? You're going to love getting fucked. Just like your cunt mother."

A sound blocked out my pleas. In the next moment, my father uttered a curse and I heard a loud thud. I cringed and flipped over to see my father staggering as though the alcohol had finally hit him harder than before.

I barely had time to roll away as his heavy body fell toward the floor. He landed with a grunt, face down, spittle coming out of his mouth.

Stunned, I stared up at my mother. The book she held was old and big, but it had done the trick.

"Honey, hurry. Get up."

I got to my feet, still shaking, and clutched her to me.

"Mom. He's going to kill you when he comes to."

"Maybe." Her throat moved up and down. "Yes. He probably will."

She was shaking more than I was. "We've got to get out of here. All of us." I tugged on her arm. "Come on. We have to leave now."

I'm not sure if it was what I said or my father's groan that finally got her moving. She jerked out of my hold and ran to the bedroom she shared with him. Flinging the door open, she gestured for my brothers and sisters, huddled together, to get off the bed.

"It's time. Does everyone remember what I told you?"

Each of my siblings nodded, but I was once again in the dark.

"Then get your things out of the garage and put them in the car. Hurry."

My brothers and sisters didn't waste any time. They jumped off the bed and dashed past us, running as fast as they could to the one-car garage.

"Mom, what's happening?"

She took me by the arms and made me to look at her. "I'm finally doing it. I'm finally leaving him for good."

She sounded on the edge of hysterics. "Really, Mom?" Oh, how I wanted to believe it. And yet, it was so hard.

"Your sisters and brothers have some clothes hidden in the garage. We had to be ready to leave as soon as we got the chance. Honey, I'm sorry, but I couldn't tell you because…"

"Because you were afraid he'd make me tell him." She must have heard him in bed with me as he fondled me and tried to coax me into telling him the secrets my family kept. Secrets like where Nate Jr. hid his drugs. Secrets like if my mom was planning on running away. Either I refused to tell him or I'd make up a lie. Half the time he was too drunk to remember later anyway.

"I never told him anything, Mom."

"No one would've blamed you if you had. But I couldn't take the chance."

"Where are we going?"

She didn't quite meet my eyes. "Your brothers and sisters and I are going to a shelter for women and children. But you're not coming with us."

"Why not?" Didn't she want me? Was I so bad that even she'd turn against me? "I'll get my backpack."

She took hold of my arm as I turned to go.

"Listen to me, Mia Elizabeth. I want you to go to that place on the invitation you showed me. You go and you pick the man or the money. Whichever one will make you happy."

After all she'd been through for the past twenty years, how could she believe a man could make any woman happy? She'd only married my dad because he'd knocked her up with me.

If she didn't stop tearing up, I was going to cry, too. Hell, I might cry anyway. "This isn't making any sense. I have to go with you."

"No you're not. This is your chance for a better life. And I know you, Mia. You'll feel trapped at the shelter with all those people."

My heart broke, both at the thought of leaving her, and at the sacrifice she was making. My mom was the strongest woman I'd ever known. It didn't matter that she'd put up with so much hell. It didn't matter that she hadn't left him sooner. To have endured so much for so long proved she was as brave as anyone. She straightened up and gave me the same look that had always gotten me to obey her.

"Mia, once you get through with the games, or the challenge, or whatever it is, you come and find us."

"But I can't, Mom. Shelters don't give out information. And what if he comes after you? You know he will. What if he finds you and—"

"He won't. I promise. You aren't the only one who's been planning to get out. Now stop arguing and go." She turned me around and shoved me toward the bedroom I shared with all my siblings. Mattresses covered most of the floor. "Get your things and leave. You're wasting our time and yours."

I grabbed hold of the doorknob, then looked back at her. "Thank you, Mom. I'll send you some money soon."

"Then send it to your Aunt Brenda, honey. As soon as it's safe, I'll get in touch with her. She'll know how to find me."

"Okay. I will." I pushed open the door and rushed into the bedroom. Yanking up the floorboards, I tugged the backpack out.

By the time I'd made it back into the living room, my mother and my brothers and sisters were gone. I paused, standing over my father, who was beginning to groan and move around. It was an awful thing to do, something he would've done, but a switch flicked on inside me and I couldn't help but let a little of the ugliness I'd lived with come out. For once, the man who'd done us all wrong had to pay a price. Even if the price was only a small one.

I kicked him hard, straight into his crotch, and my foot sank into his soft package. He was still moaning as I flung open the front door and ran outside.

Chapter Two

Mia

"Sweetie, are you sure you're being safe?"

Miss Charlotte, the older waitress who manned the counter at Hugo's Truck Stop just outside Atlanta, gave me a worried look then slid a slice of apple pie in front of me. After eating a huge hamburger and a gargantuan pile of fries, I wasn't sure how I'd get the pie down. But I was damn sure going to try. Miss Charlotte had refused to let me pay while assuring me that Hugo wouldn't mind "one damn bit." I'd thanked her, but I'd had no idea she'd give me so much to eat. After growing up in a house where meals were often meager if not missed, I figured if someone put food in front of me, I'd chow down. Who knew when I'd get another chance?

"Yes, I'm being safe and I haven't run into any trouble so far. Most truckers are nice family men." I gave her a comforting smile.

So far, I'd hitched my way through Mississippi, Alabama, and part of Georgia. Getting from Biloxi to Atlanta was only a six-hour drive, but I'd had to hang out overnight in Montgomery, Alabama after getting away from a handsy trucker. No way would I tell her how he'd held me down and shoved his hand up my shirt. He'd had me pinned down, but when he'd reached to undo his belt, I'd seen my chance and had taken it. I'd kicked him in the balls as hard as I could. Just like I'd finally gotten to do to my lousy father. He was probably still clutching his junk and hollering his head off. Hiding in a cold, wet sewer pipe, I'd had to wait most of the night until he'd finally gotten tired of hunting for me and pulled his truck back on the road.

I'd never really cared before about owning a cell phone. Who would I call anyway? But I sure could've used one then. I'd have called the cops and sent him scurrying away like the rat he was.

The next trucker I'd ridden with had been more of the fatherly type. He'd talked a lot, but he hadn't disturbed me even when I'd fallen asleep while he was talking. When he'd dropped me off at Hugo's, he'd insisted on giving me his cell phone number in case I needed a ride back to Biloxi. I didn't bother telling him that I didn't have a phone.

Hopefully, my luck was still looking up. Another trucker had just agreed to take me all the way to Greenville, South Carolina. From there, it would be a little over an hour ride into Asheville. After that, I'd have to figure out where Cripple Creek was. The town had to be tiny since it wasn't listed on any map. But I figured the closer I got to the mountains, sooner or later, I'd find someone who'd know how to get there.

If I'd had my own car, I could've made the entire trip in one long day. Hitching wasn't a reliable source of transportation. I'd done it before to get around town. Often getting from one place to another meant going on a drive that took me out of the way. Then I'd have to find another ride that would put me back on track. It was like taking two steps forward only to have to take one step back. And sometimes, even with the big windows of the cab all around me, I just needed to get the hell out before the ride was over.

It's like people said. Shit happens.

Miss Charlotte leaned on the counter, flopped the cleaning towel over her shoulder, and studied the man paying for his meal at the register. She hadn't offered to take care of his check, too, and he hadn't taken it well. I guess he figured if she could give me free food, then she could do the same for him.

"I don't know, sweetie. I haven't seen him before. Maybe you should hang out until someone I know comes in. Then I won't have to stay up all night worrying about you."

I got it. Really I did. I looked like I was still in high school even though those years were behind me. I was on my own hitching across several states. Any self-respecting older woman would be concerned for me. As irritating as it was, I realized it came from her heart.

"I'm a pretty good judge of character. And I can handle myself." At least most of the time.

"Well, okay." She glanced at the driver again. "You'll keep your phone nearby, right? In case you need to dial 9-1-1?"

Although I hated lying to her, I nodded, pushing the guilt aside. If I told her I didn't own a phone, she'd probably freak out and tie me down to keep me safe. My family hadn't been able to afford phones for their kids and I'd never seen much use in handing over hard-earned money for one. Whenever I'd needed help, a phone was the last thing I'd grabbed for. A bat or a gun would've been my first choice.

"You ready, girl?" Jimbo, the trucker headed across the state border, motioned for me to follow him out to his eighteen wheeler.

I crammed a big bite of the pie into my mouth, then lifted my hand in farewell. Sliding my butt off the stool, I snatched up my backpack and hurried out to meet Jimbo.

Mia

Jimbo turned out to be a huge prick. Once he found out that I didn't think Ronald Reagan was the best president America had ever had or that I didn't know one single Johnny Cash song, he'd pulled over on the side of the highway and ordered me out of his cab.

It took me another two rides and one night sleeping on a bench at a roadside rest stop before I finally made it into Greenville. If I'd gone any slower, I would've made better time walking backward. But no one, not even any lecherous truckers would pick me up. I'd have to catch a break or I'd never get to Fang's on time.

I was walking as fast as I could down the highway on the other side of the city, my hand out as the trucks and cars passed me by, when I saw a huge roadside sign for Maggie May's Roadside Diner, a half-mile down the road. I figured I could use a rest. And, if I was lucky, a free breakfast along with a ride into the mountains.

I walked into Maggie May's, and as I figured I would, ended up meeting the lady herself. She was a vivacious forty-something-year-old who would've looked more at home selling upscale real estate than sliding hamburgers across the Formica counter. To my delight, she'd followed in Miss Charlotte's footsteps and had set me up with a good meal. Then she'd handed over a clean towel and told me to wash up. I'd finished eating and was just coming out of the ladies room when I saw him.

Oh, hell, yeah.

I wasn't the type of girl who gave a shit what a guy looked like. I generally went for the personality, the funny guy who'd keep me laughing. If a guy could make me giggle, then he had a better than even chance of getting between my legs. But this guy? He didn't even need to crack a smile, much less tell a joke. He wouldn't need to say one damn word.

It wasn't about the sex. Not really. I used guys as a release valve. Sex was my way of letting off steam and taking control of my body again. I decided when and how much sex I wanted.

Thankfully, my father's drunken groping hadn't gone as far as fucking. He was almost always too drunk to get it up. Those awful times had always left me with a freaky kind of pent-up energy. Kind of a whirlwind of anger mixed with the need to be with someone. Of course, if the guy was good-looking, it helped.

And the guy getting off the motorcycle and walking into the diner was as good-looking as a man could get.

"Oh, my word. No helmet. Gotta wonder if some folks have the sense God gave them." Maggie May's booming voice hadn't bothered me until now. Had he heard her? Yet, if he had, he didn't show it. "Although it would be a shame to hide that head of hair under a helmet."

No helmet. Yeah. I like a guy who breaks the rules.

His blond hair feathered around his neck as he strode into the diner. He was tanned, his skin a burned reddish-brown after long hours in the sun. His face was the perfect picture of a hero with its square jaw and high cheekbones. Blond eyebrows ducked toward the bridge of his nose as he scanned the other side of the large room. Looking for what, I didn't have a clue.

The black T-shirt he wore was skin tight, showing every muscle. The black jeans weren't too tight or hanging off his hips like a lot of guys wore them. I hated the slouchy look. Like I could give them a little tug and pull their pants down.

But not this guy. His jeans were a perfect fit for his rounded ass, hugging them just enough to show what he had. The black boots he wore had small silver buckles that matched the big buckle at his waist.

I stopped and watched in awe as he strode to the counter and sat down on the stool right next to mine. Or at least where I'd been sitting. My empty plate and half a glass of milk were gone. Maggie May fell on him like a cat on a June bug.

I frowned, thrown by the stab of jealousy burning within me.

"What can I get you, handsome?"

Eck. Maggie May sounded like one of those older ladies people called a cougar, looking for a new boy toy.

"Coffee. Black."

"Coming right up, big guy."

Big guy? Double Eck.

Maggie May reached for the pot behind her and caught my eye. With that one look, I knew she didn't want me anywhere near the hunk. I would've done what she wanted, but the irritation that came over me whenever someone tried to order me around flared to life. Instead of staying away, I swayed my way back to the counter.

I held up the towel she'd given me. "Thanks, Maggie May. I needed a quick clean-up." I held it out to her and felt the biker's cool gaze rake over me.

All at once, the place got really, really hot.

"Just drop it in the trash outside. I don't want it back."

No wonder she didn't have many towels. Much less clean ones. "Okay. Whatever you say, Maggie May." I put on a pleasant smile, skimmed it over her, then brightened it and gave it all to him.

Blue-silver eyes met mine and promptly took my breath away. Who had eyes like those?

"Like I said. Put it in the trash." She took my arm, jolting me out of my trance, then pointed outside. "The trucker who offered you a ride is waiting on you. You'd better get a move on."

Shit. It figured. My timing sucked.

The biker guy was hot enough to make me forget about my time crunch. Who knew? Maybe he'd let me hop on his motorcycle? Riding with him would be a thrill and a half.

"Yeah. I know." I couldn't help but see the biker's gaze make another slow, easy trek down me then back up. From the gleam in his eyes, he liked what he saw.

"Honey, you'd better hurry." There was the slightest hint of a threat in her voice.

As if she had a chance. His hungry gaze said otherwise. But I couldn't afford to miss getting to Fang's on time. "Yeah. I know. I've got to run." Reluctantly, I tore myself away and went outside.

Mitch was an older man who obviously lived a lot of his life on the road. He was chewing his tobacco a mile a minute by the time I trashed the towel and made it out to his truck. "'Bout time. Time's a-wastin'."

"Sorry." I nodded and headed around to the passenger side. I was just reaching for the metal handhold and stepping on the running bar so I could haul my ass into the cab when Mitch grabbed my backpack and tore it away from me. I fell backward, landing on my butt, the air forced out of me.

"What the hell?" It took a moment before I could get to my

feet. I grabbed for my backpack, but Mitch easily held it out of my reach.

"Just hold up."

"What do you want?" I didn't have much. Just a little food, a bottle of water, and forty dollars left over from the fifty-five bucks I'd started out with. I'd squirreled away as much money as I could during the past six months, stashing it in my hidden backpack. I'd also kept a little of the plane ticket refund, too, but most of it I'd given to my mom.

He pulled out the small wad of cash, then dropped the pack. "This'll do for a start. We'll call it gas money."

"You're making me pay to hitch a ride?" I snatched up my backpack.

"Yup. Though there ain't much here." He opened the cab door. "Hop in. I'll take the rest out in trade."

"I don't understand." Sometimes playing dumb was safer.

"Uh-huh. You girls are the same. You act all innocent, but you know the score." He scowled. "A fuck and a hand job and we'll call it even."

Playing it dumb idea went out the window. "Fuck you."

He laughed, then reached out and pinched my tit. A hard slap didn't do much to discourage him.

"Come on, girl. Like I said, time's—"

I'm not sure what happened next. A dark shadow appeared behind me and then a huge body was past me and holding Mitch by the back of his shirt.

"Give it back."

The hot biker had Mitch against the side of the truck. Mitch had to outweigh the guy by fifty pounds just counting his belly alone, but he was helpless against the biker.

I would've thought it'd take more to make a big guy like

Mitch give in, but there must've been something in the way the biker looked at him. Mitch's angry, ready-to-fight expression changed. His eyes widened and his mouth dropped open. He held out the money, his hand shaking.

I reached around the sexy biker guy, snatched the money, then tucked it back into my backpack. "Thanks."

"Get back inside the diner."

I didn't want to, but there was a quality, an extra something in his voice that made me obey him. Mitch's wide eyes got even bigger as I threw the pack over my shoulder and took off, hurrying to get inside. If Mitch's reaction was any indication, I didn't want to be around to see what the biker did to him.

"What are you doing back in here?" Maggie May frowned at me, then gazed past me to the outside. "Where's the good-looking motorcycle guy?"

As far as I was concerned, it was none of her business. Instead of heading into the ladies room, I kept going and pushed my way out the back door to the smaller parking lot behind the building. Once outside, I leaned against the wall, dropped my backpack, and closed my eyes.

Lots of other girls went nuts over guys, but I'd never been one of them. But this biker guy? He was the type any girl would go gaga over. He was sexy, hot, dangerous, and a hero all rolled into one.

He had my body sizzling, stirring me up inside like no one had ever done. He kind of scared me and thrilled me all at the same time. I didn't know what it was, but it was more than simply turning me on big-time. My heart was racing and I felt like I was about to jump out of my skin. If he'd touched me, I was sure I would've gone wild.

Crazy wild.

It was the truth. If he'd given me so much as a flick of his finger telling me to spread wide I would have. And not just to ease the growing tension inside me, but because I truly, undeniably wanted to fuck him.

"You need to be more careful."

I sucked in a breath, opened my eyes, and found myself staring straight into those strange blue-silver eyes.

Holy shit.

He narrowed them, studying me in a way that wasn't the least bit unpleasant, then tilted his head. "Did you hear me?"

I nodded, unable to find the right words. It was as though he'd stolen my ability to speak English. Hell, to speak at all.

And then I noticed it.

He was breathing as fast as I was. Quick, shallow breaths like he'd run a long way really fast.

"Are you okay? I wouldn't put it past that asshole Mitch to pull out a gun."

"Shut up."

"What?" I was too stunned to get angry. "Where do you get off—"

His mouth pressed against mine, stealing away what little breath I had. His hands yanked at my T-shirt, tugging it out of my jeans. Lust hit me like it never had before, burning outward to fire through every inch of me. I clutched a hunk of his hair in both hands and kissed him back, hard, needy, wanting his body to melt into mine.

He moaned—or was it a strangled growl?—and answered me by shoving his hand under my shirt, then yanking my bra off. I heard the tear of material then felt it brush against my legs. His hand covered my breast, his thumb doing its work to change my already peaked nipple into a tiny mountain.

Arching, I pushed my breasts against him, urging him to do more, to put his mouth where his hand was.

A smile came to me as he seemed to hear my thoughts and shoved my shirt out of the way. His mouth left mine to travel down my neck and onto my boob. He sucked in my nipple and I laid my head back, my mouth open as I gasped for much needed air.

We were moving fast, but I didn't care. I couldn't have slowed down if my life had depended on it. I was feverish for him. Turning loose of his hair, I found his shirt and wished I had the strength to tear it in two. "Damn."

His chuckle swept warm breath over my skin. Yet instead of helping me get his shirt off, he took hold of my jeans, popped the button, then roughly yanked them along with my thong over my hips and down to my ankles.

"Shoes."

He didn't need to say anything more. Hating like hell to let go, I pushed him away, then lifted my foot, intending to yank off my shoe. With one quick tug, he pulled my shoe off and jerked my foot free of my jeans. We didn't bother with the other shoe.

Picking me up off the ground, he slammed me against the wall, then with his arm muscles bulging, he gripped my ass and pushed me higher. Surprised, I yelped as his face pressed to my pussy. My surprise didn't last long. Nothing could once he sucked in my clit and dug his fingers into the flesh of my ass. All I could do was grip his shoulders and hang on.

Fuck, yeah.

The guy was strong as hell and knew how to use his tongue.

His tongue moved quickly, skimming over my clit then sliding down to drive into my pussy. He pushed back and forth, moving me up and down the wall, his arm supporting and protecting my butt from the rough surface. He pumped first his tongue into my sheath, then added fingers to plunge in and out of me. His mouth went back to torture my throbbing clit.

I moaned and thrust my hips forward, asking him to do the impossible and go deeper. The harder he sucked, the stronger he thrust his fingers into my pussy, the louder I became. But I didn't care. All the truckers in the world could've stood there and watched, and I wouldn't have stopped him. I couldn't have stopped him.

"Ah, yes. Oh, shit."

He was unlike all the guys I'd slept with before. I wasn't using him to relieve stress or to take control of my body. He was using me, taking me as a man should take a woman. I had no control over what he did and didn't care. He was in complete command and I was his willing slave.

Whimpering, I clutched at him, afraid the dizziness would spin me away. The whirlwind inside me had started out as cloud of dust, but now it had grown into tornado. I was riding along in the frenzy of it, my climax tugging me closer and closer to the center where it would burst free and pull me into the safety and calm of the storm.

And then he turned me loose.

I cried out as my feet hit the ground, but the sound was lost as his mouth found mine. The taste of my pussy flowed over my tongue and I drank it in, wanting to get past it to find his flavor. Keeping me pinned to the wall, he brought my legs around his waist. Juices flowed over my inner thighs.

All at once, he broke the kiss and stared into my eyes. Gone was the blue-silver I'd seen before. Instead, his eyes appeared more silver.

"Please."

He smiled, then put his cock at my entrance. When had he gotten his jeans down?

He pierced me, driving his cock into my pussy with enough force to slam my body and head against the wall. I reached around and put a hand on his tight ass. The muscles rippled under my palm and I tried to grab hold, to squeeze it, but it was impossible. Like trying to squeeze a rock. I searched for a handhold, trying first his shoulders, then his arms. But once again, I reached for his hair. If I didn't hold on to some part of him, I was sure we'd break apart all too soon.

He was huge, like a battering ram trying to fit into a small hole. The friction was amazing, driving me insane. Harder and harder he pounded. Faster and faster he went. I tried to match his movements, but couldn't keep up. His mouth found my other breast, giving it the same treatment as he'd done before. My body had come alive in his hands, and for the first time, I knew what real sex, pleasurable sex was like.

Squeezing my legs around him as tightly as I could, I bucked back, thrusting my hips toward him, matching my rhythm to his. I made no more sounds. I didn't have the air or the strength to make them.

Just as my climax was about to rip through me, he stopped, then rammed against me again, pulling me toward him. He ground into me. Then, as I hung on, he took my head in his hands.

Silver. His eyes are almost all silver.

He grabbed my hair and jerked my head to the side. Something sharp, like eye teeth, pushed against the flesh of my neck. I stilled, waiting for whatever he'd do next.

In the next second, he groaned, letting go of my head, and

shoved his cock into me, harder, deeper than I thought possible. The force of it banged me against the wall, sending a sharp, stabbing pain into my back. But the pain and the raw sexuality of it combined together and sent my orgasm flying.

I gripped him as hard as I could as he ground out his climax. We rocked, both of us working through our releases, clinging to each other like two people trying not to drown in a sea of their emotions. My body shuddered out the climax as I skimmed my fingers over his shoulders and vowed that the next time, he'd be naked.

The next time?

The thought came and went as he lowered me to my feet again. For a while, all we could do was rest against each other, seeking support.

I didn't know what to say. Instead, I tugged my jeans up as he did his, giving me only a fleeting glimpse of his massive cock.

He zipped up his jeans, then brushed back his hair. "I found you another ride."

"What? How'd you know where I'm going?"

"Let's just say Mitch was in a talkative mood."

He'd found me a ride? When did he have time? And shouldn't he have said something else? Like "what's your name?" or "let's get together again soon"? Instead, he was telling me about a ride? Did he mean a ride with him?

"There's a family seated at one of the tables. Parents and two kids. Wait for them to finish eating and they'll take you up the road."

He caught my head between his hands, putting his face a few inches from mine. "And for fuck's sake, don't take a ride from just anyone. Ask the waitresses for names of truckers. They'll know the regulars and who you can trust. It's better to wait than to take the first trucker who offers."

It was true. I hadn't asked about Jimbo. Maybe if I had, I wouldn't have ended up stranded on the side of the road. Then again, if I hadn't gotten tossed out of Jimbo's truck, I wouldn't have met the biker. But who had I met?

"What's your name?"

"Go wait for them. Their names are Todd and Susan Williamson." He let me go and started to walk away.

"I asked you what your name is." All the wonderful sensations coursing through my body rushed out of me, replaced by both hurt and anger. So that was it? Just fuck and run? He wasn't even nice enough to want to know my damn name?

He pivoted on his heel, turning back to face me just as I was going to ask him again. And tell him mine whether he wanted to know it or not. "Thanks."

That just pissed me off even more. "Yeah. Sure. You're welcome. Asshole."

One of his eyebrows jumped up, and then a small smile formed. In the next minute, he was around the corner of the building and gone.

I wasn't an easy lay. Not really. I'd known and liked the guys I'd had sex with. Most of them were friends. Guys I'd met and gotten to know. They hadn't been just any guys who'd whispered in my ear. To hook up with a complete stranger at the back of a diner wasn't like me.

But then again, the biker guy wasn't like anyone I'd ever met.

Logan

Fucking A. She's hot.

I wasn't sure what had come over me. When she came up beside me in the diner and looked at me with those big green eyes, I thought my heart had stopped. She was walking sex appeal. My lion had roared to life so hard and fast that I'd barely been able to stop it.

If I hadn't kept it down, it would've been a disaster.

Keeping our existence unknown was hard enough without one of us shifting in front of a bunch of humans at a truck stop. We lived high in the North Carolina mountains in a remote part of the land that was hard to get to and away from the usual hiking paths and camp sites. The people of the nearby town of Cripple Creek knew what we were and helped guard our secret. So far, only a few outsiders had ever seen one of us after shifting. Those poor souls had paid a heavy price, but what choice did we have?

I'd wanted to talk to her, to watch her green eyes flash with arousal, but I hadn't had time. She'd already started getting into an eighteen wheeler before I'd figured out what to say.

I'd had no choice. I'd had to follow her.

When I saw the trucker robbing her, then telling her she'd have to fuck him to pay for the ride, I'd gone a little nuts. I fucking hated it when men pulled that shit on women, but with her, it had been a hundred times worse.

Taking care of the trucker had been easy. Not following her into the diner, then out to the back had been impossible. I'd managed to pause long enough to ask the family of four to give her a ride and then I'd had to see her again. The mother had seen her face as she'd rushed back into the place and had readily agreed to give her a lift. Telling her about the ride was my excuse to go and find her.

I should've known better. Fucking her was a crazy thing to do. And dangerous as all hell.

Even now, with the roaring power of my bike underneath me, I couldn't wipe away the remnants of her. I could still feel the soft silkiness of her raven hair. The fullness of her breasts against my chest. My cock still ached, missing the sensation of her pussy walls wrapped around it.

I should've sniffed her when I'd had the chance. Not in the diner where others might see, but once I'd had her against me. But the heat inside me, the need of my lion to take her had been too urgent. Instead of the long, slow sniff that would bring her scent deeper inside me and tell me if she was my mate, my breaths had been shallow, puffed gasps of air as I'd pounded her against the wall.

The long highway stretched out before me and I picked up speed. The Claiming Games would start soon. I'd find my mate in the games, just as all the members of my pride did. And yet, I had a feeling that, no matter who I found, I'd never forget the beautiful girl I'd fucked behind the diner.

My lion didn't care about the games. All it cared about was getting more of the girl.

"Screw the games."

I took the next exit, knowing what I had in mind would go against the rules the pride had put into place. Mates were chosen at the games, not elsewhere. But I didn't care.

If I was lucky, she'd still be waiting for the Williamsons and their kids to finish their meals.

And if I wasn't lucky? I didn't even want to think about that.

Mia

Todd and Susan Williamson took me farther than Todd wanted to, but Susan made it clear to him in no uncertain words that "we're doing this." She didn't care if it took them out of their way. She was a mother on a mission and Todd would have hell to pay if he didn't do as she said.

I had hoped they'd know where Cripple Creek was, but they were going through North Carolina on their way to Boston for an extended vacation and didn't have a clue. The small town didn't even show up on her phone's navigation app. If they hadn't been going close to Asheville to visit the Biltmore Estate, they would've taken another route.

After Susan had given him the final word, Todd had grown quiet and tossed me irritated looks via the rearview mirror. But he didn't complain again. It was obvious who was in charge in their family.

When I thought I'd pushed my luck with Todd far enough, I finally convinced Susan to let me off at a truck stop just outside Asheville. As I told her, it was as safe, maybe even safer, than picking up a ride from the side of the road. At least at a truck stop, I could ask the advice of the waitresses.

I considered myself lucky to have made it to the Stop and Grab Truck Stop. With one ride, I'd gotten all the way from Greenville to Asheville. From there, I hoped to find out how to get to Cripple Creek.

If I didn't, I was screwed. The Claiming Games would start

without me.

As I opened the door to the truck stop's combination diner and convenience store, I waved good-bye to the family. They were nice people, the kind whose father went to work, then came home sober and played with the two kids, Mike and Melissa. Mike was the same age as Johnny, but with a joy for life I'd never seen in my little brother. The baby, Melissa, gurgled in her car seat and gave me a toothless grin every time she caught me looking at her. Sighing for a life I'd never known, I stepped into the diner.

Truck stops all looked the same, with metal tables and chairs along with barstools at the counter. The convenience store part of the place had several rows of shelves boasting the usual chips and junk food, except the waitress's name was Lee Ann instead of Miss Charlotte or Maggie May. I took a seat at the counter like I always did and was once again chowing down a free meal. Truck stop waitresses were becoming my favorite people.

"Mia, are you sure you're safe—"

"Yes." I forced yet another smile at the same old question. If she'd noticed the snap in my voice, she didn't show it. "I'm positive. I'll be fine. But you can help me another way, if that's okay. I need to know where to go from here. And I need to find a ride. I'm hoping you'll know someone who'll take me there. Someone you think I can trust."

She sighed, reminding me of how my mother would sigh just before giving up on getting me to study harder. "Where are you headed?"

"Cripple Creek."

She blinked a second before her body went still. "Did you say Cripple Creek? As in Cripple Creek, North Carolina? The town way up in the mountains?"

Could there be more than one town in North Carolina with the same name? "Yeah. I'm going to a bar called—"

"Fang's."

It wasn't so much that she knew what I was about to say as how she'd said it. Like she'd just told me I was going to Dracula's castle. "Yeah. Do you know the place?"

"Not personally, no. And I wouldn't know how to tell you to get there." She cleared her throat, glanced around, then leaned in as though we were two international spies planning a covert mission. "Let's keep our voices down, okay?"

I couldn't help it. When a person leans toward me and whispers, I tend to lean forward and whisper back. "Why?"

She glanced around again, then visibly relaxed when no one appeared to be listening in on our conversation. "There's been some talk about Cripple Creek."

"What kind of talk?" I'd assumed it was an invitation only event. That maybe the K.O.B. Corporation—whatever that was—wanted to keep it on the down low. Which I could understand. It was probably their way of keeping uninvited girls from showing up.

"I've heard some scary stuff. Weird shit like monsters running around in the woods. Like men who turn into lions. Not cougars like a few folks have seen around here every so often." She leaned even closer. "I'm talking about real, live African lions." She flexed her fingers, then put her hands on either side of her head. "You know. With the big manes and everything."

I tried to keep from laughing by biting my lower lip, but she wasn't fooled. She rolled her eyes and made a silly face. "Oh, I know. I shouldn't have said anything. I mean, men changing into lions. Have you ever heard of anything so ridiculous?" She tried to act like she'd only been kidding, but the lack of sincerity was too obvious to ignore.

"Lions." *And tigers and bears, oh my.* "So that's it? Just a silly rumor about shifters?" I was relieved, but it didn't last long.

She gave up on trying to convince me that she didn't believe the rumors. "Look, I know it sounds stupid, but there was also talk about girls around your age going to Fang's and never coming back." Her eyebrows shot up. "Now, that one really scares me. I mean, when you go all the way up into the mountains like that you're getting up into hill country where anything can happen. Folks up there can be… different."

"And you've heard these things from… who? People from Cripple Creek?"

"No. None of them would ever say anything. They're as closed-mouth as they come. But the stories have been around for years. I figure there's got to be a grain of truth in the rumors for them to stick around so long."

"Which means they're more legends than facts." I didn't want to hurt her feelings, but did she seriously think I'd believe the stories were real? Stories about monsters, vampires and werewolves had been around for centuries, but no one had ever proved their existence. It was all just a bunch of superstitious nonsense.

"I don't know." She shook her head, denying my legend theory.

"So I might run into Big Foot?" I was playing with her, but she took it good-naturedly.

"Okay, now, there's no reason to make fun of me. I'm only trying to give you a head's up."

"Maybe the girls liked what they found once they got there

and decided to stay." I could see it happening. I'd jump at the chance to live on a mountain filled with nature and wide open spaces. I could open up my own little beauty shop with wall to wall windows and call it Mia's Beauty Box. Or Curly Locks. Something down-homey like that.

"I guess you could be right. Still, before you put me down as a crazy person, think about it, okay?"

I hadn't meant to offend her. "I'm sorry. I shouldn't have teased you. And thank you, but I'm sure I'll be fine." After what I'd been through, I could handle a few raccoons and deer. Even a bear or two if I kept my head. Did they still have bears in the mountains?

"Sure you will. But like I said. Give it some thought, okay? I mean, you know what they say. Where's there's smoke, there's fire."

Unless someone was blowing smoke up her ass. Did I have to reassure every waitress between Biloxi and Cripple Creek? "I will. But what I really need from you are the directions."

How had K.O.B. Corporation expected me to find the place? Unless they'd planned on meeting me at the airport. It suddenly hit me that I might have blown my chance of ever finding Cripple Creek before I'd even left home.

"Suit yourself." She reached into her pocket and took out a pack of gum. After offering a piece to me, which I declined, she popped one into her mouth and started chewing.

Again, I held back a laugh. There was just something about a person chewing gum that reminded me of a cow chewing its cud.

"Personally, I've never been to Cripple Creek before, but I think you just got lucky. I don't know anyone who's been there, either, except for one person. And that person's Arnie Stucker.

He doesn't come in here a lot, so maybe this is a good sign. Like you're meant to go there." She pointed at a man sitting in a booth across from the counter. "Arnie's kind of slow and he's a bit on the odd side, but like I said, he's the only one I know who's been to Cripple Creek. He's from around those parts. Maybe you could see if he's headed up there."

"And he's okay? Do you trust him?"

She gave it extra thought. "He comes in here about once every two months or so and never causes any problems. So if you're asking me if I think it's safe for you to catch a ride with him, then the answer's yes. Just take care, anyway."

"No problem. I will. And thanks again. For the food and the information." I swiveled the stool around and studied Arnie. He was dressed in faded overalls and an equally faded T-shirt. A baseball cap with the words *I Don't Swerve for Squirrels* on the front was pulled low on his forehead. He was lean and wiry, but I would've bet he could hold his own in a fight. Or pull out a jackknife to even the score.

I strode over to where he sat, then took a glance at the magazine he was studying. Not that it was meant as reading material.

Hunting and Firearms. Great.

But who was I to judge? Mississippi had a long history of gun-toting good old boys, too, so I couldn't chalk it up to being a North Carolina thing. "Hi, Mr. Stucker. My name is Mia Travers. Can I talk to you for a minute?"

He scowled as he forced his attention away from the photo of a really big, bad-looking rifle. Or was it a machine gun? I'd never liked guns much or hunting, either. The only good thing about a gun was that my dad had never owned one.

"What do you want, little girl?"

Judging by the dark brown hair sticking out from under his ball cap to the lack of lines around his eyes, I would've guessed that Arnie wasn't too much older than me. "Lee Ann said you might give me a ride to Cripple Creek."

Sudden interest sparked in his bloodshot eyes. "What 'cha want to go there for?"

I wasn't about to tell him about The Claiming Games. And especially not about the two hundred and fifty thousand dollars. He might want to stick around and hit me up for a loan. Or just hit on me. Instead, I lied. "My aunt lives there. She's, uh, been sick lately and I'm going there to help take care of her."

Arnie didn't look like he was bright enough to know the alphabet, but I was wrong. From the look in his eyes, he was smart enough to guess I was lying. "Is that right? What's your aunt's name?"

"Lucinda White." Mrs. White was my third grade teacher, but it didn't matter why I'd picked her name. As long as I could convince him of my story, then I was good to go.

"Uh-huh. Is she any relation to Buford White?"

"Not that I know of." I wouldn't fall for the old fake name trick.

He scanned me, not in a sexual way, but still it had me shifting from one foot to the other. "Okay. I'm going up in the mountains anyway so I guess I could swing by Cripple Creek and drop you off on the main street."

"Cool. Um, but I can't pay you anything." Emphasis on the *anything*.

"Don't matter none. Like I said, I'm going anyway." He seared me with an intense look. "You sure you want to go there? I can't come back and fetch you home or anything."

"I'm sure."

I stepped back as he slid out of the booth, then lifted a hand to Lee Ann. She returned his wave then gave me a quick nod.

Hoping I hadn't made a mistake, I stuck to Arnie's heels as he strode out to the parking lot. By the time we'd made it to an old, rusted-out pickup that didn't look like it had enough life left in it to make it up a mole hill much less a mountain, I'd already started second guessing my decision. With no other choice, I figured I might was well see the plan out. Besides, my curiosity about Cripple Creek, Fang's, and The Claiming Games was going full blast.

Arnie hopped behind the wheel, then waited when I paused. He leaned across the seat and shoved the passenger side door open. "You comin' or what?"

"Yeah, I'm coming." I slid onto the seat and slammed the door. Just before I'd lowered my backpack, I saw the hole in the bottom of the floorboard and the gravel pavement beneath the truck. I hugged the backpack to my chest.

Arnie turned the key and the motor kicked over. After several coughs and sputters, the engine settled down into a steady rhythm. He pulled the truck out of the parking lot and onto the highway.

"You're going to Fang's, aren't you?"

Shit. I knew he hadn't bought my story. "Do you know the place?"

"I've driven by it a time or two. Never gone inside, though." He cast a sideways look at me. "Don't want to, neither."

I could sense the question hanging on the tip of his tongue. He waited several minutes then gave in to the urge to ask.

"So why's a girl like you going to a biker bar?"

"Uh..." A biker bar? The image of the blond biker came rushing back. I hadn't stopped thinking about him since he'd left me behind. What were the chances of him being at Fang's? Probably not much since we'd met up in South Carolina and not Asheville. He was probably long gone and already fucking some other stupid girl at a truck stop.

Damn him to hell and back.

"Cat got your tongue?"

What could I say? I didn't want to tell him about the invitation. Shrugging, I tried throwing a question back. "Why shouldn't I?" If he told me he'd seen a man turned into a lion, I'd ask him to pull the truck over and let me out. Talking crazy stuff with a waitress in a crowded truck stop was a lot different than talking crazy stuff with a backwoods hillbilly in his pickup.

"I doubt it'd be safe for a girl by her lonesome."

"I can handle myself."

He skimmed his gaze over me, shooting me a pessimistic look. "Uh-huh. Just the same, what's Fang's got to do with your sick aunt?"

I waited too long to answer, confirming his suspicions. He knew I was lying, but I was already knee-deep in shit to get out of the hole I'd dug for myself. "Nothing. I figured I'd make a pit stop, is all, and check out the rumors I've heard about the bar." At least it was partly true. Even if the invitation hadn't told me to go to Fang's, after what Lee Ann had said, I'd still want to see the bar. Maybe.

"Curiosity killed the cat, you know."

"Yeah, I know." But stories about monsters and girls going missing? Come on. It was all a bunch of bullshit. I'd learned early on how to distinguish between bullshit and the truth. Bullshit stank to high heaven and what Lee Ann had said was stinking it up bad.

"You just be careful while you're in Cripple Creek and

especially at Fang's. They're mountain folk and they don't like outsiders getting into their business."

"Lee Ann said you're from up that way."

He chuckled and gave me a sly look. "Up that way and from Cripple Creek are two different things. I'm mountain folk, too, but not that kind of mountain folk."

I didn't have the nerve to ask what he meant. "Is Fang's on the main street?"

"Naw, but I guess I can take you a little closer to the bar. Not all the way, but close enough so you can walk the rest of it." His piercing look swept over me again. The man had missed his calling as an interrogator. "Looks like you've done a fair bit of walking already. Where you from?"

"Biloxi." Did I look that bad? I'd given myself sponge baths in public restrooms and rest stops along the way, but there was only so much a girl could do without soap and a proper shower.

He let out a low whistle. "Well, now, you have done some travelin'. Must be somethin' pretty important at Fang's for you to hitch all this way."

His attempt to get me to open up was subtle, but I was smart, too. "Not really. Like I said. I'm just curious." I wouldn't tell him the truth even though he knew I was slinging a load of crap.

"Uh-huh." He reached over and shoved in one of those old eight-track tapes into the player. A country singer's voice filled the cab, singing of tough luck and hard liquor. Jimbo would've loved it.

I settled into the seat and kept my attention to the side window. If I was lucky, Arnie wouldn't ask me any more questions.

Monsters. Girls going missing. It was all just a bunch of silly rumors. The locals had probably made up the stories to keep people away. But nothing would keep me from the two hundred and fifty thousand dollars. Without the money, my family would have a difficult time getting on their feet no matter where they ended up.

Logan

I settled into a crouch and waited for the deer to lower its head and munch on the grass again. As a lion, I could take the deer down with one quick swipe, but I wasn't planning on killing it. If I'd needed the food, I would have, but my pantry was full of canned goods and my freezer stuffed with other game.

I'd tracked the deer for a mile and only now had it gotten any hint that a predator was around. As far as I was concerned, it was a win-win for the both of us. I got to stretch my limbs and let my inner lion have some freedom, and the deer got a lesson on paying better attention to what went on around it. I'd frighten it and it would remember. Maybe the fear would save its life later.

I crept closer, the need for blood curling inside me, urging me to turn play time into a real attack. But my pride didn't hunt for sport. At least not the same way humans did. My ears flicked back and forth, picking up the sound of a squirrel scurrying up the trunk of a tree. Birds fluttered their wings and chirped in the trees overhead and a rabbit dashed in front of the deer, startling it.

If the deer had any brains, it would've picked up on all those warning signs. Instead, it looked up, then once again put its mouth to the grass.

Dumb ass deer.

I was close enough for it to pick up my scent. Hell, it should've been able to look me straight in the eye. But it stayed, quietly chewing, oblivious to the impending danger.

I should kill it anyway. It would die soon enough, either by my paws or another predator's. Instead, I lunged out from behind the bushes, roaring loudly enough to put a good scare into it. If I'd stretched my neck a little, I could've bitten off its ear. I landed on my feet, then threw my body to the side, dodging its hind legs as it kicked. It bolted into the forest and was gone, running to live another day.

Any other time I would've given chase just for the fun of it. But since screwing the girl behind the diner, I hadn't been able to get excited about much of anything. She'd stuck in my mind, shoving all other thoughts out of the way. Enough that I'd gone looking for her. I'd driven up and down the stretch of highway, even checking some of the side roads, but I hadn't been able to find her or the Williamson family.

Maybe Lady Luck had been with me. Fate had stepped in and kept me from making an even bigger mistake. But if so, why did I feel anything but lucky?

I still couldn't shake the thought of her. I shouldn't have fucked her, but I hadn't been able to resist. Like a rare steak, I'd wanted her so badly that I'd thrown all caution away and taken her. I could blame it on my lion, and that was part of it, but it wasn't all of it. I'd needed her as both a lion and as a man. Fucking outside the pride was okay, even encouraged to relieve sexual stress. But, hell, I'd almost bitten and claimed her. Not cool.

If I had bitten her, I would've caught holy hell from the others in my pride. Our mates came from the games. To do it any other way wasn't allowed. Lion shifters going out and claiming a mate from outside the games would have invited all kinds of trouble.

Our ancestors had found their mates by stealing them. By raiding human towns and dragging girls back with them. They'd taken the girls and claimed them whether they'd wanted it or not.

Burke, our leader, had changed all that by starting The Claiming Games. At least through the games, a girl had a choice. A girl who answered the invitation and chose to do the games could take her pick. The man or the money. But only if she completed the challenge without anyone's help. And, of course, if she survived.

I'd join in The Claiming Games this year and find my mate the right way. Not at the back of a diner with a girl whose name I didn't even know. I should've asked her what her name was, but, as much as I hated to admit it, I'd been so thrown by how close I'd come to claiming her that I'd had to get away. I'd run off like a frightened deer.

I'd fucked and then fucked up.

It was a good thing I hadn't drawn in her scent. I'd smelled her, all right. How could I not? And her fragrance had tempted me to take a bigger breath. Thankfully, the rush of excitement had kept me from making that grave mistake.

"Damn, man, are you getting slow or what?"

I spun around to find my fellow Kings of Beasts pride member Ruger Hogdon leaning against the tree. He'd gotten his name because of his fondness for Ruger guns. I didn't like guns and I definitely didn't need one. Then again, I didn't frequent human bars any longer and didn't need protection like Ruger did. Not after what had happened to Ruger's brother,

Vic.

I shifted back to my human form and shook off the lingering ache of the change as well as the bad thoughts about Vic. "Fuck off."

I started walking toward the place where I'd hidden an extra set of clothes. Most of us didn't stash clothes in various places around the mountain, but after running into a camper and his family one day after having shifted back to my human and very naked self, I'd decided I didn't want a repeat of the awkward encounter. Burke had escorted the lost camper and his family down the mountain, giving him a not-so-subtle warning not to return. We'd all gotten lucky that they hadn't seen me change. Seeing a naked man was one thing. Seeing a lion? Bad. Seeing a lion change into a man? *Real* bad.

"Now is that any way to talk to a friend?"

Arguing the point wasn't worth it. He was a pride mate and we were civil. But a friend? Not anymore. Our friendship had gone south after I'd brought Vic back home dead.

"What do you want?" It came out harsher than I'd meant, but it was getting harder and harder not to get irritated with Ruger.

"You're doing the games, right?" He tagged along behind me over to a stack of rocks where I'd hidden my extra clothes.

I retrieved the burlap bag and started getting dressed. "Yeah. It's time."

I was twenty-three and should've joined into the games five years earlier, but I'd put it off. Just like humans, we were living longer, so what was the rush to take a mate as soon as we turned eighteen? Most of the males didn't bother questioning the when of it and entered the games as soon as they were old enough. But a growing number of us wanted to wait. Like Ruger, Colter

Quaid, and myself. Even now I wasn't sure I wanted to go through with it, especially after what had happened behind the truck stop. Still, to keep Burke off my back, I'd check the girls out. If none of them caught my interest with either her looks or her scent, then I'd pass them by and wait for the next year.

"So what type you hoping for? A redhead, a blonde? Big tits or little ones? Although I don't get why any man would want a girl with small titties. Gotta have something solid to bury my face between."

"I don't care what size her tits are. As long as she's smart and easy to get along with, who cares what color her hair is? Besides, you never really know if it's her real hair color or not. Or, hell, even her real hair." I detested girls with fake anything. Hair, nails, personality, whatever.

"Which is why we need to check them out first before they decide to do the games. Or at least before they finish getting to their destination."

I led the way back toward Fang's, trying not to tell him to shut up. I'd heard the same thing too many times already. Ruger wanted to "get to know the girl" before he chose her to participate. He wanted to know she was a good lay. It was an excuse for him to fuck some random girl and we both knew it. It sucked, but I wasn't going to butt my nose in his business. We already had a hard enough time getting along.

"Getting to know the girl" ahead of time, however, couldn't happen. As soon as a male picked the girl he wanted, the girl immediately started the challenge. Then, if she completed the challenge and wanted the man instead of the money, he was hers for life. It wouldn't matter if she was a good fuck, sweet as hell, or a real bitch.

"That's not going to happen and you know it."

The girls had to make their way through the forest to a pre-determined destination. For my mate, she had to go to a cave my parents had used during their games. The girl I chose would stay in the cave two nights where, if I wanted, I could get to know her, including fucking her—as if I wouldn't want to—then she'd make it back to Fang's. If she survived those three days and two nights, and made it back to our hangout bar, she'd have a say in which prize she wanted. Choose the money or choose the man.

Most of the girls who'd received invitations never got started in the games. If they'd dared to show up, a lot of them would leave as soon as they heard what was involved. Among those few who took up the challenge, some never made it back to Fang's, falling victim to injury as well as wimping out. If they didn't make it back, they were either left alone to survive on their own in the woods or, if they got lucky, were found and sent away. The pride didn't accept any girl who didn't pass the challenge. We only wanted strong and capable females.

"Yeah. It's fucked up. I don't want to pick some girl and then find out after the challenge that she's a bitch. Or lousy at blowjobs."

I shrugged. "Then you'd better make sure you go for her based on her scent and not on her boobs. The boobs could be fake, too, you know."

"Who cares as long as they're huge?" He cupped his hands and held them in front of his chest. "As long as she can walk and not fall over, I want them humongous."

I chuckled, enjoying Ruger's dilemma. We hadn't had a good conversation like this one since Vic's death four months ago. Was Ruger finally coming around? He'd never said it straight out, but I knew he blamed me for his brother's death.

And the truth of it was, I believed I was to blame, too. Maybe not in a logical kind of way, but at a gut level. If I hadn't stepped out of the bar in Greensboro, maybe Vic wouldn't have gotten a bullet through his head.

I'd gone out to get something out of my truck. By the time I'd made it back inside the bar, Vic was shit-deep in the middle of a fight. Five guys had him on his knees, but I threw my body into the mix and took out two of them, freeing Vic to send the other three flying. I knocked the two guys out and turned to see another guy pull out a gun and press the barrel against the back of Vic's head.

If one of the shooter's friends hadn't canned me with a barstool, I would've lost it and shifted. I went down, my brain scrambled, the world spinning. Before I could get back on my feet, the bartender and the other customers had wrestled the gun away and restrained the other fighters. But by then, Vic was already gone. Having Vic's killer behind bars helped a little, but not enough.

It took a lot to kill a werecat, especially a lion shifter. We could heal our bodies—up to a point. But a bullet to the brain? That would drop us like dead weight.

"Better sniff her hard then and be sure. They should be showing up soon."

Ruger grumbled all the way back to Fang's. Was I ready to make a choice? What if he was right? What if I sniffed her, got her scent embedded in me, and then found out she was a real bitch?

What if I found out I wanted the girl at the truck stop instead?

Mia

Arnie's driving was freaking terrifying. He took the mountain roads going faster than any of the truckers had driven on straight flat highways. Too many times, I thought he'd lose control and send the truck flying over the edge.

By the time we'd made it up the mountain and almost to Fang's, I was ready to get out and kiss the ground. True to his word, he didn't take me all the way to the bar. Instead, he stopped, pulling the truck over onto one of those lookout areas made for tourists to park and take photos of the luscious green scenery. Weird thing, though. It didn't look like anyone had made use of the lookout area in a long time. No car tracks. No litter. No nothing. I guess Cripple Creek wasn't a popular tourist destination.

The road had been cut out of the mountain. One side was a rock wall and the other, the one with the lookout area, had a cliff that dropped off straight down into the forest below. A fear of heights had never been a problem for me, but I wasn't about to get close to the edge.

"Here you go, little girl. This is as far as I'm going."

I tugged my backpack next to me and shoved my shoulder against the door to get it unstuck. "Thanks for the ride, Mr. Stucker."

"Arnie."

"Sorry?" I slid off the seat and onto the ground.

"Call me Arnie."

"Okay. Thanks again, Arnie. And it's Mia. Not little girl." I was about to close the door when he stopped me.

"You sure you want to do this? I don't mind taking you back down the mountain with me."

"I'm sure." Granted, I'd gotten a little uneasy when we'd driven through Cripple Creek. It didn't look much different from any other small town with its mom-and-pop shops and pickups outnumbering regular cars. But it had felt *different*. Which was a stupid way to judge a town. Still, it had rattled my nerves when we'd driven by and everyone had stopped to stare at us. Only one old woman had lifted her hand in greeting and she'd done it half-heartedly, as though she didn't want to get caught being friendly. I'd probably gotten more spooked about the monster thing than I'd thought.

"Mia?" It was the first time he'd called me by my name.

"Yeah?" My stomach did a little flip-flop at his worried expression.

"You take care now, you hear?"

He wanted to say more. It was written all over his face, but he held back. "I will." Okay, now I really was nervous. But I'd come so far already, I wasn't about to turn back. I couldn't let my family down.

According to what Arnie had told me earlier, it wasn't much farther to Fang's, although it was all uphill. I slung my backpack over my shoulder, then waved good-bye as Arnie turned his truck around and started down the road. When I looked up the road again, I knew that, one way or another, going to Fang's would change my life.

The problem was, I couldn't stop thinking that my life had already changed. Not only because I was out of the hell hole I'd called home, but because I couldn't stop thinking about the biker guy. Thinking he'd influenced my life was stupid. He was gone and only a memory now. Unless, of course, he'd knocked me up. Then I'd have a living reminder of him for the rest of my life.

Talk about stupid. Having sex with a guy I'd just met. I'd literally fucked up.

Yet I couldn't have stopped myself even if I'd tried. As much as I realized how dumb a move it was, I still didn't regret it. If I never saw him again, I'd relive our quick hook up every time I got lonely. And horny.

I moaned, a different kind of warmth heating up my body. He'd left me with a wonderful sense of satisfaction. Like I'd finally been fucked and fucked right, and left feeling like a real a real woman, all sexy and desired. Feeling a hell of a lot better than I'd ever felt with any of the other guys.

He'd left me wanting more.

Maybe if I'd gotten his name I could track him down after my trip into the mountains was over. But I hadn't even gotten his first name, much less his last. And he hadn't even asked for mine. Hadn't even acted like he wanted to know who I was.

Shake it off. You both got what you wanted and it's over.

Instead of lusting after a guy who'd come into my life and was gone forever, I'd be better off focusing on my goal. Whatever I had to do, I had to win The Claiming Games and make a better life for myself and my family. Everything else, including sexy guys, wasn't important.

After an hour of trudging uphill, I finally saw it. Fang's Bar and Grill. I wasn't sure what I'd expected, but it wasn't much to look at. In fact, I had to read the sign twice to make sure. The painted-on words had faded and shingles hung from the dilapidated roof. Motorcycles were lined up in two not-so-straight lines with a few pickups thrown in for good measure. It didn't take a genius to know it was a biker bar. But what would bikers have to do with The Claiming Games? Or had they chosen the place, like the vague warnings in the invitation, as a means to scare off any girl who wasn't dead set on doing the challenge?

Three girls stood outside the place. The brunette kept walking toward the front door then retracing her steps back to the other two girls. She was pretty in an off-beat kind of way, but she lacked confidence. One of her friends had an amazing body, tall with all the curves in the right places. She was beautiful, but her confidence seemed forced, like she really didn't believe in herself. The third one had red hair that glistened like fire under the sunlight. I wondered if it was her real color or out of a bottle. Either way, it was pretty awesome. She was nervous and shifting back and forth on her feet.

The invitation hadn't said we'd be competing against each other, but if it was a competition, I figured I could hold my own with all of them.

Might as well meet them.

I started toward them, putting on a smile. The brunette turned my way, her steady gaze sliding over me.

"Hi. I'm Mia Travers. Are you here for The Claiming Games? Did you guys get an invitation, too?"

"Yes. No." The brunette was as nervous as her red-haired friend. She just showed it in a different way. "Hi, I'm Erin Pierce."

I laughed, trying to ease their jitters. And mine, too. "O-kay. So which is it? Yes or no?"

Erin blinked, obviously unsure how she should take me. "Yes. That's why we're here, but after getting a look at this place, we're ready to take a cab back to the airport."

She looked around and, for a minute, I thought she'd take

off running. "Did you come in a cab? Is it still around here somewhere?" Her gaze slipped back to me.

I wished I'd taken the time to stop and clean up in Cripple Creek. To at least brush my hair and wash my face. I liked her and, for some reason, I wanted her to like me. Although she was nervous, she had a way about her. Like she'd seen some bad shit and had made it through. I could sense she was strong. Probably stronger than she knew she was.

"Nope. I hitched my way up from Biloxi, Mississippi."

"You did? But why? Didn't they give you a plane ticket?"

Her gaze raked over me and, for a moment, I was sure she was putting me down. At least, mentally. But when I checked the other two girls, I didn't pick up that vibe. Maybe I was just sensitive with my nerves jumping like they were. "Yeah, they did. I cashed it in and gave the money to my mom. She's got seven other kids to clothe and feed. I'm hoping whoever sent it won't mind as long as I showed up on time."

"Wait. So you're saying you took rides from strangers to get here? Damn, girl. Either you've got a ton of guts or you're just plain stupid."

The pretty, tall one scrunched up her nose. Like the first girl, I didn't think she meant it as harshly as it had sounded. I smiled bigger.

"Maddy." The redhead stared pointedly at the tall girl, then at me. "I'm sorry. She speaks her mind, but she's really a nice person."

"Nina's right," added Erin. She lifted her hands to ward off her friend's glare. "Hey, I'm agreeing that you're nice."

"Don't worry about it." I didn't want to start anything. Not with the unknown coming up fast. Instead, I kept the smile and shifted my backpack from one shoulder to the other. "I like people who say what they mean."

The tension eased, giving me a little breathing room.

Erin tugged at her hair. "I've got to ask. Do you think this is legit? And even if it is, why meet here? Why not at a local hotel? You know. Some place nicer than this." She frowned. "Some place that probably has a clean toilet."

At least it had a toilet. I'd seen some places without one. And even some others that did, but I wouldn't have set foot in them for anything.

"Aw, it doesn't look so bad to me." The one called Nina tossed her hair over her shoulder. "I'm Nina Winters and this is Maddy Wheller."

"Nice to meet you." And it was. They were a tight-knit trio. I bet they stuck together and I was envious of their friendship. I'd never bothered getting too close to anyone at school. How could I when I was so busy hiding my bruises? What would I have told them? My father's a drunk who likes to hit me? Oh, yeah. And he likes feeling me up, too?

A few minutes of awkward silence came next. I was about to say we might as well see what was going on, when Erin beat me to it.

"Come on. Let's go inside and get this over with." She grabbed her suitcase and started toward the door.

I took a step before I noticed that Nina and Maddy weren't following. Had they changed their minds?

Erin finally caught on and came back. "We might as well find out what this is about. What else are you going to do? Hitchhike like Mia?"

I was about to agree when Maddy chimed in. "She's right. Let's do this."

Letting Erin take the lead, I gathered my shaky nerves and headed to the front door.

Chapter Three

Mia

Stepping inside only confirmed what I'd thought. I'd found my way into similar bars when I'd had to take what little money my mom could spare to my dad to pay off his tab. She figured it was worth giving him the money he demanded if it kept him drinking instead of coming home.

Erin murmured something I didn't catch. My attention was riveted to the men standing against both walls.

"Yep. Typical biker bar." I shrugged. "I've been inside a few."

I took the lead when Erin and the other two girls didn't look like they were going to go any farther. My nerves were gone, replaced by excitement. I'd made it to Fang's and I couldn't wait to find out what would happen next.

I'd gone only a few feet before I realized that the place didn't have any windows. Not a single one. I wasn't sure how I kept my legs moving, but I managed it. The old familiar feeling of being trapped hit me, warning me to run before the walls started closing in.

Why had they built a bar without any windows? Were they getting broken in a bar fight every Saturday night? Yet the reason didn't matter. I was already inside with nowhere to run except back out the front door. I dragged in a long breath and forced the fear down.

Crap. This is not good.

"The girl definitely has guts," whispered Erin.

If only she knew. But I was determined not to let them see the swirl of emotions starting to choke me.

It's okay. Don't freak out.

I took another deep breath, practicing the calming techniques the school nurse had taught me, and moved toward the one remaining empty table near the center of the room. As long as I could keep away from the walls, I just might be okay. At least, for a little while. Sooner or later, however, I'd have to get outside, away from the crushing walls and ceiling.

Concentrate. Think about something else.

Other tables surrounded the empty one. Around thirty girls, all of them close to my age, occupied the rest. Many of the girls fanned themselves with the same invitation I'd received. Men stood on the outskirts of the room, leaning against the walls. I caught their underlying curiosity mixed with a weird kind of sexual tension. They wore the usual biker clothing, most of them in black. Although it was warm outside, a few of them wore leather vests with the emblem of a roaring lion on the back. Their club name, *Kings of Beasts MC*, was emblazoned under the lion's head.

Although they dressed like bikers, they were different than other bikers I'd seen. I didn't see one with gray hair, not even at the temples. Instead, they were like the women, all within ten years or so of my age, and they were the best-looking guys I'd ever seen. Maybe some of them weren't handsome like the models in a magazine, but they all possessed a regal quality about them that made them even sexier. They looked like they could take on men twice their size—if bigger men even existed—and whoop their asses with one hand tied behind their backs.

Now I wasn't just nervous, I was a little afraid. If they wanted to, they could take us girls and do whatever they wanted to us. But then, if that was their goal, why hadn't they already done it?

One girl who sat near them said something to the man closest to her, tossing her hair in a flirty kind of way. But he, like the others, remained quiet. They were dead serious. As if their lives depended on it.

As if our lives depended on it, too.

My gaze flicked to the wall on my right, then to the other on the left.

It's okay. Just breathe. It's a big room.

"Oh, shit. We're going to get gang raped. Gang raped by bikers and left for dead in a ditch."

The idea was ridiculous and I wanted to laugh at Nina, but I couldn't. It was too close to what I'd been thinking.

"I say we run and don't look back. Every woman for herself."

Was Maddy serious? Or was it her nerves talking? I kept taking in as much air as I could. Living with my father had taught me how to be quiet and check for signs of looming trouble.

"Thanks, Mad. Good to know you have my back," answered Nina.

The three of them kept on talking, but my attention shifted as I concentrated on the girls around me. If I could keep my mind occupied elsewhere, I might be able to relax about the place having no windows.

Except for our age, we didn't have much else in common.

We were a diverse group. Some of us were girly-girls who spent a lot of time in front of a mirror. Others, like me, were more involved with just keeping on keeping on. We didn't have time to make our lipstick perfect. If we even bothered to wear lipstick.

Would that make me less attractive to the men? Did I care? After all, I was there for the money.

"This is degrading."

Maddy again. I guess she was the unofficial spokesperson for their trio. But I understood what she meant. Not that it bothered me. Life was about being sized up and I was used to getting put down. I'd had to face my father's rejection every damn day since I could remember. What did I care if some biker guys didn't like what they saw? I didn't mean anything to them and the feeling was mutual.

"It's like we're cows and they're picking out the ones they want to buy."

No one could've mistaken the anger in Maddy's voice. A few of the men heard her and shifted their attention our way. Not something I wanted them to do. At least not until we found out what The Claiming Games were all about.

"You're right." I reached out and patted Maddy's hand, hoping to keep her quiet, then wondered if my hand was sweaty. I didn't want her drawing anyone's attention. "But don't worry. We're sizing them up, too. They can't buy us, no matter how much they may want our milk." When Maddy pulled her hand away, I knew I'd failed.

Oh, well. I tried.

I turned back around, distancing myself from her. If she wanted to cause a problem, then let her handle whatever came next.

And then I saw him. I no longer heard what anyone else was saying. I couldn't, with the roar of my blood pounding in my ears. Even my leeriness of walls had taken a back seat.

His blue-silver gaze met mine, and just like before, it stole my breath away. Seriously. Just like in those stupid romance novels my mom liked to read. But it was true. Dragging in air became my priority. Right after keeping my gaze locked to his.

He was just as amazing as before. Extraordinary, just like the invitation had said. I hadn't given the finding love thing much thought. Money was my goal. But now, looking at him, I couldn't keep my thoughts from going there. If there was ever a man to drool over, it was him.

And on the plus side, I already knew how amazing he could make a woman feel.

He leaned against the wall, arms crossed, watching me like some wild animal who had found me wandering the forest. And he was ready to protect his territory. The *Kings of Beasts MC* logo fit him. If I could imagine any man as part animal, then I could easily imagine him as a lion. He was strong, fierce, and more regal than any real king could ever be.

He possessed another quality, too. One that had me getting wet between my legs and squirming in my chair. One that took me right back to behind the truck stop.

No wonder I'd wrapped my legs around him without knowing even his name. The man had straight in-your-face sex appeal.

Yeah, that was him all right. He oozed sinful, carnal, raw sex appeal like no one I'd ever met. When he let a small smile lift the corners of his mouth, and nodded at me, acknowledging having already met, I was glad to be sitting down. If I hadn't been, he would've floored me with that simple gesture.

Yet simple wasn't right. I doubted anyone had seen him do it, but its effects hit me hard, like an explosion in a gunpowder factory. His smile was monumental, possessing every drop of magnetism in the world. Compared to him, all the others were just flesh and bones.

The black-haired man next to him bumped against his shoulder, drawing his attention from mine. I blinked, suddenly aware that my mouth was parted. It wouldn't have surprised me to find drool on my chin.

What the hell is wrong with me?

He was just a guy. A little older than me, that's all. And hot as hell. But hot as hell didn't pay the rent.

I jerked my gaze away from him—not without some effort—and focused on the front of the room. "Holy shit." Thankfully, I'd whispered. Unnerved, I forced myself not to look back at him. It helped calm me down, but not by much. Not when I could feel his penetrating gaze back on me.

No. Don't look at him.

But it was so hard not to. Everything in me wanted to get another look. When would I see a man like him again? Running into him after what we'd shared was more than I'd hoped for. Was it a sign? I'd never been a big believer in fate, but I suddenly wanted to believe.

I couldn't help it. As though my eyes had a mind of their own, my gaze jumped back to him. His smile grew a little stronger.

Hell, yeah.

Not thinking, I started to smile back, then caught myself.

Oh, fuck.

I glanced away once more, the heat of my blush rushing to my cheeks as I warned myself not to be stupid—again. Dating had never been my thing. Having a father like mine, I hadn't had any interest in any guys other than to use them for sex. Sad, but true. But I didn't make any bones about what I'd done. A girl had to do what a girl had to do to stay sane.

In fact, I'd only been out on two real dates and both of those had ended up with me fighting to get away from their pawing hands. Although I didn't blame them for cussing at me and calling me a tease, I was the one who decided who I screwed. Not them.

I'd always figured that if I ever found a man strong enough and worth my time, he'd have to be able to dominate me. Not in a bullying kind of way like my dad, but in the way a girl wanted to be dominated. Dominated so she felt like the man couldn't resist her. Dominated in a way that made her feel treasured, desired, and even loved. Could the blond sex god be that guy?

Take it easy. One fuck is not worth throwing away two hundred and fifty thousand dollars. No way, no how.

I had to remember what I really wanted. And the two things did not mesh.

As terrific-looking as he was, he was, after all, just a man. Nothing more.

And the Hope Diamond is just a sparkly rock. Yeah, right.

I groaned and kept my attention on the bar. Maybe he was more than just an average man, but it didn't matter.

I glanced around me, studiously keeping my gaze from going anywhere near him. Was there another spot in the room where I could get farther away? But Fang's wasn't very big. The place would have to be the size of a football stadium to be big enough not to notice him, not to keep my eyes on him. Unless I decided to leave, I'd just have to keep my head and not let him get to me.

I did my best to act as though nothing bothered me. To stay calm and focused on the goal. That was my motto. And yet, the more I tried to ignore him, the more I tried to resist him, the harder it was not to turn and look at him. He was a piece of delicious chocolate cake just waiting for me to eat it and my sweet tooth didn't want to say no.

Suddenly, the country song playing on a jukebox in the corner ground to a halt, catching everyone's attention. Something was about to happen and I was ready for it. Anything to get my mind off *him*.

Like every other girl in the room, I watched as a man appeared in the doorway of the hallway leading to the back of the bar. He was tall, taller than all the men standing near him. But was he as tall as the sexy blond guy? I couldn't help it. I had to check.

Nope. My guy was a few inches taller.

My guy?

I groaned and shifted in my seat again. Letting myself think stupid thoughts would screw up my game.

The man standing in the doorway was as tanned and muscled as the others, but there was something more about him. He was older and exuded an air of authority. His eyes, the same strange blue-silver, swept over us before he took hold of his handlebar mustache and gave it a short tug. Black hair, slicked away from his forehead, gave him a frame for his stern, almost-menacing face.

A woman with long, white hair followed him to the front of the long wooden bar, then turned to face us when he jumped on top of the counter. She had the same air of authority mixed with an easy confidence that came from years of giving orders and having them obeyed. The man took his time, looking from table to table, before finally stretching his arms out in what seemed like a welcoming gesture.

"Welcome, bitches, to The Claiming Games."

I heard exclamations from a few girls, but most of them remained silent. The men, however, clapped and cheered as though a football game had just started. I remained silent, concentrating on making my breathing as steady as possible.

Was this for real? Although the group didn't look as though it had enough money to splurge for a meal at a fast food restaurant, I knew better than to judge by appearances. The old lady who'd lived down the street from us had died, leaving over a million dollars to a charity for cats. Fucking cats. Most of us in the neighborhood had figured she was living on food stamps or eating canned dog food. My mom had even taken her part of our dinner every so often.

But shit. Fucking cats.

I couldn't help it. Once again, I looked at the blond god. Strangely, I wanted him to keep staring at me and yet I wanted him to stop. Most of all, I wanted him to touch me again. To take me as he'd taken me before. He had a primal air about him that had awakened my inner cave woman and I wanted nothing more than to have him take me by my hair and drag me into his cave.

He was all male, rough, tough and ready to do whatever the hell he wanted.

Who could blame me for staring? My interest was understandable. He was the kind of guy girls would scream and throw their underwear to. And I knew what he had between his legs. Did he want another go? But I couldn't do that. Not and keep my head in the game. My fingers were halfway through a tangle in my hair before I realized I was primping for him.

All at once, I was angry. What was with him anyway? Was he trying to get to me, to psych me out? Did he get a prize or reward or something if he fucked my mind as much as he'd already fucked my body? Why was he studying me like a bug under a microscope? I scowled at him, not caring if he thought I was a bitch or not.

Tossing him yet another glare, I turned back to face the man at the bar. He'd already begun talking about the challenge, which made me even angrier at myself for not paying attention.

Forget the hot blond guy. I was there for the money.

Logan

So far, no good.

From the expressions on most of the girls' faces, they knew we were checking them out. Although checking them out wasn't exactly the best way to put it. We were doing more than looking at their bodies and faces. Sure, we did that, too, but we also watched the way they walked into Fang's. Did the girl act like she was sure of herself? Or was she easily intimidated with only one hard stare? Did she have a lot of luggage with her? A girl hauling along a couple of suitcases, a purse, and maybe even one of those bags Roberta called a "makeup bag" was bound to be high maintenance. I doubted any man among us would go within ten feet of a woman like that.

I hadn't paid much attention to them as they'd filed inside. My heart just wasn't in it. From what I'd seen, these girls weren't anything special.

Woman. Girl. I wasn't sure which term fit. A few looked

like they knew the score. Way too many of them looked like they'd been around the block and had let too many men get between their legs. They were the ones wearing the tight shirts or shorty-shorts with their ass cheeks hanging out. I wanted a confident woman, but I didn't want one who'd open her legs to any male.

Thinking like that, of course, brought me back to the girl at the truck stop. It didn't matter that she'd opened her legs for me. I knew she wasn't like them. We'd shared more than a need for sex. Now that I'd had time to think about it, something more had been at work. I wished I'd gotten her name or, better yet, gotten Burke and Roberta to hand deliver my personal invitation to come to Fang's.

If only I had. But at the time, my brain had flat-lined from mind-blowing sex and was unable to realize what I was walking away from. She'd scrambled my brains, all right, and it had taken a good while before they'd gotten unscrambled.

Although I knew it wouldn't do any good, I did what was expected of me. I scanned the room, going from one table to the next. If a girl caught my eye, I studied her, giving her a hard, challenging stare. The way I figured it, if she had enough confidence to stare back, then she might have enough guts to make it through the games. But my heart really wasn't in it. Every time I saw dark hair like hers, I'd stop, excitement bursting through me, only to see the girl's face and be disappointed.

How the fuck did I leave her behind? But what choice had I had? Claiming a mate outside the games wasn't allowed. Still, she might've been worth taking the risk.

When I saw her, I froze.

She's here.

Suddenly, I couldn't hold back the grin. There she was. Like my wishes had suddenly come true. I'd been right to think there might be more between us than just a quick fuck. What I'd felt, the need I'd fought against to stay with her, had been real. She had to be the one for me.

Slow the hell down.

I needed to sniff her and draw in her aroma first. Then I'd know for sure if she was the one I wanted. Until then, it was just my cock doing the picking.

Cock, my ass. She's it. She's got to be.

Sniffing a girl's scent was how we'd know if we were compatible. If my inner lion didn't draw in her aroma and take it for his own, then we'd never have a chance. It wasn't love at first sight, but it was damn close. From the moment a man took in a woman's scent, he was committed to her. If she turned him down at the end of the challenge, he could take another's scent, but it was damn hard to find another woman he'd want. Possible, but damn hard.

My grin faded. Had I already messed up by fucking her? We weren't supposed to have actual intercourse before our mates made it to their destinations. Did it count if we'd screwed that rule to hell and back before the games had even started? Before we'd known we were breaking the rule? How could I have known she was coming to the games? I wasn't sure, but I wasn't about to ask anyone, either. As soon as I could, I'd tell her to keep quiet, too.

Had I already met my mate? Ruger would blow a fuse if he knew. After all his talk about checking the girls out sexually before the games, I was the one who might actually have done it.

Her appearance was rough, as though she'd had a tough

time getting to Fang's. Like she'd been on the road a few days. But so what? Didn't that mean she wanted it more than they did? Didn't that mean she could take whatever happened to her in the games?

For whatever reason, she must've cashed in the ticket and pocketed the money. It wasn't like it hadn't been done before.

She wore the same T-shirt and jeans with running shoes that she'd had on earlier. From the way she sat in the chair, she had enough self-esteem to know what she wanted without being an ass about it. Her raven black hair was tousled, giving her a just-fucked kind of appeal. My cock ached thinking about waking up to see her look like that, her hair all messed up, her eyes sleepy, but soon filled with yearning.

I groaned as my cock pushed against my zipper and I did a quick adjustment. I wanted to walk over to her right then and there and toss her on top of the table. If I could've, I would've torn her clothes off her and slammed my shaft as far and as hard as it'd go inside her pussy.

I tucked my chin and stared at the floor, waiting for my need to ease a little. Keeping my attention off her would help, but I couldn't do it. I had to look again.

She was lean and fit, exactly the way I liked a girl to look. I guessed she was a solid eight inches shorter than my six-foot-four-inch frame. Tall or short didn't matter. Her body was nicely proportioned with all the right curves. She didn't think much about how good-looking she was. Instead, I got the impression that what mattered to her came from the inside. She had an air of I-don't-give-a-fuck-what-you-think that I liked. Hers was the perfect attitude for a lioness.

I'd liked her from the start and I liked her even better now.

And then, finally, she saw me.

I started to grin again, then morphed it into a small smile. Just enough to show I remembered her, but not big enough to let her see how much I still wanted her. After all, I didn't want to give anything away. Not yet. But I was pleased when she met my gaze. And held it. And kept holding it.

Yeah. She's a lioness, all right.

My cock twitched again, growing harder just thinking about talking to her. If I thought about fucking her again, I'd have to go jerk off in the restroom.

She is so unbelievably hot.

About the time I'd decided to risk giving her a wink, she glanced away. At first, her looking away hurt like hell. Like she'd just taken my balls and squeezed as hard as she could. But I knew what she was doing. She was trying to psyche me out. Or trying to keep from getting turned on.

Yeah, baby. Go ahead. Try to ignore me. You couldn't do it before and you can't do it now.

She tried, but judging by the way she squirmed in her chair, she was failing and failing hard. By the time she couldn't resist any longer and had to look my way again, I was ready. I widened my smile. Not too much, but enough to make her fidget in her chair again.

I was having a good time rattling her. She acted like she wasn't bothered by me, but I knew when a female was getting hot between the legs and starting to burn. I watched and waited. She'd turn back to me soon enough.

And I was right again.

It threw her. Her eyes widened as they met mine.

I stayed as still as possible, like she was a deer and ready to bolt. But she wouldn't leave. I had no doubt she'd seen enough of me to want to see more. I sure as hell did. I let my focus drop down her body then back up. She sat up straighter, crossed her legs, then uncrossed them. Her hand went to her hair then stopped when she realized she was getting pretty for me.

I smiled a little bigger, just enough to encourage her to keep watching. But not too much.

Burke's appearance was the only thing that could've made her look away. He commanded a room and when he jumped onto the bar, there was no way she couldn't have watched.

I waited, knowing not even Burke would keep her distracted for long. And sure enough, I was right again.

This is fun.

Her hard stare hit me and if she could've knocked me upside the head, I had no doubt she would have. I irritated the shit out of her and it made me happy as hell that I did. My mate, whoever she was, had to have some spunk. If she couldn't take a little in-your-face taunting, she'd have no chance in the woods.

At last, she'd gotten so pissed off that she glared at me, searing me with yet another scowl. When she realized it didn't bug me, she jerked her head to stare at Burke again. As if she wasn't thinking about me so hard her brain was about to melt down.

But she was strong. Strong enough to finally stop checking me out. I chuckled, although I was disappointed when she locked onto Burke and started listening.

Burke Ryder, the leader of our pride, had just finished introducing himself and welcoming the girls to the games. He was a flamboyant kind of guy and he liked having all the girls' attention. He also tended to talk too much and drag things out.

I was more than ready to get closer and give her a good, long sniff.

"Damn, what's he want? A fucking crown?"

I didn't bother telling Ruger to keep his trap shut. It wouldn't have done any good. Burke droned on, telling them what a pride was. I sighed and wished he'd just get on with it.

"What does he think he is? A wolf?"

Fuck.

Although she'd spoken in barely more than a whisper, it was loud enough for every shifter in the place to hear it. I bit back a groan when Burke tilted his head and stared her down.

"Aw, sweet thang. You got a problem with wolves? I don't blame you none, but let's get this straight. We aren't a bunch of mangy mutts."

Shut up. Don't say anything else.

"No. I mean—"

Damn it. Shut the hell up.

Burke's expression went darker. He didn't like being questioned. Not by us and definitely not by one of the girls. They hadn't earned his respect.

Burke kept at her, telling her how we were a family and how we always stuck together. As usual, he got dramatic when he told her "we'll go down fighting until the very last one of us is dead." He was right, but couldn't he have said it a different way? A less macho, in-your-face kind of way?

My inner lion came to the surface, ready to defend her, as he continued to hound her. "Is that all right with you, sweet thang? Or do I need to stop and answer more of your questions first?"

She'd squirmed in her seat, but with Burke coming at her, she got really nervous. I wanted to grab Burke by the neck and slam him against the wall when she slumped lower in her chair, cowed by his attack. My lion roared, demanding I take action. I bristled, the fangs pushing to get out. The guys standing near me sensed my struggle to keep my lion contained. They were always up to watch a fight and would love it if I turned my beast lose. A fight between Burke and one of us? That was prime time entertainment.

I shoved my beast back down, for her sake as much as for mine. I wasn't stronger than Burke. To start a fight with him was just asking for a beat-down. He was older and wiser, too. Besides, he tended to fight dirty. I had to admire and respect him for all those reasons.

She looked at me as though for reassurance, then glanced away before I could send her a comforting smile. The whole thing made me regret how I'd teased her before. Still, if she was going to become one of us, she needed to be able to handle our alphas, Burke and his mate, Roberta. And I needed to keep my cool and let her do it.

Burke went on as he took a mug of beer and downed most of it. After going over how he'd started The Claiming Games over twenty years ago, he continued on until Roberta finally chimed in and told him to get to it. Everyone in the pride knew she could only push him so far before he'd put her in her place, but she knew just how far and how hard to do it.

At last he told the girls about choosing to stay or to go. He hadn't told them everything. If he had, the place would've emptied out fast. But he'd told them enough for them to make their choice. Risk doing the games and survive, and claim a prize. The man or the money.

Burke jumped off the counter then sauntered among the tables. I was more than ready when he finally announced the next step.

"Men, you're up. Stake your claim."

I was halfway to her table when Ruger grabbed my shoulder. "If you're thinking about going after the one with black hair, then think again."

I knew who he was talking about, but I had to make sure. "Which one? Her?" I jerked my chin toward a girl with dark hair at a nearby table. "Go ahead. She's yours."

Sometimes I hated it when Ruger did his crappy chuckle. Like he was so damn sure of himself. I'd never met anyone who had the right to be that cocky. "Naw, man. You know the one I'm talking about. The one who thought we're a wolf pack."

Shit. I took his hand and yanked it off my shoulder. "Too bad. She's already claimed."

"Really? I don't see any bite marks on her. Or did you bite her where the sun don't shine?"

He was right. She wasn't claimed until she'd been bitten and changed. But he knew what I meant. I shoved him back and strode toward her. If one of the girls at a different table hadn't snagged my hand, I would've made it to her first. Instead, I had to stand there, half listening to the girl rattle on about what she wanted to give me, and watch Ruger slide over to the girl from the truck stop.

What was he doing? He didn't give a shit about the games. He'd said often enough that he didn't want a mate. He wanted to fuck every pussy he could, but if he got mated, his fun was all over. Lions didn't cheat on their mates. I couldn't remember any male ever doing so. Once a male got his female's scent embedded in him that was it. He wouldn't want anyone else.

So why was Ruger going after the same girl I was? He could take her scent, too, but it wasn't likely. The thought of possibly sharing a mate with him made me want to hurl.

As I had several times in the past few months, I wondered if he was trying to get back at me. To exact revenge. Maybe it was stupid not to have done so before, but I hadn't asked him directly if he blamed me for Vic's death. I guess I hadn't really wanted to know.

"Are you listening to me?"

The girl who'd taken my hand seemed put out. As if I cared. Irritation whipped through me, bringing out the tips of my fangs. Her eyes widened as I met her gaze. "No. I'm not."

She turned me loose fast, like she'd grabbed hold of a hot poker. "Oh."

I didn't have time to wonder if she'd seen. If she had, I'd fucked up and I'd hear about it soon enough. She'd probably talk herself into thinking she hadn't really seen anything at all. At least, I hoped she would. But I didn't have time to worry about her. I needed to stake my claim as fast as I could.

"Damn, girl, you smell good. What's your name, sugar?" Ruger leered over my girl and drew in a long, slow breath with his face inches from the side of her head.

Before he'd finished sniffing her, before she could answer him, I took hold of his hair and jerked him back. "Damn it, Ruger."

"Fuck, man. Back off before I kick your ass."

It was a challenge, but Ruger didn't back it up. Instead of coming back at me, he only growled, low enough for me to hear him, but not any of the women.

She'd leaned as far back as she could, her hands held up in front of her in fists as though she was ready to throw down with the huge man. I liked her spunk. If my mate needed to fight, I wanted to be sure she had it in her to do exactly that. *After* I changed her. If she tried before she became one of us, she'd have no chance in hell of surviving.

"Both of you hold up." Her green eyes flashed, giving me yet another reason to want her.

"Shut up, bitch." Ruger added a low snarl to emphasize his order.

I almost laughed at her surprise. She recovered fast, though, making me think she'd been told to shut up by someone else and hadn't liked it much then, either.

"Back off, Ruger." I didn't shove him this time. Instead, I flattened my hand on his chest and eased him away, hoping to avoid a real fight. If he decided to go at me, I'd have to defend myself. And once the adrenaline got pumping, we might shift without even thinking. Not only would shifting show the girls what we were and send them running in panic, it was against the rules of the games. Only after they chose us over the money could we tell them about our inner beasts. If they made it through the games and took the money instead, they'd never find out what we were.

The slight pressure I put on his chest dared him again to back up his words with his fangs. "Don't go scaring her."

Ruger snarled at me, his nostrils flaring and his eyes growing more silver. His inner lion was close to the surface, but he held it back. Its power wafted off him, flowing over me, giving my lion another reason to scratch its way toward freedom. I tipped my head toward Burke, who stood nearby, his piercing stare waiting to see just how far we'd take it. If we shifted in front of the girls, we could call it quits with the Kings of Beasts MC.

At least Ruger was smart enough to catch my subtle warning. If she'd noticed, she didn't let on.

She dropped her fists. "I'm not scared. Just annoyed as hell. I don't know who you think you are, Ruger—"

I chuckled, loving the way she'd made his name sound like

scum on the bottom of the lake.

"—but don't get in my face again. Got it?"

Ruger and I turned toward her. I'd bet he was thinking the same thing I was.

Good. She's a fighter.

Except we thought of her being a fighter in different ways. I wanted a strong mate, a fighter who'd help get us through tough times. Ruger had always liked a girl who fought back during sex. He liked it rough, with some BDSM thrown in, but sometimes he took it too far in dominating a girl. Anticipation was his game. Tying the girl up and playing with her before finally fucking her turned him on. Sometimes I thought he liked tormenting the girl more than he liked fucking her. The thing was, he didn't care if it was consensual or not. Hell, he liked it when they said no.

"Sugar, we're the Kings of Beasts. I'm Ruger Hogdon and this asshole is Logan Kessler. Don't go telling us what we can and can't do."

So suddenly we were on the same side? I ached to slam my fist in his fucking face, but I stayed silent and kept my hands down. I could sense Burke's eyes boring a hole in my back.

She glared at him, but she was smart enough, intuitive enough not to say anything. Whether she'd obey any orders more than that was still up in the air. If I was a betting man, I'd put a wad of cold hard cash on her not obeying either one of us.

Ignoring her warning to stay out of her face, I pushed Ruger aside, then put my hands on the back of her chair, capturing her between my arms. Daring her, I put my nose a couple of inches from hers. Her green eyes held intriguing bits of gold and I wondered what she'd think when her eye color changed from green-gold to blue-silver. Would she like the change? Not that she'd have a say either way. All the pride's eyes were the same color and would change to a bright silver color when their lion rose to the surface.

"What's your name?" I made sure I'd asked in a different tone than Ruger had. Hopefully, she'd catch my unspoken message to pretend we hadn't already met. Fact was, we didn't know each other and that's how we'd have to play it.

She shot me an unmistakable look of *"Oh, so now you want to know my name?"* and deepened her scowl. Thankfully, she followed my lead and answered the way I'd hoped she would. "Mia Travers."

"I'm going to sniff you, Mia Travers."

Those beautiful eyes widened. "You're going to do what?"

"I'm going to sniff you." She began to say more, but I didn't wait to hear any protest. "Quiet."

Unlike Ruger's blunt order, mine was softer, a whisper that held as much power as his growled command had. She didn't like me telling her to be quiet, but she didn't argue, either. She relaxed her hands enough to grip the arms of her chair as I tilted my head, closed my eyes, and drew in her scent.

The spicy fragrance I'd gotten when she'd had her legs wrapped around mine tickled the inside of my nose. I relished it, just taking regular breaths, and savoring the smell. The scent alone took me back to behind the diner. I had to use all my determination to keep from pulling her legs around me and fucking her again.

"I don't—"

"Shh." I put my finger on her lips and got a shock of sexual recognition. If she'd tried to deny it, I still would've known. She wanted my cock inside her as much as I wanted to feel her pussy around me.

Then I did it. Closing my eyes, I took in a long, slow breath, letting it glide into my nostrils then down and down until it made its way throughout my body.

Although her fragrance was amazing, it was still like any other woman's at first. Filled with a sweet aroma. Then, slowly, it changed, drawing from her pheromones and rising to the top of the layers of scents. She was spicy, sassy, with an underlying of... *something*... I couldn't pinpoint. Maybe I'd figure out what it was later and maybe I wouldn't. It didn't matter. All I needed to know right then was that she was the one for me.

Hell, yeah.

Just to make sure and just because I wanted to, I let out a sigh, then dragged in another long, slow breath.

Yeah. She's perfect.

"Back off, Logan."

I ignored Ruger and took in yet another long sniff.

Her mouth parted just enough for me to catch a whiff of her breath. I smiled and kept my face close to hers. "Let him sniff you, Mia. It'll get him to calm down. But don't worry. It won't matter either way. You're mine."

I had to believe that. Had to believe he wouldn't catch her scent the way I'd done.

Straightening up, I gave Ruger a look telling him to go ahead and do his best. He frowned, catching my confident attitude, my way of telling him I'd already drawn in her scent. He mimicked my hands on the chair and got even closer than I had.

As usual, he was determined to get his way.

I couldn't deny my satisfaction when she leaned even farther away from him. She hadn't leaned away from me at all. If Ruger had any sense in his head, he would've noticed it and moved on to another girl.

But that was the way it had always been. Although Ruger and I had grown up together, had always been at each other's sides, we'd had our tough times, too. He never would've admitted it, but I'd always had the feeling that he was jealous of me. I had two parents, both still alive, while he and his brother had been orphaned at the age of eight when his parents had died in a flash flood. My parents had taken him and his younger brother Vic into our home and raised them like they were their own sons. It wasn't uncommon in our world. We were a pride and the pride looked after its own.

Even when I'd started acting more like Ruger and Vic, getting into trouble as a teen, my parents had stuck by all three of us, loving and punishing us as equals. My younger sister Kyla had, at one time, thought of Ruger and Vic as her brothers. Still, there'd always been something off between Ruger and me, and I'd grown closer to Vic. Ruger was a part of my family, but he'd never stopped wanting whatever I had. He didn't care if he didn't want it. He'd try and take it from me, then lord it over me, taunting me. I hadn't understood it then, and I still didn't.

Then Vic had gotten shot and the gap between Ruger and me had grown even larger. Too large.

Ten minutes earlier it would've turned my stomach to see Ruger getting close to her. Now that I'd already sniffed her, it was worse, sucking big time. My chest tightened as he put his nose next to her hair, even pressing it against the silky strands. Not wanting to scare her, I hadn't gotten that close. I'd heard it was better to take it easy with the girls. Why spook them when it wasn't necessary?

I doubted she would've minded. The memory of her face, filled with desire as I plunged into her, made me feel a little better. No, she wouldn't have minded at all.

Ruger being Ruger made a huge show of getting a good whiff. If the other girls at her table hadn't been involved with the men around them, they probably would've gawked at him. Why was he such a fucking showoff anyway? I gritted my teeth to hold back my fangs. If he didn't stop soon, I'd have to do something. Pull him back. Rip off his nose. Tear his head off. Something.

At last she couldn't take any more. She pushed him back, then gave him a hard look that would've made any human man think twice. But we weren't just any men. We were the Kings of Beasts.

When Ruger faced me, I knew we were in for it. He'd sniffed her, but her scent hadn't meant anything. I didn't see the same look of recognition and pride in his eyes whenever a male found a woman who could be his mate. But, fuck it all, I knew in my gut he was going to lie about it.

Taking hold of my arm, he dragged me toward the sidelines. "She's mine."

I shouldn't have laughed. Ruger hated anyone laughing at him. But it was ridiculous. I'd sniffed her, drawing in her breath and letting it soak into me until my lion had taken hold of it. "Look, I know you're only lusting after her because she's mine, but this isn't the time to play your damn games. I took her scent in and you didn't. You have to let it go."

He was earnest. A little too earnest, just confirming what I'd already guessed.

"I'm telling you, she's mine."

Was I wrong? Had he really gotten the same reaction I had? I'd heard of more than one man wanting a girl at the games, but it was rare. I'd never considered sharing my mate and I wasn't about to start now. Just as the older pride members had always told us, I'd drawn in her scent and known she was the one for me.

"You're wrong, Ruger. I already told you. I took in her scent."

"I'm telling you the same thing, man."

Was it possible? He had me doubting my instincts. "No you didn't. No way. I'm not sharing my woman."

He got in my face, pressing the issue along with what remained of our friendship. "Back off, man. Just do it."

"Sorry. Not happening." My lion roared, ready to spring into action. If I had to, I'd drag him out back and tear into him.

His eyes flashed silver. His lion sensed mine. Both animals were determined to take over and deal with the conflict in the lion way.

"Let her go."

Even if he'd really taken in her scent, why would I let her go? No male would do that. At least, not without a fight. I had just as much right to her as he did. Yet I knew fighting him wouldn't solve anything. He was too stubborn to give in. "What about Sally?"

Sally was a human girl Ruger had dated for the past six months. She lived in the small town of Cripple Creek just down the road from Fang's. She knew what we were and was eager to join us. Almost all the residents knew about the pride. Hell, half of the pride members had homes in and around the town. Even though we kept to ourselves and only shifted to run when it was safe to change into our lion bodies, the citizens of Cripple Creek had found out. Fortunately for both them and us, they were willing to keep our secret. Maybe willing wasn't the right word. They had to keep our secret or else.

"Come on. You know that little town whore means nothing to me. I'm just having fun with the little bitch."

I did and I'd never liked the idea. Having sex with a willing human female was one thing. But everyone knew Ruger had let her talk about joining us. Had even encouraged her. He'd led her on because it was easier than telling her the truth. He'd always planned to choose his mate from the games like most of us did. If and when Burke and the others forced him to. I'd suggested to Burke that Sally be brought into the games, but he'd refused, saying she didn't fit the requirements. The only so-called requirement she didn't fit was that she had family. The girls selected for the games had little to no family, or came from homes where no one cared if they went missing. Or they were too poor to get any attention from the authorities.

"Whatever. Sally's your problem. But don't play around with this girl. The games are too important."

"I'm not, man. She's my mate." He started toward Burke, ready to tell him how he'd found his mate.

Fuckin' A.

I took another look at Mia, not questioning my decision, but needing to get a hint of what she was thinking. She met my gaze dead on and didn't flinch. A human girl didn't take in a lion's scent, but most of them had a quick instinctive, primal feeling toward the man who was her future mate. I couldn't believe she'd gotten a gut reaction to both of us. Not the way she'd reacted to Ruger. Girls thought he was handsome, but attraction wasn't the same thing.

Tilting my head toward Ruger, I lifted my eyebrows and sent her a silent question.

Him or me?

She glanced at Ruger, then frowned and slowly, almost

imperceptibly, shook her head.

Relieved, I nodded, then made my way toward our pride's leader.

Mia

What the hell just happened?

I kept my eye on the blond hunk of masculinity as he headed for Burke. Ruger made it to Burke first and was already whispering to him. Logan got on his other side.

Damn it. Say something. Do something.

I wasn't sure what I wanted to happen. I didn't even know for certain what was going on. But I didn't like that Ruger guy and I wanted nothing to do with him.

Still, what did it matter? It wasn't like I was there for even one man, much less two. So what did I care if they'd both sniffed me? And why the sniffing thing anyway? It was downright freaky.

Freaky awful with Ruger. But freaky awesome with Logan.

Logan getting so close to me had sent me into automatic turn-on mode. I could still remember how his cock felt inside me and I wanted more. So much more. I wanted a long, slow time together so I could relish sliding my tongue over every part of his hard body. So I could get a better look at what I'd had so fast and furious. So I could ask him why he hadn't told me his name or wanted to know mine.

I was still pissed at him, but my irritation wasn't as strong as my craving. And, man, I craved him like crazy. From the second I'd seen him standing against the wall, I'd realized just how much I'd thought about him. Until that moment, the slow burn he'd left me with had been just that. A slow, but very intense burn. Now it was an out-and-out forest fire burning me up from the inside. A fire only he could extinguish.

Just because I was here for the challenge didn't mean I couldn't have a little fun, did it?

Then there was the other guy. Ruger with his short dark hair and an abrupt manner had caught me off guard. My head still swirled with unanswered questions. In his case, not pleasant ones.

Would I say yes and do the games? Of course. Why else had I come? Whether Ruger or Logan wanted me wasn't part of it. They could say whatever they wanted to Burke. In the end, I'd take the money, wave them a good-bye, then be on my way to my Aunt Brenda's in Jackson, Mississippi. Knowing my mom, she'd do her best to get to Aunt Brenda's. Hopefully, someone at the shelter would help them.

Okay, maybe I'd give Logan more of a good-bye than just a wave.

After forcing my mind back where it should be, I'd listened to Burke explaining how things were going to go. He didn't give us a lot of information and neither did Roberta when she stepped in to answer one of the other girl's questions. After Burke heard my sarcastic question about his being a wolf—*how the hell did he hear my whisper, anyway?*—I'd settled down, keeping my mouth shut until I heard more.

He congratulated us for coming, although saying we were either brave or "just plain stupid" hadn't set well with some of us, including me. Did I want to be one of the "chosen" girls, as he'd put it? If the way Ruger and Logan had acted was any indication, I'd already made the cut. I guessed it was just part of the games. A man had to choose you or you were automatically out. So okay. Let them choose me. I was the one who'd make the final call and take the money.

A pseudo history lesson came next where Burke gave himself credit for starting the games. Yet even as he continued to talk, he wasn't saying much. Maybe I should've done more research before coming, but getting out of my home as fast I'd done had left little time or means to search for info on The Claiming Games. Besides, I'd had a gut feeling I wouldn't have found out much, anyway.

Then when Burke had told the men to "stake their claim," he'd pitched me a curve ball. I still hadn't recovered by the time Ruger and Logan were in front of me sniffing away.

Sniffing me. I couldn't get over it. What kind of weird shit was that?

And yet, once Logan had put his nose close to me and had inhaled not once, but three times, I'd been so turned on, so wet between the legs I'd had to fight to keep from grabbing his shirt and pulling his mouth to mine.

I was still reeling when Ruger had put his nose way too close to me. Instead of getting hot and bothered in an oh-so-good way, I'd gotten chilled and irritated. The two men were as different as their coloring. Ruger was dark and foreboding. His laugh was anything but humorous and I couldn't shake the feeling that he was like my father. A man who wanted everything his way and wouldn't take no for an answer. He'd expect prompt obedience even when what he wanted didn't make any sense. Like getting sniffed.

Or worse.

Logan, however, was the flip side of the coin. He was powerfully built like Ruger, like all the other men, but his confidence and masculinity came from an inner source of power. Just like Ruger's, his arms bulged with muscles and rippled with power. Both of them dressed alike, but I was drawn to Logan with his blond hair and sparkling eyes. He was taller than Ruger. Taller than most of the other men. Not that I'd taken time to study the rest of them. Once I'd laid eyes on Logan, I hadn't bothered to check out anyone else.

And when he'd leaned over me, then put his mouth close to my ear? Damn if I hadn't felt like I'd been hit by lightning. The deep, rich voice I would've expected from a much older man flowed over me like melted chocolate over vanilla ice cream. It seeped into me, spreading its intoxicating sensuality throughout every inch of my body. He could've made millions with his voice doing commercials. Women would've lined up to hear him talk. It wouldn't matter what he said, just as long as they could listen.

His body was incredible, but not even his physique could match the animal-like energy pouring out of him. He was like raw sex personified, every woman's wet dream standing right in front of me and dragging in a long smell.

He was so fucking hot I even forgot to worry about my own personal hygiene. I'd tried to stay clean on the trip, but was I clean enough for someone to sniff me? Especially someone like him? But it was too late to do anything about it now.

And his eyes. Blue-silver eyes like one of those dogs that pull sleds in Alaska. I'd never seen anyone with similar eye color, and yet both Ruger and Logan had the same strange eyes. Were they related? And they weren't the only ones, either. Were the Kings of Beasts one big family? I didn't think so, but then what else could explain it?

I glanced at Ruger, then back to Logan. Other than the eye color thing and their amazing bodies, I didn't see any similarity between them.

I'd never gotten turned on by a handsome face and a great body. Both were good to have, but if I wanted a guy long term, he'd have to have more than that. After all, looks fade, but smarts stay.

Logan had both looks and intelligence, but it was something more that attracted me to him. He possessed an underlying quality few men possessed. The other men in the room had the same kind of dominating air about them as though they knew they were the best in the world and no one and nothing could change their minds. But Logan had gotten more than his share of the indefinable quality. I studied him as he let Ruger talk to Burke. He pushed his hair behind his ears, his muscles moving like well-oiled machinery with the simple move. On most other men the tousled mass of blond might've seemed effeminate. But not on Logan. Nothing about him could ever be thought of as girly. Not a damn thing.

I let out a breath I hadn't realized I was holding. Yet when Burke finally turned to Logan and he looked up from checking the notepad Burke was holding, I almost forgot to breathe again. What would he say? Would he tell Burke he wanted me? Or was he giving me up to Ruger?

It doesn't matter.

At least that's what I told myself. Now if only I could believe it.

He said something to Burke. Burke's smile didn't make me feel any better, but as long as Logan was there, I felt safe.

Feeling safe was an odd thing for me. If it wasn't my father terrifying me, it was getting stuck in a place and feeling trapped.

Which reminded me of how I'd felt earlier. Had I really forgotten for a while? I tore my gaze back to the walls. Had they gotten closer?

Hang in there. It can't be much longer.

But they're moving closer.

It's getting harder to breathe.

I stopped letting the awful thoughts take over and focused on my breathing. And on trying to realize that I was okay. I was still unnerved, but not freaking out like I could have. Like I normally would have. Was it because Logan was close by?

Stupid. He has nothing to do with it.

Still it was weird. Every time I looked his way, I felt less anxious.

Erin and her friends talked about the men who'd come by them, but I didn't pay enough attention to remember what they'd said a moment later. By the time Burke held up the pad, I was sitting on the edge of my chair, dying to know what had gone on between Logan and Burke. I was more than eager to get out of the bar and back into the parking lot. Would they disqualify me if I stepped out to calm down and "get some fresh air"? No way would I tell them why I really wanted outside.

"Quiet." Burke waved the notepad in the air. "Okay, bitches, listen up."

Oh, I was listening all right. My body tingled with the knowledge that finally my life was about to begin.

"If I call your name, you leave. No bitching. Roberta will meet you outside where she'll give you enough money to purchase your return trip home. Ask no questions before getting into one of the cabs. And remember this"—he gave us a hard, hard look—"do not speak of this to anyone. Not once you leave." His blue-silver eyes narrowed. "Not ever."

Why not? Yet as soon as the question flitted through my mind, I came up with a good reason. If anyone and everyone could do The Claiming Games, the little town of Cripple Creek, not to mention Fang's Bar and Grill, would be overrun with women seeking true love. Or, like me, cold hard cash. Sometimes the best things in life had to be kept quiet.

"Aren't you going to tell us what this means or how this works? What is K.O.B. Corporation? You've told us basically next to nothing. What happens during The Claiming Games? Are we chased and locked up? Claimed by these men? Is that the claiming part of it?"

Unlike everyone else, I didn't bother shifting my attention to the girl who'd asked the questions. Instead, I was too focused on Logan to care about anyone else. How could any man seem so laid back and yet give the impression that he was coiled and ready to spring into action? He reminded me of a tiger I'd seen at the zoo. Primitive power contained in muscle and fur, ready to reach out and tear out my heart. I'd watched for a solid hour as the tiger paced back and forth, beautiful and magnificent even while trapped in a cage. I could sense how he felt, locked up in such a small space. If I could have, I would've set him free.

Nothing so amazing should ever be confined. I zoned out, imagining Logan pacing back and forth in a cage. Then, all at once, he broke through the bars and landed on top of me. He pinned me down, his handsome face over mine. And then he started changing, his face growing wider while his jaw and nose jutted forward. Golden fur spread over his skin. His mouth opened, exposing large, dangerous-looking fangs.

I jolted, aware that some of the girls were staring at me. Had I said something out loud? I checked Burke, ready to see him coming at me, and was relieved to see that he wasn't paying any attention to me.

"For those of you who aren't called, remain where you are. And keep your mouths shut."

What had Burke said? I was sure I'd missed a lot of info I'd need later on, but I sure as hell wouldn't ask Burke to repeat himself. Why was I having such a hard time holding it together? The answer was clear enough.

Logan had me spellbound.

Another girl dared to ask questions, but it was Roberta who hurried through the crowded tables and grabbed the girl. I turned to watch, then felt the urge, like a compulsion to turn back to Logan as Roberta tore into the girl. She spoke of real men, the men of our dreams, and whether or not we were brave enough to find them.

Was I brave enough? I guess I'd soon find out. My mother had told me to choose whichever one I wanted. The money or the man. To do that, I'd have to be brave.

"A hot man is a lot better to hold on to than a cold dollar," warned Roberta.

I had to agree, but in my case, I wasn't the only one who needed the dollar. Even if I wanted Logan instead of the money, my family was depending on me. Roberta's voice faded to a background noise as, yet again, I couldn't focus on anything but Logan.

Once I came out of my zoned-out state and realized I was missing valuable information, I turned back to Roberta. Who knew what else I'd missed? I was frustrated and angry at myself. It wasn't like me to get distracted. No matter what, I always did my best to keep a clear head. At least most of the time.

My gaze skipped to the walls again. Anxiety clutched at my heard and squeezed.

Keep it together. They're not moving. They can't.

Breathing grew harder. I glanced up to the ceiling. Was it closer, too? I closed my mind and stayed in control. One look at Logan helped push away the fear.

Listen to Roberta. Concentrate on what she's saying.

"How many of you can say you've had a man like that?" asked Roberta.

The vise around my heart eased a little and I dragged in a good, long breath. My attention stayed on Logan. What had she said? A man like what? Virile, strong, and sexy as hell? If those were how she'd described the man of our dreams, then I was staring right at him.

The buzz of people talking around me came in and out of my consciousness. Even Nina dared to ask a question, but none of it concerned me. All I wanted was to get on with the games and get the hell out of the bar. Everything else was unimportant.

All at once, the tension in the room doubled. Either I hadn't heard or I'd already forgotten. If I heard my name, did I stay or go?

"Listen up," shouted Burke. "The following bitches need to get the hell out." He glanced down at his notepad. "Lilly Mathews."

The first girl called wasn't happy to hear her name. I guessed that not having my name called meant I was in the games. The games that would lead to winning the money.

Or Logan?

What choice did I have? As much as I would've liked to get all romantic and choose him, I'd take the money and run.

Lilly was beautiful and obviously not used to being turned down. But her complaining didn't help. She was sent out the front door with a firm "get out" from Roberta.

More names were called. Some of the girls left, obviously relieved, while some grumbled, bitching every step of the way out the door.

I darted my gaze away from Logan for a moment to see if Erin, Nina, and Maddy were still there. Pleased that they were, I came back to see Logan, a slight, yet smug smile on his face.

Maybe I was stupid for staying. Especially when I'd missed most of what Burke had said. But without any real option left, I'd have to stick it out. I smiled back at Logan. And if I got to spend a little time with him, then why not go for it?

Glimpsing him from the corner of my eye, I saw Burke lower the notepad. The excitement coursing through me whipped into a frenzy.

"Congratulations, bitches. You've been chosen."

Chapter Four

Logan

The choosing hadn't gone exactly the way I'd hoped. Although I'd wanted to beat the shit out of Ruger many times in the past, I couldn't remember being this angry at him. I went back to the same wall while Ruger moved to the other side of the room. To my relief, Mia kept her attention on me and didn't look at my so-called friend.

The real question was whether or not she'd still be interested once she found out what she'd have to go through in the games. I was already looking forward to the moment when I could rid her of her clothes and enjoy having her body next to mine again. Not just for a few minutes with her clothes shoved out of the way, but for a long, slow night with both of us naked, our bodies pressed together in sweaty sex. I'd take her time and again until she could barely stand the next morning. If I had it my way, I'd wake up with her scent in my nostrils and her juices still on my lips and cock.

Her scent had been layered with some unappealing smells, but if she'd had a rough time getting to Fang's then I wouldn't criticize her. If nothing else, it showed she was the type of girl who could get down and dirty.

Burke was ready to lay it out for the girls. "Listen up. Here's how it's going to go down. One or more of the men have decided that you're the woman they want. You should consider yourself lucky."

He made his way to the center of the room. If nothing else, Burke had a way of putting on a show, getting and keeping everyone's attention. Every one of the girls waited for what he'd say next. Everyone except Mia.

She needed to pay attention to Burke. Otherwise, she'd be going into the games not knowing what she'd be in for. And yet, I couldn't help but feel pretty damn good when she couldn't keep her eyes off me.

And it didn't hurt that Ruger noticed the same thing.

"It's up to you to decide to continue."

I cringed when he flung his arms outward to point us out to the girls.

"These guys aren't ordinary men. They're not the weak-willed, soft-handed college boys you're used to screwing." He chuckled. "Naw, bitches, these men are more than just human. They're fucking animals."

Funny, Burke. If they knew we really were animals, how many of them would stay? Would Mia?

Mia Travers.

I liked the name almost as much as I liked the independent streak shown in the thrust of her chin and the straightening of her shoulders. And yet, every once in a while, I'd see fear on her face as she glanced around at the men. Did she expect them to jump on her? And why did she keep looking at the ceiling?

Burke continued, letting them know what K.O.B. stood for. As the Kings of Beasts MC, we were proud of everything we were and considered ourselves not only brothers in a club, but a true family.

I studied Mia's expectant face as the Kings of Beasts alpha

told them that, if they made it through the games, they'd have the honor of becoming one of us. Or the girl could choose the money instead.

Would Mia choose money over me?

Almost as though she'd heard me, she glanced at me, then looked away, and I knew.

Shit. She's going to pick the money.

My skin prickled as I picked up the sensation of being watched. Ruger grinned at me from the other side of the room. He'd noticed, too.

Fucking asshole.

It wasn't often that a girl had more than one man vying for her in the games. Most of us didn't like the idea of sharing. But Burke hadn't told Ruger or me if one or both of us could claim her.

If he let Ruger have her... But I couldn't believe he would. Letting Ruger co-mate with Mia wasn't going to happen. The thought made my stomach churn. No way could I handle seeing him touch her.

I hated the way I was thinking. He was, after all, my friend, my pride mate, and my pseudo-brother. But loving someone and liking him are often different things. I'd always love him as the adopted brother I'd grown up with, but as the man he'd become? It sucked, but that was a lot harder.

Nacho, nicknamed after his favorite food, nudged me. "You find your girl?"

I wasn't sure I wanted to admit it. Yet the pride would know soon enough. "Yeah."

"Hey, cool. Which one?"

I tucked my head toward Mia. "The one with the black hair."

"No shit? She's hot."

"Thanks." As if I'd had anything to do with her looks.

"You?"

"Naw. I got a good sniff at a lot of them, but I just didn't catch a scent I liked."

"Sorry. Maybe next year."

"Yeah. Maybe."

Nacho was getting older, though. Most of us found our mates during the games and didn't have to worry about it. However, a few men, having reached the age of thirty and their last chance at the games, would claim any girl. It was better than living a life without a woman. Rarely, a man could choose to leave the pride and go out on his own to find a mate, but he was never allowed to return to the mountains.

Nacho drifted away. I didn't like it much when Ruger sidled up next to me. "Okay, man. Burke's on the last part. As soon as he puts that mouthy girl in her place, we're outta here. So what's it going to be, man?"

The last thing I wanted to do was argue with Ruger. But I knew him well enough to know he wasn't about to lay off. "She'll choose me. I took in her scent." I confronted him, letting my lion come to the surface enough for him to know I meant business. "And you didn't."

He frowned, not getting the answer he'd wanted. "If you don't want to share her, then why not give her to me? Back out now while you still have your dignity. Or take one of the others."

"Fuck off."

Damn, how I hated his cocky chuckle.

Our inner lions would've liked to have a pride full of females for their own, but our human sides fought against it. As men, we knew the value of sticking together instead of breaking off and forming separate prides. Unlike our African lion ancestors, we could share. If we wanted to. The thing was, I didn't. Especially not with Ruger.

I had a feeling he'd push me into a fight whether I wanted it or not. Part of me, the human side of me, didn't want a fight. As a human, I'd try and reason with him even when I knew it was hopeless. The other side of me wanted nothing more than to rip my claws across his tender belly and open him up. My lion growled inside me, urging me to give in to its need to protect its female.

Several of the men nearby caught the tension between us and started easing closer. A good fight was always fun. Just the thought of digging my claws into Ruger gave me a quick flash of excitement, but I shoved my lion back down, refusing to give in to its demands.

"I'm telling you, Ruger. Back the fuck off." I strode away from him, hoping he'd take the hint. He didn't, staying right on my heels. I kept my gaze on Mia, but, at last, she was putting all her attention on Burke.

"Come on, man. She's not going to pick you. Not over me."

Ruger was an arrogant jerk, an asshole. "Don't push me on this. I took in her scent." I kept repeating it. Not that it would do any good. Once Ruger got his mind set on something, he'd chomp down and hold on as hard as he could. I turned, catching him off guard. "I swear, Ruger. If you fuck this up, I won't hold back. Now get away from me."

He got in my face, threatening me. "You wanna make me?"

I could've told him he sounded like a high school bully, but again, I tried to keep the peace. "We don't have time for this. They'll be going outside any minute now."

Burke was telling the girls the men would meet them in the parking lot, but I couldn't stay next to Ruger a second longer. I'd wait for Mia outside. Fighting back the bloodlust of my lion, I strode out of Fang's and into the sunlight.

I wasn't sure what would happen once we were told to go to our mates. If Ruger started toward Mia, then I'd have to take a stand.

Mia

"The man, or men, who have chosen you will meet you outside and tell you what to do next. Your body, your mind and your guts are going to be tested. He'll tell you where to go, but wherever it is, you'd damn sure better get there before nightfall. If you don't, you're out."

No. I wouldn't be out. I didn't want to put any of the other girls down, but if anyone could make it, it was me.

It'd been hard to do when Logan was still around, but he'd already gone outside. At least now I could pay close attention to what Burke was telling us. From the sound of it, I hadn't missed much while I was drooling over Logan. At least I hoped not.

"Once you're there, you'll have two nights to survive on your own. Your man might show up and he might not. It's up to him. But he can't leave you supplies, water or food, or you're out. Got it?"

So it was a kind of survival game. Which was fine with me. I'd survived a lot worse. My gaze slipped to the walls again. With Logan outside, the tension set up shop in my neck, tightening my fear.

Hurry up. I need to get out of here.

"It won't be easy. If you're weak, if you can't handle yourself, you're fucked. There will be obstacles along the way, from traps to animals. It'll be up to you to overcome them."

Animals? What kinds of animals? We had snakes and even a few gators in Mississippi, but what kind of animals lived in the mountains? Mountain lions? Bears? I had to believe the animals would more than likely stay away from humans unless provoked. I wouldn't let myself worry about them. Although from the way Nina gasped, she already was.

"So it's like a survivalist training course?"

I swiveled in my chair to see a determined Maddy scowling at Burke.

"Yes and no. We don't care about whipping you into shape. Either you're already strong enough or you're not."

He moved closer and I picked up a weird sensation from him. The feeling was similar to what I'd felt from Logan, yet lacking any sexual attraction. Instead, the vibe coming from him was all business mixed with a readiness to do whatever he had to do. He wasn't a man who liked to be questioned. But how far would he go to silence her?

"We live on the outskirts of civilization, off the grid as much as possible. If you hope to stay with your man and become one of us, you'll have to fit in. We don't make any allowances for the weak. It's survival of the fittest and only the best among you will make it to her destination and back. If you don't, then you get kicked to the curb. If you can't make it on your own steam, don't expect us to drag your ass home. You understand?"

Maddy meekly nodded, then he turned away from our table. I breathed a sigh of relief to be out of his line of fire.

"If you do get through the challenge, you'll have the

ultimate choice to make. Keep the man or keep the money. And just so you know, you can't choose the money, then meet up with the man later. We'll know and you'll both regret it."

Had someone tried to do that? I could see why they might, but I could also understand it from the Kings of Beasts' point of view. What was the purpose of making the choice if the girl could have both in the end?

When Maddy spoke up again, asking if we had to fight for our man, I thought Erin would jump out of her skin. I smiled at her, trying to keep her calm.

Yeah, like I'm not about to jump out of my skin, too.

"If he's the man for you, then that's what you'll do. If you don't, then it wasn't meant to be." He came back, getting closer to Maddy. "It's the challenge that'll either bring you together or split you apart."

Split us apart. But how could two people get close in only three days?

My thoughts whirled as Maddy asked a question about soul mates and something to do with romances. To my way of thinking, she was stalling, trying to make her decision to stay or to go.

Burke's tone deepened, a signal of his growing annoyance. He turned around, slowly, taking in all of us. "Anyone want out? Now's your time to do it."

Finally.

At first, there was an uncomfortable silence. Then, as if on cue, girls began pushing back their chairs and getting up. They didn't wait to be asked again. They didn't hang around to talk. Instead, they rushed toward the door as though a pack of wolves nipped at their heels.

Burke crossed his arms over his broad chest and nodded at

the few girls who had remained. "Good to see some of you have the guts to give it a try. Okay, then, leave your suitcases, purses, and whatever the hell else you brought. Roberta will watch over them until you return. Or contact your next of kin if you don't."

He had to be kidding. Or trying to scare a few more of us off.

"The man, or men, who decided you're worth a chance will come to you outside." He nodded at the group of men, signaling them to go.

When he turned back, his smile was chilling, giving me my first real doubt. Was I making a mistake? And yet, I didn't think I was.

"Time's up, bitches. Get moving."

Nina, Erin, Maddy and I stood up, then paused as we searched each other for our decisions. Part of me wanted to get away from the place, while another part of me couldn't wait to see what would happen.

But Maddy had a different idea. She snatched up her suitcase. "This is unbelievable. I'm out of here."

The girls argued with her, trying to get her to stay. I followed the conversation half-heartedly, but couldn't help but feel more anxious about getting outside than trying to talk her into staying. If she wanted to go, then she should go.

We finally made it out the door and into the parking lot. I was more than happy to get out of the windowless bar. As far as I was concerned, I'd made it through a battle, staying when I'd wanted to get out of the big box. Taking a deep breath, I scanned the wide open area around me then over to the forest. I'd been in the woods once before and it had kind of set my claustrophobia on edge where the trees grew closer together. If whatever we had to do had us traipsing around in the deep woods, then I'd have a tough time of it.

I wouldn't think about it. Not until I had to. *If* I had to.

The men formed a semi-circle around us, like predators ready to attack a herd of gazelles. Cabs waited by the side of the road, but I wouldn't need one. I was sticking it out.

Burke stalked past our small group, not giving us a single glance as though we were nothing to him. I wasn't sure I'd ever like the guy, but who cared? Once I got through the challenge and got my money, I was out of there.

Like the grandstander he was, Burke crossed his arms and glared at first the girls, then the men. "Well, all right. What the fuck are you waiting for, guys? Claim your mates."

I hated the word *claim*. It made us sound like we were slaves up for auction. Like back in the olden days when men thought they owned the women in their life. Stupid. But when in Rome—or in this case, Fang's—then it was best to do like the rest.

The men moved closer. A couple of the girls freaked out a little, stepping back like frightened rabbits. I stood my ground, determined not to let them see how much my nerves were jumping. A huge blond man took Nina's arm and tugged her away. She didn't put up any resistance other than a quick yelp, so I didn't try and stop them. Besides, what chance would I have against a brute like him?

Maddy was still insisting on leaving and trying to get Erin to go with her. "Erin, are you coming with me or not?"

For some strange reason, Erin turned to me for help. But I wasn't about to make the decision for her. Mine was already made and she could make her own. I shrugged, trying to be nonchalant. "Do what you want, but I didn't come all this way to hitch a ride back home."

As soon as I'd finished answering, I felt a firm grip on my arm. I spun around to find Logan, his blond hair shining in the sun like he was a Nordic god. I could see the tip of his tat peeking out from the loose collar of his shirt and recognized it as the roaring lion of the Kings of Beasts MC. The lion tattoo fit him perfectly. If any human could ever seem like a lion, it was this guy.

Logan had tightened his hold on me. I kind of lost my cool then and craned my head around toward Erin. All I had time to do was to shoot her a look before getting hauled off around the side of the building.

By the time we'd made it away from most of the others, I'd regained enough sense to yank my arm away. "Don't touch me."

"Shit, sugar, where's the fun in that?" Ruger's voice flowed over my shoulder as he stepped up behind me.

I jumped, hated myself for it, then stepped away from him, putting myself closer to Logan. Between the two huge men, there wasn't much room to move. Both of them were amazing men, one light, one dark. Their bodies were the perfect blend between toned and not too muscled like bodybuilders. They had matching lion tattoos—I guessed all the men in their group did—with Logan's on his chest and Ruger's higher up on the curve of his neck. They oozed power and self-confidence, but they weren't overbearing like some guys got. Instead, they made me feel safe—at least Logan did—something I haven't felt in a long time. Hell, maybe in forever.

Ruger's blue-black hair glistened under the sun. He kept it swept back in the way I'd always liked. If I'd had two photographs, one of each man, and had to say which one I found more attractive, I might have picked Ruger. But in person, there was just something about the guy that made my stomach queasy.

Logan was the opposite. He was handsome and masculine, but he was also the one making me feel safe. I don't know what it was about him, but he put off a hero kind of vibe. He was the kind of guy in the movies who always came to the girl's defense even when it might cost him his life.

Checking out guys as a more than just a one-night fuck wasn't my style. What was the point anyway? I'd always figured I didn't have much of a chance of finding one who'd want to deal with my family and my emotional baggage. It was easier to push ideas of love and romance out of the picture. Some people might've said I'd built a wall around my heart, but I thought it was more like a cage. A cage had bars so my heart could see what was coming before it got hurt. Unlike most people, I knew a cage didn't just keep someone inside it. It could keep someone safe from others getting in. Like the cages divers used to keep sharks away.

My style or not, I checked Ruger and Logan out. Not once, but twice. Down and then back up to their blue-silver eyes.

"What's with the eye color?"

They both blinked, like I'd caught them off-guard. But surely someone else must've mentioned it before? Even Burke had the same blue-silver eyes.

"It's a family thing," answered Logan.

"Huh. So all of you are related?" Kissing cousins maybe? I cringed inwardly. The jokes about mountain folks inbreeding had been funny. But not now. Was that the real reason behind The Claiming Games? To bring in fresh blood?

"Nope."

I wanted to get into it more, but Ruger's twisted grin stopped me. If they were into incest and the like, it wasn't my problem. As long as their check cleared, they could do whatever they wanted.

"Why did you sniff me?" All of a sudden, it seemed like I had a lot of questions. And yet, as fast as they were coming, I could only get hold of a few of them. A few more were the type I wouldn't have asked anyway. Like if it was true that if a man had big feet, then he had a big dick. Or was it his hand?

"Because you smell good, sugar."

I didn't care what Ruger said. I'd really asked the question of Logan. "And you?"

He had a majorly awesome way of looking at me. I'd heard other girls describe feeling tingly and all that girly stuff, but I'd never experienced it. Until now. Logan turned me on with only one look. And I knew where that look could lead.

"Sniffing you is how I knew you were my mate."

Okay. A little creepy. And yet, a little exciting, too. "So you like the way I smell?" It was hard to believe he could since I hadn't had a real shower for a while.

He caught the caution in my tone. "Everyone, everything has its own unique scent. If you didn't like the way someone smelled, you wouldn't want to be near them." He zeroed in on me. "Am I right?"

"Yeah. I guess so. I mean, I've never thought about it." I inhaled before I realized what I was doing—sniffing him. Worse, he knew what I was doing.

Hmm, but he smells good. All manly and strong.

I couldn't let myself continue to think about him. If I did, I might not put all my effort into getting what I'd come for. I needed to get off the subject fast. Problem is, I should've thought before I jumped.

"I like your hair." *Shit. Talk about lame.*

My sudden appreciation for his blond locks threw him. "Thanks."

"No problem." I suddenly found the gravel at my feet interesting.

"I like yours, too."

I nodded, thinking he'd only said so out of the need to say something nice back.

"Don't you like my hair, sugar?"

Actually, I did. Too bad I couldn't stand the rest of Ruger. "It's okay." I almost laughed at his surprised look. "So what's next?" Even though Ruger kept trying to move closer to me, I did my best to ignore him.

"If you go through with the challenge, you choose the money or me."

Ruger's laugh didn't make me feel like laughing along with him. "Logan's right. Except you're my mate. Not his. I offered to share, but he's afraid you'll compare my huge cock to his tiny one."

Did Logan just snarl? "Look, guys, I'm flattered and all, but I'm nobody's mate. I'll do the games and all, but I'm taking the money."

"No, you won't." Logan took hold of me by my chin, startling me enough that I didn't think to react. "You're my mate. Once this is over, you'll know it."

His strange eyes locked to mine, diving into me, sparking that same instant need for him that I'd felt at the truck stop. Moistness hit me between my legs and I could hear my heart beating in my ears. I might've stayed like that, him holding me still with only his fingers on my chin, if it hadn't been for Ruger breaking the spell between us.

I sighed when Ruger tugged me around to face him. Before I could step back, he tried to do the same thing Logan had done. But his touch had me jerking away. Instead of a need to have him, all I felt was a wave of revulsion. Anger flashed in his eyes and I would've sworn the blue got lost in a burst of silver.

I wouldn't have admitted it to anyone, but he scared me. "Just tell me what I'm supposed to do, okay?" Acting tougher than I felt was my go-to place. I'd had to face my father down often enough. Sometimes it had even worked.

"Go on, Logan. Tell her what's what. It'll be the last thing you get to do with her." Ruger skimmed the back of his fingers along my cheek. "I'm the one claiming you, sugar. You can count on it."

I started to tell him I'd rather mate a pig, but it wasn't worth the effort. Let them both think what they wanted. Besides, I had the awful feeling that I was getting into the middle of a long-standing argument. One not solely about me.

"Like I said before, Logan. If you're nice about it, I might just share her with you."

Damn, what a douche. "Seriously? I get to have both of you?" I put on an exaggerated expression like poor pitiful me would be so honored to have the two of them.

"It's not going to happen."

Again with the snarl? If Logan didn't watch out, I might start thinking he was more animal than man.

"Come on, man. It's not like others haven't done it."

"Forget it."

Okay, I had to admit. It was kind of nice for both of them to want me. Even if Ruger wasn't getting anywhere near me. Logan, on the other hand…

He hardened his glare at Ruger, but then focused his attention on me, his eyes softening at once. I could sense the waves of anger rolling off him, but knew they weren't directed at me. If things didn't calm down, they might end up choking each other. I was just about to suggest I leave when Burke's booming voice dragged their attention to him.

"Ruger, get over here." Burke waved him over to where he stood with Roberta.

"I'll see you soon, sugar." Then he licked his lips.

Yuck.

"Forget about him."

"That may take a while. Which is why I don't watch horror movies." I shook myself, earning a small chuckle from Logan.

"Here's what you have to do." He pointed up the hill. "You and the others will walk up the road. At the top of it, you go into the forest—"

Aw, shit.

He paused and studied me. I made sure my dismay didn't show on my face. At least, not any longer.

"Anyway, once you're at the top, go down a little ways then off to your left and into the woods. Go several yards and you'll see a large tree with a hole in its trunk. Attached to the tree will be a paper with the directions on it. Follow the directions up to a cave."

"A cave?" Caves didn't have windows. Caves were often small and cramped. This was so not good. But he hadn't said I had to go inside.

He lifted an eyebrow. "Once you're at the cave, you'll stay there for two nights."

Shit. Inside?

"If you make it through those two nights, then you have to

make your way back to Fang's."

I did my best to act like the cave thing didn't bother me. "That's it? All I have to do is walk up a mountain and spend two nights in a cave? For two hundred and fifty thousand dollars?" It couldn't be that easy. Even with a cave involved, it sounded too easy. "What's the catch?"

"No catch, but don't go thinking it won't be hard." His gaze shifted to Ruger, then on to the woods beyond. "There are a lot of things in the woods. And a lot of things can happen. Accidents. Animals. And no one can help you. You're on your own. Did you pay attention to what Burke said?"

"Sure." He didn't need to know how much I'd zoned out while staring at him.

He narrowed his eyes and gave me a suspicious look. "I'm serious. Don't go thinking this is just a hike in the woods."

Granted, what he'd said was kind of ominous, but I wouldn't let it get to me. "Okay, I get it."

"If you don't make it to the cave by the time the sun sets, you're disqualified. If you get hurt, don't count on anyone hauling you to the emergency room. Understood?"

"Yeah. Like I said, I get it." How hard could it really be? It's not like we were in the middle of the jungle. Bears might be a problem, but I doubted many people ran into them.

He tilted his head toward Ruger. "He's not your mate. No matter what he told you and no matter what he's saying to Burke. Don't worry. I'll make him understand and accept it."

Yet he didn't look like he believed he could. Still, it wasn't my problem. They could duke it out over me and I'd still end up taking the money. "Like I said, it doesn't matter."

A slight curve of his mouth told me he didn't agree. "Right. I get it. But I'll see you at the cave, anyway. You'd better get going."

His hand cupped against my cheek sent flares speeding through me. How could he turn me on so fast? Was there something to this mate thing?

Yeah, right.

"Be careful, Mia."

His heartfelt words touched me. When had anyone except my mother ever said that to me?

"I will."

"Good." He started to lean forward then caught himself. "If I kiss you, I might not stop."

Then kiss me.

Instead, I stayed quiet as he turned on his heel and strode away.

Once he'd stepped into the trees, I turned to see some of the other girls already walking up the hill. "Okay. Here goes everything."

Chapter Five

Mia

I hurried to catch up with Erin and Nina. Their friend Maddy had gone, leaving them confused. The best I could do was to try and get their minds off her. "I didn't know what to expect, but I sure as hell didn't think some guy would lean over and sniff me."

"You too, huh? Yeah. That was really weird."

Erin gave me a searching look as though she wanted me to take what she'd said and run with it. I got the feeling she wanted me to say I'd liked getting sniffed.

Nina made her way back up to us. "Mine, too. But you know what? I kind of liked it."

"I guess they all took whiffs of the girls." I kept my attention on the road ahead of me. "Mine told me thanks for liking his hair."

"His hair?"

"He wears it kind of long. A little shaggy. And the color went well with his eyes." I cringed, thinking I'd just developed verbal diarrhea. And girly verbal diarrhea at that. But who could blame me? After growing up with so many brothers and sisters, having someone actually listen to me was a nice change. Hell, even getting to talk was good. At my house, we'd all stayed as quiet as we could, hoping not to upset our father.

"Were they blue with silver?" asked Erin.

"Yeah. And yours?" I only asked to confirm what I already knew. But why did they all have the same eye color? Logan hadn't given me an answer.

"Same thing. Freaky, huh?"

Yeah. Freaky. But I kept my mouth shut. It was a ridiculous idea, but I suddenly felt like I was betraying Logan by talking about his strange eyes.

Nina agreed, confirming that her man had the same blue-silver eye color, too. We finally reached the top of the rise. "He told me to go into the woods here and find a map and directions stuck to a tree."

"Did he tell you his name? My guy didn't."

"No." I don't know why I said no. Was I trying to protect him again? Like he had secrets I needed to keep? Or was I just trying to go along with the other girls? Maybe standing out at the games wasn't a good thing to do. Not even in a small way.

"Mine, either. Okay, this is getting scary," said Nina.

"He told me to do the same thing. Except to go to the right side." Erin didn't look very confident as she watched other girls walk into the forest. She shifted back and forth on her feet, as though she expected Burke and the other men to burst out of the trees and attack us at any moment.

"We should go home."

I was surprised at Nina. She didn't seem like the quitting type.

"We should."

Erin's agreement, however, didn't surprise me. At times she acted really determined, then, in the next, she was ready to give up. I wondered if it had anything to do with the scars on her ankles. Her jeans hadn't covered them as she'd stretched her legs coming up the hill. She was probably pretty good at hiding them, but then, I was the observant type, especially at noticing weird shit. The girl had issues, but I didn't have any right to judge.

"Then why aren't we?" Nina bit her lower lip.

"Money." I shrugged.

It was the truth as far as I was concerned. I didn't care what their reasons were, yet from the way Erin glanced away, I figured money wasn't her only reason. Maybe not even her biggest reason. It just didn't ring true.

"But what if they want us in the woods so they can do horrible things to us?"

I didn't tell Nina I'd had the same thought only a minute ago. What good would it have done, anyway? Except to make her even more nervous than she already was.

Surprisingly, Erin was the one to try and ease her friend's concerns. "Like I said before. If they wanted to hurt us, they've already had plenty of time to do it."

"Maybe they'd rather play cat and mouse first."

I had to smother a smile at Nina's comeback. Unless they really were playing with us. Then the idea wouldn't be funny at all.

"Maybe. But if you really think so, then why don't we get the hell out of here? Why are all these girls taking this risk? It can't just be about the money."

I studied Erin, almost expecting her to admit that it was definitely not just about the money for her. But she stayed quiet.

"We came this far." I was eager to get going. The longer we stood there and yacked, the later it would be by the time I made it to the cave. Going into a cave was bad enough. Going into a cave in the dark would be straight-up hell.

A cave? That alone was weird enough. I should've mentioned it to them. Should've asked what their destinations were, but again I chose to keep what I knew to myself. Were they doing the same thing?

And yet a part of me yearned to tell them more. To make them understand. To help them feel better and me along with it. "I came because I need the money and because I've always dreamed of an adventure like this. I want to try my luck at being alone, out on my own, instead of trapped in a tiny house filled with all my brothers and sisters. Or where my father..." The tremble worked its way through me. I couldn't make it stop and had to ride it out. And then came a real burst of honesty. "This is the most exciting thing to ever happen to me."

But did I mean the challenge? Or Logan?

"I could say the same thing."

I guess Erin and I have some things in common. She has her secret and I have mine.

I turned my gaze to the woods, sensing that they needed time to themselves, time to reassure each other in a way I couldn't. They lowered their voices, but they didn't have to. Living with as many brothers and sisters as I had, I'd learned how to tune people out. I started listening again when Nina's voice grew louder.

"Okay then, I guess this is goodbye. For now." Nina fell against Erin.

Jealousy hit me so hard I rocked a little on my feet. What would it be like to have a close friend? Because of my father, because of the bruises I'd had to hide from not only my teachers but from everyone else, I'd never gotten too friendly with anyone from school. What was I supposed to do? Say "You can't come over. My dad's drunk and he might want to grab-ass you"? No way.

"You take care of yourself, okay? Keep on going. Stay safe. Don't do anything—" Nina stopped. Something passed between her and Erin.

Erin did her best to cover Nina's mistake. I figured it had something to do with Erin's scars.

"You, too. And you, too, Mia."

It was time. We all had to get going. The other girls had already gone into the forest. We were the last.

I lifted a hand in a farewell salute, then started walking down the other side of the hill. I'd cut to the left and into the woods after I got a few feet away. "See you back at Fang's to claim the money." Watching Erin, I wiggled my eyebrows, guessing at what she really wanted. "Or the man."

By the time I'd stopped laughing, I was already at the edge of the woods. I wasn't laughing any longer as I stared into the dimly lit forest.

"Just take it easy." I drew in a long, slow breath and told myself not to let it get to me. A forest was still an open place. I had to remember that. It was nothing like our house and definitely not anything like the closet. And yet I knew the trees could get so thick in places, along with the underbrush, that they'd feel like walls closing in around me.

I couldn't stop. I couldn't give into the fear. The challenge was my only way of helping my family. Whatever it took, I had to keep going.

Logan

I didn't like to fight. But the lion inside me sure as hell did.

Meeting Ruger head on, I opened my jaws wide and clamped down on his shoulder. Ruger let out a roar, then jerked his body away. Part of his fur and flesh came away in my mouth and I spat them out. His tail whipped across my face as he spun around, ready to attack again.

Ruger struck out with his paw, digging his claws into my mane. I didn't feel it as I rose up on my hind legs and threw my body at him. The double layer of fat under my skin added protection against his attack, but not enough. Another swipe and I felt the searing pain slice though the flesh of my side. I roared, more out of anger than agony, and threw my body against his, forcing him to fall backward. He landed on his back with a thud, his sharp fangs flashing under the sun.

We'd fought many times during our lives, but this was different. This time wasn't for fun or to assert dominance over the other. This time my instincts took over, flooding my mind with emotions instead of thoughts. He was my rival for my mate. As his brother, as a human, I didn't want to hurt him. As a lion, I wanted to shred his meat from his bones, then roar my victory over his dead body. Growling, I slashed at his underbelly, but with a quick move I should've seen coming, he rolled out from underneath me.

Again, we came together, claws finding skin, teeth sinking into fur and flesh. I tasted his blood in my mouth, but had no regrets. He'd attacked me first and I had a right to defend myself.

The other men of the pride crowded around us as we battled. Lionesses, the few who had shown up after the girls had gone up the hill, backed away, unwilling to get involved. Unwilling to get between two strong males.

We were a pride, both as humans and as lions. But, unlike our wild counterparts, we were a team. Territory was shared, and sometimes women, but I wouldn't share Mia with anyone, not even Ruger.

"Break it up, you two!" Burke strode toward us.

It was dangerous to do, but several of the others grabbed first Ruger then me and dragged us off each other. Burke stepped between us, a brave yet foolish thing to do. Still growling, I stood my ground, ready to go on the defensive if Ruger kept fighting. To lose to him would mean losing Mia. I'd die before I'd let him have her.

Ruger spun around, throwing off the men who'd tried to restrain him. He snarled, shaking his darker colored mane and moving his tail back and forth. He kept his ears flat against his head, not attacking, but not ready to stop, either.

Burke had seen us fight enough to know I'd be the one who'd listen. "Knock it off, Logan. Shift back. Now."

If I did, I'd be risking Ruger not doing the same. If he really wanted to wound me, he'd get his chance once I changed back to my human form. I growled, resisting Burke's command. Going human with Ruger still a lion went against both my human and animal instincts.

"Logan. I'm not asking again."

Damn it. Fuck off, Burke. Let me finish this.

I'd keep fighting until one of us lay bleeding on the ground, unable to rise. Killing wasn't allowed, but maiming, crippling was.

Burke hadn't asked to begin with, but that was his style. If I wasn't careful, he'd set the whole pride on me for not obeying him.

Again, I snarled, but I backed off, putting distance between Ruger and me. Not a lot, but enough to make me feel safer.

I had no choice but to obey Burke and take the risk. I sure as hell knew Ruger wouldn't back down unless Burke ordered him to. Maybe not even then. He was tough and had never walked away from a fight. If someone didn't stop us, or get me to stop first, we always kept going until we were both too exhausted to lift a paw.

I growled then shifted. The world of gray-scale hues drifted into the full spectrum of color as my silver eyes gave way to the blue-silver. The aches of the transition wracked through me, but I was used to it. I'd been shifting since I was a year old.

I straightened up, my gaze set on Ruger still in his lion form. If he jumped at me, I'd have to hurry out of the way or hope one or more of the others would get between us.

"Ruger. Now."

He snarled, showing his fangs again.

"Ruger, I said now."

At last, he obeyed Burke and started changing. By the time he'd finished, my wounds had already started healing. None of our wounds were too serious.

"She's mine, Logan."

"That's bullshit and you know it." Two males rarely took in the same female's scent and I didn't believe it had happened now. Ruger was up to something.

"She's mine."

"Why are you doing this?" I was pretty sure I knew why. Yet, I wouldn't call him out on it in front of the others. Year by year he'd started getting more jealous of me. I was the one with the family. I was the one Burke turned to when he needed something done right. I was the responsible one.

To make things worse, I was the one the females liked best. In the lion kingdom, the lion with the darker mane, with dark fur running down his spine was the one the females were drawn to. My own mane was light with dark golden strands mixed together while Ruger's was a rich dark brown. He should've been their first choice if they'd listened to their animal instincts, but the reverse had happened.

It wasn't hard to know why. Ruger treated all females like shit and they knew it. Why the hell would they want anything to do with him?

I'd had plenty of girls. But they were mere distractions, ways of letting off steam and sexual frustration. As a lion, I could fuck any free female, if I wanted to. But I wouldn't take a girl that way. Not like Ruger would.

Those reasons would have been bad enough, but there was one more reason. The reason neither of us would speak of.

I was the one who'd let his brother die. As much as I tried telling myself that it wasn't my fault, that I hadn't been inside the bar when the fight had started, I couldn't shake the guilt. And Ruger hadn't let me forget it, either.

A part of me had died with Vic. Ruger wasn't the only one who'd lost a brother. Why didn't he get that?

He glared at me, never letting his gaze waver. I couldn't look away. To do so would be admitting defeat. But I grew angrier, knowing our fight had kept me from tracking Mia.

"You won't follow her."

Ruger narrowed his eyes at me as we pulled on our clothes. "It's not your say."

"But it is mine." Burke planted his feet apart, his head held high, a silent show of his command. "Which of you took in her scent?" He turned to Ruger, catching him before he could answer. "The truth this time."

Ruger wanted to lie. I had no doubt about it. But he wouldn't. Not with Burke asking him a direct question. Still, he tried to get past saying it.

"I sniffed her."

"But you didn't draw in her scent." Burke arched his eyebrows, turning the statement into a question.

Lions have a very good sense of smell whether in our human or animal forms. Just smelling her meant nothing. But when a lion drew in the scent of his mate, it went deeper, as though her aroma permeated every part of him. I'd felt it when I'd taken in her fragrance. And if I had, then it was doubtful Ruger had. "Damn it. Tell the fucking truth."

"Back off, Logan, and let me handle this."

I glanced from Burke to Ruger. The anger I saw in his eyes shook me. No matter how many fights we'd gotten into, I'd never seen real hate there. When had he started hating me? Had it started with Vic's death? Or before, arising out of jealousy? Would it ever end?

"Damn it. Tell the truth, Ruger. Did you draw in her scent or not?"

He spat on the ground. "No."

"Then it's settled. She's Logan's mate."

Even Ruger knew better than to argue with the facts. And especially not with Burke.

"Then fucking stop fighting. First Shayna offers herself to Colter and gets rejected, and now you two idiots go at each other. Hell, the girl might not even make it through the challenge, so give it a break until she does."

Ruger growled and I gave him a snarl in return. If he shifted, I'd shift, too. No matter what Burke said.

"I told you to knock it off." He stayed between us, daring us to disobey him. "If you two kids are through having your little squabble, let's get out of here." Burke started to walk away, then confronted Ruger again when he growled once more. "I mean it. Let it drop."

Although Burke stayed where he was, waiting for Ruger to nod his agreement, it never came. The surprised and annoyed murmurs of the others had no effect on him. I was ready to shift and go at him again, but when Burke didn't react, I had to let it pass. At last, Burke shot me a hard look, a silent warning to watch out for my former friend, then stalked away.

Ruger and I stayed where we were, each of us unwilling to be the first to turn their back on the other. I wanted to ask him why he was doing this, but I couldn't. In the end, it didn't matter. Instead, I backed up, keeping my eyes on him until I was far enough away.

My stomach tightened, paining me as much as the ache in my heart did. I hadn't wanted to believe it before, but now I knew for sure. I'd lost first Vic and now Ruger. Both of my brothers were gone.

I had to get out of there. Mia would be all right on her own for a while. I couldn't help her, anyway. Before I could follow her, I needed to get the rest of my aggression out of my system. But a run wasn't what I wanted, especially not with the girls in the forest. Stalking to my ride, I swung my leg over and got it going. Fuck wearing a helmet. Part of the release a ride gave me came from feeling the wind whip through my hair. I turned my bike toward the uphill road and left gravel flying into the air behind me.

Mia

It didn't take long to find the map. In fact, it was so easy I had to wonder why they hadn't just handed it to me. Had the others found their maps as easily? Maybe they'd made us search for it to add to the mystique of the challenge. I was just happy I didn't have to go too far into the woods to find it.

The note was simple enough. It was a hand drawn map along with directions. All I had to do was to turn back around, go farther down the incline of the hill, then take a sharp right when I found a gravel trail.

I studied the drawing. According to the map, the gravel soon ran out as the path started going higher up the mountain. I had to pass over a dry gulch then make my way around a rock outcropping. Once I'd made it there, it looked like easy walking higher and higher. Then I'd hit the rocks separating the forest below from the trees growing thicker on the mountain. If the drawing was accurate, the path would curve around the side of the rocks and lead straight to a cave.

Why did it have to be a cave? Tension tightened an imaginary bolt in my neck. A cabin would've been better. At least cabins had windows. But a cave? Caves were windowless dark places with usually only one way in or out.

Just like a closet.

A noise behind me had me jerking around. Although it didn't make sense, I almost expected to see my father standing behind me, the evil grin plastered to his face, and his dirty hands reaching out for me. In that moment, the forest disappeared and I was back in our house, trapped in my bed with his hands roving all over me.

No. Never again.

I shook off the vision, even welcoming the thick forest surrounding me. I'd been lucky. Somehow, I'd kept him from raping me. Or had I been spared because he couldn't get it up? Whatever the reason, the sensation of his hands groping me still lingered.

I forced my attention back on the map, studied it one more time, then slipped it into the front pocket of my jeans. My father and my time in the closet were a thing of the past. If nothing else happened, and if for some reason I didn't win either the man or the money, at least I was free.

I started walking, thankful I'd worn my favorite broken-in boots. Running shoes might have been a better choice, but my boots were what I always chose to wear whether I put on jeans or a skirt. The brown leather was soft and cracked, the soles broken in yet not worn out, and I liked the look of the brass buckles on the sides. They went up to my calves, high enough to keep the thorns and branches from scratching my ankles, and loose enough to give an inch between the top of the boots and my shins.

Back on the road, I stood at the height of the rise and looked down at Fang's again. I couldn't make out anyone's face, but what I did see had me wondering if the hot summer's day had already taken its toll on me. I suddenly wished I'd thought to take the water bottle out of my backpack before I'd had to leave my belongings behind.

I squinted, sure I was seeing two large dogs fighting. But those weren't two dogs. I squinted harder, shielding my face from the glare of the sun.

Dogs.

It had to be. What else could get so big?

But no. They weren't dogs.

I rubbed my eyes, then looked again.

Cats.

But not just any cats.

They rose up on their hind legs, their thick amazing manes moving in golden waves as they struck out at each other. Enormous paws tore through the air and long tails whipped around as they came at each other again and again. The sounds of growls and roars drifted to me.

I stared as hard as I could, unwilling to believe my eyes until I had no way to deny it.

Lions.

Holy shit. There are two lions fighting at Fang's.

And yet people stood around them, watching them as though they were just two drunks brawling outside the bar. But how? Where had they gotten the animals? Who would have the nerve, hell, the stupidity to turn two lions loose?

Kings of Beasts. That's what they call themselves.

The gang, the club, the family, whatever K.O.B. wanted to call its group, had their own lions. Like the animals were their own real, live mascots. And as if that wasn't incredible enough, they had the lions fighting outside, in the open, with no cage or chains or anything to keep them in check.

Lions.

As much as I ran the word over and over in my mind, it just wouldn't stick. It was impossible. And yet, there they were, right in front of my eyes.

I was torn. I wanted so much to run down the hill and watch. Maybe even get them to stop the animals from fighting. Was this their version of dog fights? Yet even dog fights were normally held in an enclosure. Who would even dream of letting lions walk free? No, I had to be missing something. Surely, they had safety measures. Like a tranquilizer gun or something in case the lions started attacking the humans.

The rumors Lee Ann had told me about had gotten it half right. There were definitely at least two lions in the mountains. The crap about men changing into lions was probably an exaggeration that had turned into folklore.

This I have got to see.

Yet as soon as I'd taken a few steps back down the hill, I stopped, realizing I might be tossing away my chance at the money. Would I be disqualified if I went back to Fang's? Would it take too much time, time that was already running out? I had to make it to the cave before the sun went down.

In the end, the need for the cash prize won out over my curiosity. I wasn't happy about turning away from such an incredible sight, but I made a promise to myself to ask them about the lions when I returned. By then, I'd have had time to make up my mind. Should I leave it alone? Or should I report the gang to the authorities for having real lions? Whatever authorities were available. Small towns, especially those in out of the way places like deep in the mountains, didn't always have law enforcement of their own. At best, maybe a sheriff. I'd have to contact the highway patrol or the FBI... or what? The nearest animal control? A traveling circus?

Who the hell knew?

I turned around and headed back down the other side of the hill. Before long, I was walking on the side of the road, my attention focused on finding the gravel trail. When I finally did, I was a little let down. Wasn't a gravel path bigger than this thin strip of land?

I checked again, walking down the hill a little farther, then giving up and going back to the path. None of the other girls were around. I had to be way behind them. But I'd thought the path, especially being gravel and obviously manmade, would be a nice three-foot wide area leading into the trees. And, as I'd also assumed, with a path like that, the trail would be uncluttered with underbrush and tree branches.

I was dead wrong.

"Damn."

I stared into the dimly lit forest and tried to see how far the trail would take me before stopping. But the thickness of the trees made it too difficult to see.

"Damn it again."

Still, why had I expected it to be easy? Logan had warned me. Sure, it had sounded fairly simple, but wasn't that the way things always went? I should've hoped for the best and expected the worst.

Into the forest I went, my boots crunching on the gravel. The trail wasn't so bad. I didn't have to watch out for any large potholes or the like. And the trees weren't too close to make me feel trapped. At least not until I'd gone maybe half a mile.

The gravel became less and less, the brown of the forest floor peeking through more and more until, at last, I stood at the end of the gravel path. I felt like Dorothy traveling through the woods on the way to see the Wizard. But where was my Tin Man who'd help me along on my trek?

"Come on, Mia. At least there aren't any flying monkeys." I cast my gaze skyward, into the canopy of trees. "Not yet anyway."

I took a deep breath, glanced at the light coming through the leaves above me, and put one foot in front of the other.

Chapter Six

Mia

I drew in a long, slow breath and tried to think of anything besides the way the trees were getting closer to me. The tightening of my shoulders didn't help. It was like my body was warning me to get ready to run, even though my mind kept insisting that everything was all right.

Just breathe.

If I could keep taking nice, even breaths, then the feeling of getting trapped would go away. Or at least, stay away for a little while longer.

Breathe.

I was making good time. Not being a great judge of time or distance, I couldn't be sure, but unless I started running, I wasn't going to make it any faster to the cave.

Why did I have to go to a damn cave anyway? Had the Kings of Beasts MC known about my problem and chosen the cave because of it? Staying inside a cave for two nights wasn't going to be an easy thing. So was that the real challenge? Had they given every girl the worst possible place to go? One that would feed on her fears?

But how? No one but my family knew about my problem with tight places. And the school nurse after I'd freaked out that day. Had I unknowingly given up information when I'd filled in a random sweepstakes on the library's computer? Maybe it hadn't been a smart thing to do, especially on a public computer, but my fascination with trips and travel had gotten to me. Besides, the only info I'd given them was my name and address. What did I have to lose anyway? No one could hack into my nonexistent bank account. And I sure as hell never wrote anything about my problem.

I shook my head, swatted at a bug, and kept going. What kind of cave would it be? If it had snakes or bats or whatever the hell else lived in caves, then I'd have a hard time toughing it out. Those things creeped me out. I didn't even like small animals like dogs and cats.

But I did like big animals. They appealed to me because they were big enough that I could see them coming from a distance. I realized it didn't make a lot of sense, but there it was. Big animals were good. Little ones? Especially flying and crawling ones? Not so much.

An image of what I'd seen outside Fang's hit me again. There had to be a good explanation. Either the hot sun had gotten to me in record time... Or I'd seen two honest-to-God lions fighting.

I laughed. No one would ever believe me if I told them what I'd seen. Hell, I'd seen it and I still didn't believe it.

That had to be what Lee Ann had been talking about. Could others have seen the lions and called them "monsters"? Had the girls gone missing because they'd been eaten by lions? What if the motorcycle club used the girls in the games as prey for the lions? Was I their next meal?

Oh, shit.

"Hey, sugar."

There was no mistaking the voice. I whirled around to find

Ruger standing behind me with a shit-eating grin on his face. "What are you doing here?"

"I thought I'd better check in on you and make sure you're doing all right." He came closer, and as I'd often done with my father, I stood my ground. But I didn't look him in the eye. I didn't want to give my father, and now Ruger, any excuse to start on me.

As much as I tried not to, I couldn't keep my breath from coming too fast and too hard. My heart thudded in my chest so loudly I was sure he could hear it. When he leaned over, putting his face an inch from mine, it seemed like he was listening to it. Either that or he was going to sniff me again.

I swear if he touches me, I'm going to go bat-shit crazy on his balls.

I wished I felt brave enough to do that, but I wasn't. Something told me not to let him see how afraid I was. Faking bravery with my father had worked. Sometimes.

He sniffed me again.

I figured him sniffing me was better than having him touch me. "I'm fine. Thanks for asking. You can go now."

"Aw, shoot, sugar. How about getting to know each other a little?"

"No thank you."

He laughed as he circled me. Like an animal staking out its prey. I shoved down the urge to bolt. If I took off running, he'd catch me before I'd gone three feet.

"Well, aren't you the polite one? Still, you need to learn what to call me."

What? I jerked my head up, forgetting not to stare him in the eye. Not to challenge him. "I know your name."

"Good, then you've got it half right. But that's not what I'm talking about."

His eyes had changed color. Silver dominated them, forcing the blue away. But how could eyes change color? As curious as I was, I wasn't about to ask him. He'd probably take my question as encouragement to hang around.

"I don't get what you mean." I shook my head, slowly, deliberately. As for being brave, I'd fake it until I made it. "What I call you doesn't matter. Once I get through this, I'm going to take the money and get out of here. You'll never see me again." I repeated it, just for his sake. "What I call you doesn't matter."

"Sure it does. You can call me Ruger when we're around the folks in town." He caressed my cheek as he'd done at Fang's.

I shouldn't have recoiled at his touch, but I didn't catch myself in time. He noticed my correction as I startled, then gritted my teeth. I think he even enjoyed it.

"Take it easy, sugar."

I stayed still, almost like he was one of the lions about to attack me.

"When it's just you and me? You need to call me *sir*."

I couldn't help it. Even my father hadn't asked me to do that. "*Sir*? Are you serious? Why the hell would I call you *sir*?"

He snagged me by my hair and yanked me closer. I yelped, then closed my eyes as he put his face an inch from mine. The fury, the anger I saw there reminded me of my father. But my father had never possessed the power and brute strength Ruger had.

"You want to know why, sugar? Because I'm your mate and your master, that's why. You do whatever I say. You live to please me. If I tell you to lick my boots, then you'd damn well better get your tongue moving. If I tell you to suck my cock, then you'd better say *please, sir* and wrap your mouth around my dick."

He chuckled, then swept his tongue along my cheek. I went cold and stayed as still as I could. "I'll bet you've sucked a lot of cock, haven't you? Yeah, you're the type. You know what I'm talking about. The type who thinks they're too good to fuck, so they'll give head instead. Is that you, sugar? Do you think you're too good to fuck me?"

What the hell could I say to that? Instead, I kept my mouth shut. His grip loosened on my hair and I eased out of his hold, letting out a breath when he didn't grab hold again.

"And if you don't do what your master tells you to do?" He shrugged as though what he'd say next was of no consequence. "If you don't, you won't like what happens next."

Fear is an ugly thing. It wraps around the spine and takes control of even the simplest of movements. But I was all too familiar with fear. And because of my familiarity, I'd learned to keep it down just far enough for me to react. I'd learn the hard way how to push back.

Problem was, I tended to push a little more than I should.

"Is your dick long and thick?"

I had him. His sick smile became even sicker. Like my dad, he was a sick fucker.

"You bet, sugar. The biggest."

I gave him a sick smile in return. "Good. I hope it rips your ass apart when you go fuck yourself."

I couldn't even get out a scream before he had me on my knees in front of him. Pain splintered into my head as he buried his hand in my hair. He shoved my face against his crotch.

"Listen up, little bitch. Whether you like it or not, no matter what anyone else says, you're my mate. And as my mate, you're going to learn how to behave."

I wouldn't give him the satisfaction of speaking. Besides, the only thing coming out of my mouth would've been curse words. I grabbed at his wrists and tried to make him turn me loose, but it was impossible. He was too strong.

He thrust his crotch against my face again so hard I was afraid he might break my nose. I let out a cry, then felt my head jerked to the side when he flattened his opened hand hard against my cheek. If he'd hit me with his fist, I doubt I would've stayed conscious.

"Undo my jeans, little bitch."

My head swam as pain threatened to take hold and never let go. I was almost sorry he hadn't knocked me out. Yet, as had happened with my father, the fear swallowing me was replaced with anger. But it was different with Ruger. I didn't have to hide my fury to keep my siblings and mother safe. I didn't care what he did to me. I was through taking shit from men like Ruger and my father. As long as I got in one good hit, it'd be worth it.

"Do it."

I swear he growled at me, but I didn't look up to see his face. I didn't want to see what was there. Instead, I took hold of his shiny silver buckle with the lion head on it and pulled it free. He planted his feet farther apart and did a couple of pelvis humps toward my face. I pulled back as far as I could and kept working on loosening his belt.

"Now that's how a mate should act. Hurry up, sugar. Unzip me."

I undid the button then took hold of the zipper. My fury had my body shaking as I pulled it down. Another whimper came as his long, hard cock thrust outward to hit the end of my nose. I choked back the bile rising up my throat. His hold tightened even more, bringing stinging tears to my eyes.

"Give it all you've got."

I'd give it all I had, all right. Just long enough to bring my teeth down on it as hard as I could.

Logan

After going for a ride, I'd come back to Fang's and had headed for the woods. We couldn't interfere with the girls, but we could follow and watch them. Once she made it to the cave, then I could get to know her. Claiming her would come later, if she chose me. *When* she chose me. I couldn't wait to sink my fangs into her shoulder and turn her. But before all that happened, she still had to make it through the challenge on her own.

I froze as a scream broke the peacefulness of the forest. Turning around, I tried to determine which direction it had come from. Someone was in big trouble, but could I help? I shouldn't get involved, but the voice behind the tortured scream sounded familiar.

Helping any of the girls, especially my own mate, was against the rules. If Burke or any of the others found out, I'd risk getting thrown out of the pride. She'd be disqualified. Worse, I'd never see her again. I couldn't imagine a crueler punishment.

But I couldn't let it go. What if it was Mia? Anything could happen to her in the woods. She could've come across a mountain lion or a bear. Or fallen and injured herself. I paced around in a circle, then made my decision. A decision I'd made once before, after leaving her behind at the truck stop.

Screw the rules.

I dashed through the trees, the slashes of the branches whipping against my arms and hands. Normally, I could run for miles without getting winded, but with my chest tightening and my gut turning into a heavy rock, I found it harder to breathe. But I wouldn't, couldn't stop. I'd keep going even if I had to crawl on my hands and knees.

When she didn't scream again—was that a good or a bad sign?—I quickened my pace. Had she stopped screaming because the danger had passed? Or because she was no longer able to scream? Unable to draw in a breath.

I lifted my nose to the breeze and sniffed. She was near. I could smell her.

Hang on, Mia. I'm coming.

If I was too late, I'd never forgive myself for going for a ride instead of following her. I already had enough regrets in my life.

I burst onto the gravel path, then cut a hard right and started down it. The gravel surface soon gave way to hard-packed earth. Her scent grew stronger, and along with it, the smell of her fear.

But at least she was still alive.

I don't know what I expected to find. But what I did find tore through me, almost bringing me to my knees.

Mia on her knees facing Ruger.

Ruger, with his jeans pulled down, his back to me and his cock pointed at her.

I slammed to a stop, too stunned to do anything more than let my mouth drop open. The rock in my gut morphed into an agonizing ball of fire.

It can't be.

She's not blowing him. She can't be.

My eyes told me one thing, but my mind refused to believe it. Mia had her luscious mouth open, her gaze fixed on his cock as she leaned forward and…

"No." The sound strangled in my throat.

But I'd spoken loud enough for them to hear me.

Her mouth widened into an even bigger *oh* when her gaze met mine. The fear, anger, and shame I saw there quickly morphed into shock.

"What the fuck, man? Can't you see my mate and me are busy?" Ruger released her hair, then tugged his jeans up as he turned to face me.

My hands fisted and my eyesight wavered. I wanted to hurt him. Bad. But more than the need to hurt Ruger was the need to understand how she could get on her knees for him.

"Mia." I didn't have to ask the question. The pained tone of my voice did it for me.

She pushed onto her feet. Her eyes were wild and her hair mussed. And yet, she was as beautiful as ever.

"Logan, he—" She shook her head, knowing what I was thinking and denying it. "No. I wouldn't—"

She didn't have to finish. I could see it in her face. She wouldn't have given him head. Not on her own. Still, my loyalty to my pride mate made me ask. "Ruger, what the fuck are you doing? You can't. Not to her."

"Logan, you don't think—"

"Shut the hell up, bitch." Ruger cupped his crotch. "Yeah, man. She was just about to suck me off before you showed up. Do us all a favor and go the fuck away. Me and my girl want some privacy, ya know?"

I wouldn't have put it past him to force himself on a girl.

He'd done it before. Not to any of the girls in previous games, but to human females. He preferred to force them. If they offered on their own, he didn't get as turned on. Belittling the girl, tormenting her was more fun to him than fucking her.

And yet, she hadn't looked like she was fighting it. Doubt and hurt raked through me, deeper and more painfully than any claws could have.

His smile faded. "Why do I have to keep telling you? She's my mate. I'm just taking what's already mine. Now back the fuck off."

"Go to hell." I wouldn't let him have her. No way. No how.

Ruger stepped away from her. I watched him, certain he was angling for a better shot at me.

"Mia, get out of here."

"Aw, come on, Logan. Don't be an ass. I tell you what. I know you said you didn't want to, but come on. Let's share her." He chuckled and circled around her, his lion stalking its victim. "She obviously can't wait to have me. You can have the sloppy seconds."

She hadn't done what I'd told her to do. Maybe she was rooted to the spot, either too afraid to move or to curious to find out what would happen next.

I shifted, enough to let my inner beast deepen my voice. Because she was my mate, my voice would reach into her instinctual need to please me and make her obey. I spoke softer, leaving a break between each word. "Mia. Leave. Now."

She blinked as though my voice had suddenly awakened her from a trance. Tilting her head to the side, she frowned, not understanding what was going on inside her. Still, she stood and pivoted on her heel to start down the dirt path again. She'd only gone a few feet before she turned back. I didn't respond.

Instead, I had to keep my attention on Ruger. She took off running.

Be careful.

I wanted to shout at her, but didn't. Hopefully, she wouldn't trip over any branches or stones. Running down an uneven trail wasn't the safest thing to do.

"Why are you doing this, Ruger?"

"Damn it, man. I always knew you weren't the brightest light bulb in the carton, but I figured you were smart enough to get this through your thick head. I want her and I'm going to have her. One way or another." He took a step toward me, his eyes changing over to silver.

I accepted his challenge. It was either that or give her up. If he thought I'd let him claim her without a fight, he didn't know me at all.

But did I know him? He wasn't the guy I'd grown up with. Once Vic had died, he'd changed. "You can't have her. I took her scent." With any other pride member, that would've been enough. He should've backed off the first time I'd told him.

A sneer lifted the corner of his mouth. "You know what? I don't give a fuck what you say."

"I thought you didn't want a mate." Trying to reason with him was like trying to reason with a brick wall. But I had to try.

He shrugged. "What can I say? I changed my mind." He cupped his crotch. "Did you see the mouth on her? Fuckin' A, man. She could suck a peel off a banana."

I lost it, hurling my body at him. He should've expected my attack, but I caught him off-guard. We came together, two men growling with our inner lions roaring to get free. We rolled into the underbrush, slugging away. Ruger brought out his claws first, then came mine.

I should've shifted, but I didn't. If Mia heard our shouts, she might turn around and come back. And if she did, she'd see us.

Ruger struck my jaw then slammed his knee into my midsection. Thankfully, he missed burying it into my groin. I punched him, going for his nose and landing against his eye. We rolled again, then jumped to our feet and crouched low like our animal counterparts would have.

I tried again, needing to understand. "Why, Ruger? Tell me."

He snarled, showing his fangs. "Because I want her. Because you owe me."

Startled, I dropped my fists and stared at him. Was he finally owning up? "Why do I owe you? Just spit it out."

For only a moment, I saw the Ruger I'd grown up with. The Ruger who'd laughed and played by my side. The Ruger who'd enjoyed so many good times with me. The Ruger who'd stayed up all night watching horror movies with me. But then that brief glimpse into the man who'd been like a brother to me was gone.

"Fuck off, Logan." He whirled and dashed away, barreling through the woods.

I stayed where I was, my chest heaving. I sucked in deep breaths, letting my breathing calm down. If only I could get my mind to do the same.

I owed him. That much I agreed with.

But for which thing? For having parents who were still alive? For being preferred by the girls over him? Yet I knew the truth of it.

I owed him for letting his brother die.

Still, I never would've thought he'd turn against me. Not

like this.

Heartache burned in my chest. I'd never really believed a heart could actually hurt. Now I knew it could.

Mia

I burst through the underbrush and fought against the branches, pushing them out of the way. The sounds of the men arguing grew softer the farther I went. I would've kept on going if I hadn't had to catch my breath.

I turned back and waited. I couldn't hear them any longer. Were they finished? Were they going to follow me?

Was Logan hurt?

If he was, I wanted to help him. If he hadn't come along...

I started back down the trail and had gotten a few yards before my paced slowed. I owed Logan my safety, but could I risk going back only to find out that Ruger was still there? Or worse. To see Logan beaten or badly injured? I'd never thought of myself as weak. Hadn't I survived so much already? But I wasn't brave enough to go back.

I hated myself for it, but I'd have to leave Logan to fend for himself.

What could I do to help him anyway? They were members of the same Kings of Beasts motorcycle club. They probably had lots of fights, but that didn't mean they'd ever do each other any real harm. At least, that's what I hoped. Besides, didn't gangs have their own set of rules? I'd probably just mess things up even more.

Maybe, just maybe, they'd already stopped fighting and, having gotten it out of their systems, were doing some weird kind of male bonding thing. Talking trash about each other or me. How the hell was I supposed to know? And, other than wanting to help Logan, why should I care?

I paced around in a circle, trying to convince myself not to go back. Rationalizing was one of my strengths. Or was it one of my weaknesses?

Shit. Get going to the cave and forget about them. I would've gotten away without Logan's help.

And yet, making me believe it was a whole lot easier said than done.

Why were both of them interested in me anyway? They didn't know me from any of the other girls and I wasn't the prettiest of the group, either. But after they'd gotten close, after sniffing me, they'd seemed to want me.

And the sniffing thing. I wished I'd had more time to talk to Erin and Nina about it. The men who had "claimed" them had sniffed them, too. Was it a mountain man thing? Something to freak the girls out before sending them on their way? Was it part of the show for the whole The Claiming Games adventure?

Or had it really meant something?

And why had two men said they wanted me? Were they both allowed to choose me? I'd still take the money over either man, but it made me feel all warm and tingly inside having both of their attentions.

Okay, maybe not so much. Ruger wasn't the type of guy I'd ever go for. He was brash, rude, and, most of all, dangerous. He reminded me too much of my father. A man who took whatever he wanted. And not in the good kind of way girls fantasized about.

I knew the difference. I'd had enough of my own fantasies to know the difference.

Although the forest was warm, I couldn't help but shiver thinking about Ruger. His hands on me had been bad enough. But when he'd made me undo his jeans, I was sure I'd either vomit or pass out. Or both. The best I could've hoped for was that I'd hurl and conk out after I'd chomped off his dick.

Talk about gross.

Even now, after it was all over and I'd gotten away, I still couldn't stop the revulsion bringing my breakfast to the back of my throat. I tried to concentrate on putting one foot in front of the other and letting my mind go blank, but every time I did, his face came back at me, grinning his sick, fucked-up grin.

All at once, what had happened came back to me, hitting me hard.

His hand in my hair.

His crotch shoved at me.

His cock pointed at my face.

My mouth open and ready to take it in.

My imagination got the better of me. The memory of my mouth encircling his dick, then driving my teeth into it was the last straw. I lurched to my right and upchucked.

A few minutes later, after staying bent over for a while, I forced myself to a standing position. If I was going to make it to the cave before nightfall, I had to get going.

It was a tough thing to do. Wanting to make it to my destination, yet dreading what the destination was. A cave.

The snap of a twig had me whirling around, expecting to see Ruger coming at me. I gasped, then fisted my hands. I wouldn't be able to put up much of a fight, but at least I'd give it a good try.

When nothing happened, when I didn't see his awful grin, I started to relax.

Too bad it hadn't been Logan following me. Where Ruger reminded me of my father, all filled with evil, Logan struck me an entirely different way. Their eyes were the same, but what was inside them was as different as the sun and the blackest night sky. I'd hated it when Ruger had leaned over me and sniffed me, but when Logan had done it, I'd wanted to reach out, grab him, and pull him closer.

Had he told me his last name? Had I told him my name?

The memory of it was blurred, obscured by the rush of lust that had hit me when he'd grown close. I didn't know why. After all, I'd been turned on by other guys and I'd had sex with them, testing my willingness to be with another man after enduring my father's hands on me. Taking my body back. Cleansing my skin of my father's touch by replacing it with another's. But those times hadn't included any real feelings. Hell, I could barely remember if I'd had orgasms. They'd been more like "slam, bam and forget you, man" encounters for me.

But Logan was different. He didn't just turn me on. No, it was so much more. So different, so stirring, something on an instinctual level I'd never experienced before. I hadn't even thought it possible. He'd gotten to me the moment I'd seen him on his bike. The moment he'd captured me behind the building and taken me. He'd been like a wild man and I was the prize he wanted. The prize he'd won.

Damn, but he's amazing.

Even now, hours after he'd sniffed me, I could still feel the warmth of his breath against my cheek. If I drew in a long slow breath, I imagined I could still smell his scent. It wasn't an aroma that came from aftershave or any other manmade concoction, but a base of masculinity that permeated his entire body. I had no way to describe how it smelled, but I tried anyway.

Virile.

Hot.

Manly.

None of them did him justice. The closest I could come was... animalistic.

Not understanding it, but knowing it was true all the same, I knew the word was the right one. He gave me the impression of being an animal in a man's body. Like a wolf or a bear. Or, closer to the real thing, a very large and very powerful cat.

Maybe that was why they called themselves the Kings of Beasts. Had other people, probably mostly women, told them the same thing? I could easily see them as the human versions of the lion. Regal, fierce, powerful, deadly. Ruger was deadly, for sure, but in a physical way. Logan, however, seemed deadly in every way. Physically, yes. But emotionally deadly, too. Like he could pull my heart out of my chest and put it in a cage for his enjoyment only.

Funny how the idea of my heart being caged by Logan didn't bother me. In fact, it was exciting and strangely comforting at the same time.

How hard had Ruger hit me anyway? I must've gotten more of a shock than I'd realized if I was thinking a man was like a cat.

Enough thinking about men.

I got going. The incline of the mountain grew steeper. I leaned forward, pushing through the still remaining ache in my head. Once I made it to the cave, I'd lie down and hope it went away.

"You're going the wrong way."

Chapter Seven

Mia

Instead of whirling around as I'd done earlier at the sound of the breaking twig, I turned on my heel, taking my time, trying to act as though my heart hadn't jumped out of my chest when I'd heard Logan's voice.

He stood a few feet away. He was taller than I remembered even with him standing at a slightly lower ground level. The muscles in his arms rippled as he shoved his hands into his pockets. His blue-silver eyes were more subdued, shaded in part by the furrow of his brow. His golden hair moved with the breeze and the top of the lion tattoo peeked out from under his shirt.

Standing there with the trees as his background, he could've been any number of amazing men from mythology. Thor. Hercules. Zeus. But he wasn't. He was a guy who ran with a gang who liked to ride motorcycles and put on a challenge called The Claiming Games. As much as I wanted to, I needed to stop fantasizing about him.

He's just a guy.

A really hot, really strong, really amazing guy. Damn.

"What'd you say?" I couldn't help but scan his body, trying to find any signs of injury. "Are you okay?"

"Of course I am."

Of course he was? So he didn't even have a scratch on him? Not a black eye or a bloody nose. After hearing the way they'd gone at each other, I'd expected him to be banged up bad. Instead, he looked like he could jump in front of a camera and pose for a magazine ad.

"But how? I heard you two going at it." Granted, I hadn't actually seen them come to blows, but from the anger I'd seen before I'd hightailed it out of there, there was no way they hadn't fought.

He shrugged, sloughing off my question. "I'm fine. You're the one you should be worrying about."

"Me?" I wanted to act like Ruger putting his hands on me was nothing, but the trembles came back. Along with memories of my father. I choked back the bile. "I'm fine."

"Did he"—his gaze dropped downward, then jerked its way up again—"do anything?"

"No. Not much anyway." How long would it take me before I'd stop remembering how he'd grabbed me and thrown me to my knees? I'd learned to deal with my father's abuse, hadn't I? I'd learn to deal with Ruger's attack, too.

His expression, so concerned, so open, hardened. "So you were going to blow him?'

"What?"

He came closer, almost in a threatening manner. Yet, I didn't think I had anything to fear. And I was good at knowing when to fear a man.

"You were on your knees. You had your mouth open and ready to suck him."

Did he really think I'd have gone through with it? "That's not the way it was, Logan." Anger flashed inside me. He didn't know me and didn't know what I'd do, but I couldn't help being hurt by what he thought. A stranger would've given me the benefit of the doubt.

"Sure looked like it."

I was at him then, moving as fast as I could. Everything from fear to anger boiled inside me, forming a churning need to strike out. The sound of my slap echoed in the woods before I realized what I'd done. Not that I would've stopped. Hell, he deserved it and more.

I'd hit him as hard as I could, but it had barely moved his head to the side. He locked gazes with me, his blue-silver eyes appearing more silver than blue, the intensity of his stare driving into me.

"Did you get it out of your system?" He lifted his chin and offered me his other cheek. "Or do you want to slap me again?"

I surprised both of us by whipping my hand out and striking him again. The second was a lot harder than the first. Especially since this time I used my fist instead of my palm. This time his head turned farther to the side.

When he faced me again, his eyes had changed almost completely to silver. "Do you need another one? How about kicking me in the balls? Anything to make you feel better."

I learned a quick lesson. It's not half as much fun hitting someone when they gave their permission to do it. "Nope. I'm good."

He worked his jaw back and forth. "You pack a good punch."

"Thanks." I held my head high, ready to take whatever shit he'd dole out.

"Now that you're over your tantrum, can you answer the question? Were you going to blow Ruger or not?"

Oh. My. God. "Not."

He didn't react. At least, not as far as I could tell. Aside, maybe, from a glint in his eyes that was gone in the next second.

"Then what were you planning on doing? Kissing the tip of it?"

The urge to hit him came again, but I resisted it. Barely. "Not that it's really any of your business, but I was going to bite the damn thing off."

Again, he didn't react.

I gaped at him. "Nothing? Really? No reaction at all?"

He burst out laughing, doubling over then slapping his leg. "You were going to bite it off? That's fucking great."

I couldn't hold back my smile. His smile was that contagious. "Yeah, well, I was going to try. I'm not sure I could've bitten it clean off, but I figured how much more gross would it be to bite it than to suck it?"

He laughed again, shaking his head. "Damn. I wish I hadn't saved your ass now. I shouldn't have interfered."

"Yeah. I guess you sort of helped me out." He had, but the way he'd said it rubbed me the wrong way. He'd definitely shown up at the right moment, but I figured I would've had a good shot at getting away on my own after I'd taken half of his putrid cock off. Provided I hadn't passed out from the gruesome task of severing Ruger's main head from his body.

His laughter faded away. "What do you mean 'sort of'? I totally saved you. And you're welcome."

I admit it. I'm not great at saying thanks to anyone for anything. After all, I hadn't had much practice at it. We weren't one of those families who sat around the dinner table together, talking about their day and saying "please" and "thank you" to each other for passing the peas. Plus, knowing he expected me to thank him made me not want to.

Later, I was sure I'd blame my bitchiness on my headache. But for now, I couldn't let him get cocky.

"I would've been fine without your help."

I'd caught him by surprise again. And I liked it. At least it was a reaction of some kind.

"Are you kidding me? If I hadn't come along, he would've fucked you, then beaten you. Maybe not in that order, but he would have one way or another."

I wanted to pretend he wasn't right, but the churning in my gut whenever I thought about Ruger made it tough to argue. But I still tried. "Biting his dick would've had him on the ground and crying for his mother. I'd have had plenty of time to get away. You know I would have."

His frown didn't make me feel any better. I definitely preferred his smile.

"You're full of shit. You might've gotten your teeth into him, but he would've pulled your hair out when he yanked you off him. Then he would've killed you."

Would I have bitten him? Or would I have chickened out at the last moment? And if I had, could I have gotten away fast enough? He was right. I knew it and he knew it. But I was known for my stubbornness.

"Oh, trust me. I would've bitten him but good. I'd have cut it in half." I opened my mouth, then clamped my teeth together, chomping on an invisible cock.

One eyebrow went up. "Okay, if you want to think so, then fine." He pulled me closer.

I resisted—a little—but kept up my false bravado. "I'll tell you what. If you're willing to admit that I might not have needed your help, then I'll admit what you really did." I made certain he understood. "You *helped* me. You didn't *save* me."

He didn't agree. Not really. If he ground his teeth any harder, he'd crack one.

"Fine. I agree. I helped you. And you're welcome." He rubbed my arms, sliding his palms up and down them.

I'm sure it was meant as a comforting gesture, but it was so much more. Having him touch me was flat-out sensual. As though his hands contained little bonfires, he sent zings of heat racing along my skin. Suddenly, my mouth watered and the flood didn't stop there. I drew in a breath and caught his magnificent scent again. I leaned closer, easing my stomach against the front of his jeans.

If I didn't watch myself, I'd reach up and pull his mouth to mine. Instead, I played it safe, sending my sinful ideas in another direction.

"Why'd you do it?"

"Why'd I help you? Because of you. Because you're mine."

It shouldn't have affected me. I wasn't there for him or any other man. But it still made me feel all warm and gooey inside. I had to get off the subject. "Tell me about your eyes."

He batted his eyelashes at me, destroying my determination not to giggle. "They're soulful, right?"

I gave him a "seriously?" look. "Oh, yeah. You're gorg. But that's not what I want to know. How do they change colors? And who has that kind of eye color anyway? They remind me of a Siberian Husky's eyes."

"Not all their eyes are blue. And you're comparing my eyes to a dog's. I'm not sure I like that."

"You didn't answer my question. I've never seen anyone with blue-silver eyes. And especially not anyone whose eyes change to almost silver. It's kind of freaky."

Logan

I couldn't tell Mia the truth. Revealing what we were was against the pride's rules. "I don't know. I'm not a scientist." I grinned, knowing she'd focus on my mouth and, if I was lucky, forget about the eye color. "But I can tell you one thing. I'm sure as hell not a damn dog."

Crap, how I want her.

After seeing her kneeling in front of Ruger, everything had gone haywire. The world had spun around me, making me dizzy and tearing a hole in my gut. The need to hurt Ruger and keep her safe dominated the whirling mess of my mind. I'd almost shifted. If I had, I'd have attacked Ruger and wouldn't have stopped until he lay dead at my feet. Not only would I have taken another lion's life, a pride member's life, but she would've seen me change not once, but twice when I shifted back to human. I'm not sure I could've stopped myself from shoving her to her hands and knees with me ready to claim her from behind.

She was so fucking hot. I'd thought so from the first moment I'd seen her, but standing in the middle of the trees with the brief flashes of sun from above glinting off the blue highlights in her black hair made her even more amazing. Her eyes were the color of the moss on the north side of the trees and held a glint of wickedness that had my cock pushing against my jeans.

Although I knew I shouldn't, especially after what she'd gone through with Ruger, I couldn't help myself. I lingered over her breasts, the perfect swell and dip of them, and clenched my hands to keep from cupping them. A bruise marred her right breast. Would I find more bruises once I had her undressed, ready for exploration?

"You didn't answer my question. Why and how do your eyes change color? I mean, sure, eyes change color, but not like that. Not that fast or that much."

I had to remember what we'd been talking about. As far as I was concerned, I'd rather not be talking. I'd rather lay her on the ground and slide my tongue over her skin from the tip of her turned up nose down to her toes. I'd suck on her toes, then make my way up her calf, then on to her inner thigh. Then I'd make satisfied noises once I got my face between her legs.

"Look, I'm sorry about before. About Ruger." I couldn't help but play with her. Her reactions were fun to watch. "And for not giving you time to chomp down on his dick."

I almost got her to laugh again. If I had it my way, I'd have her laughing all day long. Whenever she wasn't moaning and sighing in my bed.

But I had more important things to do than to tease her. "I shouldn't have followed you. And I'm not supposed to help you. But when I saw him…"

"Yeah. I get it. But no one has to know."

"Ruger knows."

She let out a low whistle. "Will he tell them?"

"I don't think so. Ruger's a shithead, but he's not the type to squeal. Besides, that's not his end game. I think he was trying to get back at me." Worse, I doubted he was done trying.

"Back at you for what?"

Telling her about Vic was the last thing I wanted to do. "Just something I'd rather forget ever happened."

Ruger would keep quiet. He knew if he told anyone I'd

interfered, I'd tell everyone about how Mia almost bit off his itty, bitty dick. They'd have a field day with it. As much as he wanted to get back at me, he wouldn't risk getting ridiculed. Having anyone laugh at him drove him crazy-mad.

Besides, that wasn't Ruger's style. He'd meant it to hurt me, but if he was really planning on getting at me, he'd do something he could savor for a while. Forcing her into sex would've killed me, but after giving him the beat down of his life, I would've eventually gotten past it. It sure as hell wouldn't keep me from mating her.

Telling the others I'd interfered didn't seem like his end goal. Getting Mia disqualified and me exiled wouldn't allow him to enjoy my suffering long enough. We'd both be gone and that would be the end of his entertainment. If he wanted to get back at me, he'd damn sure to do something major.

She nodded, letting me off the hook. "So we're good?"

"Yeah. I think we are." Yet the awful feeling that we hadn't seen the last of Ruger wouldn't go away.

"I guess I'd better get going."

I took her arm, stopping her, but for an entirely different reason than what came out of my mouth. "Wait. Tell me about yourself."

She pulled her arm free, gently, but still firmly. "Like I said, I need to get going."

"I know, but a few minutes won't hurt. I need to know more about you."

"Why?"

Because I care. And I want to care even more.

"Just curious." I grinned, letting her in on my joke. "Besides, a guy has a right to know about the girl he just saved."

She caught the word, shot me a pointed look, but let it go.

"There's not much to tell."

"Bullshit. Where are you from?" I wanted to keep her with me. After already breaking the rule about interfering with her challenge, what did I have to lose?

"Biloxi, Mississippi."

I smiled, seeing how she was finally relaxing. "Big family?"

Her expression grew sad. "Yeah. I guess it's bigger than most. Two parents and seven brothers and sisters."

She smiled at my slow whistle. "Wow. That's a lot. So your parents must like kids, huh?"

Her reaction went even farther south. Why did talking about her family make her so sad?

"My mom does. My dad's out of the picture."

Out of the picture? As in gone? Dead? In jail? A deadbeat dad?

"It's hard for her trying to make ends meet with all of us kids. That's why I'm doing the challenge. My family needs the money."

"That's rough. I'm sorry about your dad." I was fishing, trying to find out what had happened to him.

"Don't be. He's an asshole."

"Why?"

"Why what? Why is he an asshole?"

"Yeah. Why is he an asshole?"

She started not to answer. Whatever her father had done was bad. Real bad.

"Tell me, Mia."

Her mouth parted, then closed, as though she was struggling to decide if she should open up to me.

"I want to know. Tell me." I shifted just a little and lowered my voice, coaxing her. She'd hear the lion in my tone and would trust me enough to answer. "You can trust me."

She let out a puff of air and her words rushed out. "He's a sick bastard who liked locking me in the hall closet. He got drunk every night and then got his jollies off by sticking me in the closet, beating my mom and terrorizing my brothers and sisters. Are those good enough reasons?"

That threw me. Just knowing she'd been hurt tightened my chest. "What? Why?"

"I told you. He's mentally fucked up." She tunneled her fingers through her shiny black mane. "He knew how much it—" Her next breath was even more ragged than the first. "I have a thing about closed-in places."

"You mean like being claustrophobic?"

Her gaze met mine, defiant, challenging me to make her feel ashamed. "Yeah. I kind of freak out whenever I can't see out." She glanced around her. "Even having the trees this close together bugs me. Which is why going to this cave isn't real high on my list of fun places to visit."

"What do you think's going to happen?"

She swallowed, then moved her head side to side, getting rid of tension. "I feel like the trees or the walls or whatever is moving in on me. Coming closer and closer until I'm crushed." Her hard scowl was contradicted by the moisture in her eyes. "I don't know why I'm telling you this."

"Because you can. You can tell me anything."

She looked away then. "I guess."

"And your mom just let him get away with all his shit?"

She glared, hard and cold. "She didn't have a choice. A lot of women don't. They don't have the money or the help and they're afraid. What was she supposed to do? Let her kids sleep on the streets?"

"Aren't there shelters you guys could've done to?"

She laughed but it wasn't a sound I liked. "It's so easy to judge from the outside looking in. He threatened to kill all of us. She was too frightened and too used to living that way. But she finally did. She finally got up enough courage and she did it. In my eyes, she's the bravest woman I know."

I tried to understand, but it didn't make sense to me. A lion would never treat his family that way. If he did, he'd have the pride to answer to.

"Is there more?" I wasn't sure I wanted to hear anything else, but I could sense she wanted—*needed*—to tell me. I doubted she'd told many people. In fact, maybe no one.

"Let's just say he likes the way my body feels." Her voice rose in pitch and she gritted her teeth.

Shit. A drunk. A cruel bastard and a pervert. Rage filled me and it took a lot to shove it down. "He... touched you?"

She averted her gaze. As though it was her fault that her father was a pervert. "You can tell me, Mia."

She frowned at me, confused as she searched my face. "Yeah. He did."

I swallowed, finding it hard to ask the next question. But I had to know. "Did he..."

"No. But it would've happened if I hadn't gotten out of there."

I let out a breath I hadn't realized I was holding in. "But you said he's out of the picture now. What do you mean?"

"Like I said. We left him. My mom and the rest of the kids went to a shelter. Then, hopefully, on to a relative's house. I came to Fang's. That's why I've got to take the money."

Shit. How could I blame her for wanting the money instead of me? "I'm sorry, Mia. Sorry you had to take that kind of shit."

"It doesn't matter now. It's over." She pulled her body

straight and rubbed at her eyes. "And you? What's your family like?"

Unlike her, I liked talking about my family. Both my immediate one and my extended family of the pride. And after hearing about hers, it was a relief. "I've lived in our mountains all my life. I wouldn't want to live anywhere else."

"Nowhere? Like maybe Hawaii or France?" Her voice had leveled out, going back to a more normal pitch.

"Naw. Why would I want to go there? I have everything I need and more right here. Like my mom and dad. We're close. And I have a younger sister named Kyla. She's out in California, soaking up the sun while she gets her business degree. I think she's doing more partying than studying, though."

"Still. You're proud of her."

"Yeah. I am. She's pretty amazing. I still can't believe she was the little brat that was always pulling my tail."

"Your tail?"

"Uh, my hair."

A pause came then, as it often did whenever two people exchanged facts about their lives. It wasn't uncomfortable. Just part of the getting acquainted process.

"So what do you want, Mia? Other than helping your family?" I wanted to know everything about her.

She brushed her hair back. "First, I want to take care of my family. Then, after that, I'd like to go to cosmetology school."

"That's hair school, right? So you want to be a hair stylist?"

"And a makeup artist. And then, once I've gotten enough experience, I want to open up my own place. Nothing big. Just a little place in a small town."

"A small town like Cripple Creek?" I was pushing, hoping she'd want to stay. After she was changed, she would. They all did. As a new lioness, she'd want the protection and companionship of the pride.

"Uh, I don't think so. The people didn't seem all that friendly."

They hadn't been friendly because she was an outsider. Once she was my mate, they'd welcome her. Most everyone in the small town knew about the pride and they kept our secret.

"Give them time."

"I'm not planning on hanging around long enough for that." She cleared her throat and shifted from one foot to the other. "I really do need to get going."

"Yeah, you should. Listen, I'm not supposed to help you, but since I already have, I'll tell you. Like I said before. You're not headed in the right direction."

"Sure I am." She brushed away a bit of dirt on her shirt, then pulled the map out of her jeans. "Besides, I've got the map. See? I don't need your help."

I snagged it away from her, then turned it so she could watch as I slid my finger along the route. "When you took off running, you went the wrong way. This is where we are." I pointed at the spot on the map. "And this is where you should be." I slid my finger back, putting it on top of the trail. "If you keep going the way you're headed, you'll never make it to the cave. Instead, you'll wind up getting lost."

I was proud of the way she tried to hide her sudden alarm. She'd have to learn how to control her emotions if she became one of us. *When* she became one of us. Controlling my human emotions was a lot easier than controlling the lion inside me.

She squinted at the second place where I'd pointed. "Are you sure?"

"Yeah. I'm sure. I know these hills. Trust me."

"Well, fuck a duck."

Maybe it was the way she'd said the words, or it was the silly words themselves. Or maybe it was the way she'd let out a burst of air afterward, making her lips purse. I don't know which it was. Whatever the reason, I couldn't have held back if I'd wanted to.

And I sure as hell didn't want to.

I forgot about the map, the challenge and the warnings not to help her. I forgot about Ruger. I forgot about everything else. Instead, I did what both my mind and my heart told me to do.

Taking her under her arms, I lifted her off the ground, gripped her round butt with one hand and her neck with the other, and brought her to me. My mouth slammed against her pursed lips, demanding she kiss me back. Her breasts crushed against my chest and her warm crotch pressed against my abdomen.

I couldn't get enough of her. My tongue sweeping into her mouth would never bring me enough of her flavors. But then, unless I could absorb her body into mine, I doubted I could ever get close enough.

At first, she didn't respond. Not in a good or a bad way. Then, as I held her to me, she wrapped her arms around my neck and kissed me back.

As though it was our own kind of challenge, our tongues battled with each other. For a moment, I'd dive into her mouth and win. Then, in the next, she'd force it back and claim my mouth. Her fingers tunneled into my hair and she tightened her hold on me.

My lion roared, elated that I was finally listening to its call to claim her. It rose higher, pushing under the surface, demanding to show her what a lion would do for its lioness. If I turned it lose, even just my fangs, I wasn't sure I could handle it. I knew she couldn't. Driving it back into submission was harder than anything I'd ever done. But I did it for her.

Her moans gave me the added fuel to make her mine. She rubbed against me, her breasts against my chest, her crotch against my stomach. I moaned, too, answering her, telling her I'd soon have to rip her clothes away and find relief.

Instead of falling to the ground, taking her with me, I went to my knees. She yelped as we hit the ground, but I didn't let her cry stop the kiss. Nothing short of suffocation would break us apart.

But she was the one to end the kiss. Her chest rose and fell with her panted breaths. Her eyes were glazed over, lost in the same lust filling me. I took hold of her shirt and almost ripped it off her, but managed to remember that she still had most of the challenge ahead of her. Instead, I pulled it over her head and feasted my attention on her breasts. Her simple bra came off with quick work and fell to the ground next to her shirt.

I'd known she was beautiful, that her body was smokin', but when I saw her perfect, perky breasts, the brown areolas pointed directly at me, free of her shirt, I was blown away. My need for her spiraled upward, consuming me like a drug that was instantly addicting.

She tugged at my shirt and I helped her get rid of it. Yet before I could get my jeans undone, I gave in to the need to kiss her again.

She whimpered as I took her head in my hands and brought her mouth back to mine. But my kiss was only the foretelling of what was to come. I needed every inch of her as though touching her, kissing her was the only thing that could keep me alive.

I slid my mouth from her lips, over her jaw, then down her neck. Her breasts were just the right weight, just the right size for my hands. Her hair made an obsidian backdrop to her pale shoulders. Shoulders I had to nibble on.

First her shoulders, then back to her neck, trying to keep from going to the one place I needed the most. But a man, even when he's a lion, is only just so strong. I could already imagine the taste of her blood on my tongue as I drove my fangs into her, changing her. Her scent would grow stronger once she was mine. Groaning, I forced my fangs back even as I skimmed them along her skin.

I bent and took a nipple into my mouth then growled, barely keeping my lion in control. She arched her back, offering herself to me and yanked on my hair. It was a message I couldn't ignore.

As hard as it was, I lifted my gaze to hers, silently questioning. In answer, she undid her jeans and, taking her panties along with them, slid them to her knees. She kicked, taking off one shoe as she freed herself from her clothes.

In our frenzied first time, I hadn't noticed. She was clean-shaven, perfect for my mouth.

I laid her on her back, then pushed her legs apart. She laughed at me as I tried to get my jeans down while moving toward her. Just as I thought I'd get between her legs, she grabbed my arm and held me back.

"What is it?" If she made me stop, it might send my frustrated lion into a frenzy I might not be able to contain. Either way, I was screwed.

And then I saw the wild glint in her eyes. She was afraid. Even if I hadn't seen the fear there, I would've seen it in the stiffening of her body and smelled it in the extra aroma layering her scent.

"I... can't."

Damn Ruger.

He was the cause of her fear. Knowing I wouldn't have her ripped into me, piercing me like a poisonous spear. The pain radiated outward from my crotch and into my belly. But I'd do anything for her. Even stop.

I fell to the side, my breathing labored as I struggled to bring my need down. At first, I found it difficult to look at her. Not because I was angry, but if I didn't look away, I was afraid I wouldn't be able to stop again.

"I'm sorry. I just can't."

I closed my eyes for a moment, then manned up. When I faced her again, I controlled my lion and my desire. I'd always yearn for her, but that was different. For now, at least, I'd sacrifice my craving to make her feel safe.

But I had to know. If she could give me an answer, then I'd handle it better. "Tell me what's wrong." I glanced down at her smoothness just as she tugged her jeans up. The words were out before I could think about what I was saying. "You're not a virgin, are you?" I laughed. It was a stupid question. If anyone knew the answer to that question, I did.

But she didn't think it was funny. Not one damn bit. She scrambled to her feet and snatched up her bra and shirt. "Are you kidding me? Don't you remember me from before? Or was I just a fuck-and-forget girl?"

I got to my feet, feeling like I'd jumped off a cliff without meaning to. "No."

Her mouth dropped open and she backed up. "You don't remember me? Not at all?"

"Sure I do. That's not what I meant." I shrugged, but it was the truth. "I asked the virgin thing without thinking. It's kind of a go-to question for most guys. If a girl doesn't want to fuck, a guy figures she's a virgin. Or a prude. Shit. Forget I asked. I just want to know why you don't want to fuck."

"Seriously?" She shoved me away when I tried to take her arm. "You can ask me that after what Ruger just tried to do? After my father?" She couldn't have shut her mouth any faster.

I should've known better. She'd come through the ordeal with Ruger, but I'd failed to notice how badly it had shaken her. Guilt hit me, but I had no time to deal with it. She came first.

"I'm sorry. I fucked up."

"Never mind." Turning her back to me, she pulled on her clothes as I did mine, then whirled to confront me. "Since you don't remember me—"

"Damn it. I do remember you."

But she kept right on going. "—let me clue you in. I'm not a virgin. In fact, I'm damn good at sex. But that doesn't mean I want some hairy asshole pawing all over me."

I rocked back as through she'd struck me again even harder. "Hey, just wait a sec. I wasn't pawing at you. I'm not an animal." At least, not in the way she thought. I struggled to rein in my temper, then attempted to keep the trouble from getting worse. "I might be a little hairy..."

She didn't find my joke funny. If anything, it made her madder.

"Just back the hell off, all right?"

"Hey, I'm sorry, but I thought you were into it." My anger slipped through a crack in my defenses. "You sure as hell seemed like you were."

I'd kicked it back to her. Now she was the one fumbling for words.

Her fury lowered enough for her to give me a guilt-ridden look. But she wasn't about to give up the fight. "I made a mistake. Then I realized—" Her mouth twisted, working hard not to speak. "I don't have to give you a reason. Much less one you'll agree with."

"Look, Mia, as your mate—"

"Holy hell. What is it with you guys and this mate thing? What are we? Animals on a farm? I feel like I'm some mare you think is in heat."

"More like animals in a zoo." I lifted my hands, palms out, to ward off her scorching glare. "Hold on. It was just a joke." I finally got it through my head. No more jokes.

When she screamed her frustration at me, I wasn't sure whether to grab her and put her in a strait jacket or run for my life. "What the fuck's wrong with you?"

She snatched the map off the ground. "What's the fuck's wrong with *me*? Not a damn thing. Just leave me alone."

I prided myself on having a lot of patience. I'd learned to keep my cool growing up with Ruger, but she'd finally pushed me over my limit. "Leave you alone? Hell, yeah. No problem. Besides, I'm not supposed to help my mate—"

She screamed again. "Stop calling me that! I'm not yours or anyone else's mate. Got it?"

"Fuck, yeah. I got it."

But that didn't ease my craving for her. I'd heard arguing could lead to sex and I guess it was true. The more she yelled at me, the more I wanted her.

Sex was off limits with her until she made it to the cave, but I'd gotten so turned on that I hadn't cared if I broke all the rules in the world. Never mind about the truck stop. That was before the games, and in my mind, it didn't count. But I'd wanted, hell, needed to fuck her. Fucking stupid on my part.

We both jumped as one of the girls I'd seen earlier at Fang's burst through the trees and kept going. Neither one of us moved. The girl was gone before we could react.

"Do you know who that was?" The sudden appearance of someone else had broken the tension between us.

She shook her head. "No."

"We'd better hope she doesn't mention seeing us together."

"I don't think she even noticed us. She was hauling ass."

"Let's hope you're right." I pointed in the direction she needed to go. "Better hurry or you're not going to make it before the sun goes down."

Damn. The tears suddenly filling her eyes made me feel like the biggest jerk in the world. I shouldn't have touched her. Not until she'd had time to get over what Ruger had done.

I set my jaw and made a vow. One way or the other, I'd deal with him. No way would he ever put his hands on her again. "Mia, I want you to know…" The promise stalled in my throat.

"What?"

"Nothing. Get going, okay? And be careful."

She nodded, then pivoted on her heel. Before she was lost in the forest, she craned her head around, looked at me one more time, then was gone.

Chapter Eight

Logan

Fucking A.

I fought against the urge to go after Mia and make sure she was following the map again. After what had just happened, I held back. Ruger had already seen us together and one of the girls might have, too. I'd give Mia some lead time, then check on her. Without getting involved again.

No one had ever told me the games would be this hard. At least not for the men. Everything I'd ever heard had made it seem easy enough. Pick a girl. Send her on her challenge. Show up at the destination and fuck her. Then wait for her to make it back down to Fang's. It sounded easy enough, but then again, the others hadn't had a mate like Mia.

Yeah. She's an original, all right.

But damn, what a hot one. Both her body as well as her mind. And her quick-to-explode temper. She was everything I wanted in a girl. I just hadn't realized it until I'd met her. Until I'd sniffed her.

Her scent alone had been a surprise. I'd sniffed other girls before. What lion didn't? But none of their scents had seared into my nostrils, down my throat, and whipped around my gut. And none of them had taken hold of me just as surely as a lasso around my neck would have. She'd hung me up by my balls and made me hers. And now that I knew her better, the noose had tightened.

The whole thing was scary.

And exciting as hell.

I didn't understand her fear of closed-in places. Having grown up in the mountains, I'd never felt trapped. But her problem was now my problem. I'd do everything I could to help her. That, too, was scary, but I wasn't afraid of a challenge. Not even one I didn't understand.

I ducked lower as I heard another woman running down a different path. Catching just a glimpse of her, I recognized her as one of the girls who'd sat at the same table with Mia. Colter Quaid had wanted her. Why? It beat the hell out of me. She was timid where Mia was outspoken. She'd sat, squirming in her chair while Burke explained the games. Mia hadn't been afraid to open her mouth and question Burke. I hadn't wanted her to, but I'd still felt pride when she had. Of course, Burke had put her in her place, but it said a lot about Mia that she'd even had the guts to speak up. Most of the women didn't. Those who did were either brave like her or just plain foolish, like the redheaded girl who'd asked if they were on a reality show.

As far as I was concerned, I'd gotten the pick of the litter. So to speak.

I'd already broken the rules by helping her. But if I hadn't, I would've left Ruger alone letting him force her into giving him a blowjob or worse.

It sucked, but some of the old rules were still around. Another male could claim my girl as long as she hadn't already completed the challenge and chosen me over the money.

The rule was an outdated, ancient one that had been meant to test the girl's ability to fight. Some of those old rules just didn't make sense any longer, especially when they contradicted the pride's current views. We needed to change the rule, but so far, we'd just let it slide, thinking it'd become so obscure that no one would remember it. Or, as it was now, that the rule was no longer needed because no one would ever think of taking a male's mate from him. It just wasn't done any longer.

Once a male told Burke which girl he wanted, then the others knew to back off. To do otherwise would be a major sign of disrespect. Not only would he catch hell from the man who'd spoken for her, but the others would turn against him. His status in the pride would diminish and living with the pride would eventually become unbearable. Sooner or later, he'd face the same fate I'd suffer if they found out I'd interfered with the games. Exile.

Or at least that's what most of us assumed would happen. We didn't know for certain since no one had ever taken another male's mate in recent memory.

The real claiming came when I bit her and changed her into a lioness, but everyone considered her making the choice at Fang's just as binding.

Still, if I'd followed the rules, I wouldn't have interfered. But I hadn't been able to stop myself. I couldn't lose her. Not now, after I'd taken her scent and made her a part of me. To not have her become my mate would kill me.

But why had Ruger done it? To get back at me for sure. Still, I doubted he'd wanted to sink his fangs into her and claim her. Not because he respected me, but because he'd always said he never wanted a mate. If he had, he would've pounced on her, bitten her, and then fucked her. Instead, he'd wanted to see her submit to him and for me to find out about it later.

I shuddered to think it could've happened. Yet, no matter

what, there was no way I'd ever turn her away.

The question of why Ruger had done it still remained. Was it really payback? Or Ruger just being his usual asshole self? Yet unless I was his target—and my gut said I was—I would've thought he'd have attacked the first girl who'd come along. I didn't get that sense from what I'd seen. No, it was personal.

A low growl slid out of my throat and threatened to grow louder. I held it back, knowing the sound could be heard for miles.

I had to make sure I didn't slip up again. She could fall and injure herself, but I couldn't help her. A bear or another wild animal could attack her, but I was supposed to stand by and just watch. I understood the need for her to make it through the challenge on her own, to prove she was strong enough to be a lioness, but understanding the rule and letting something bad happen to her was a hell of a lot different. Now that the games had become personal for me, I vowed I'd do anything I could to get rid of the rule.

Until then, I had to hope Ruger would back off. It hurt to realize how far our friendship had split apart. But I'd never expected Ruger to hate me enough to hurt my mate.

Maybe he wouldn't try anything else. I couldn't be sure, so I'd have to stay close to her just in case. As though I hadn't already been planning on doing that, anyway. Most of us did without ever letting our mate know we were there.

So much for not letting her know I'm around.

Mia would make it to the cave. I was sure of it. She was strong and resilient. Stubborn enough not to let anything, even Ruger, keep her from getting there on time.

Once she made it, I'd show up and get to know her better. The burn I had for her that had been fueled by both our encounters sparked to life again. When she was at the cave, I'd go to her. I'd pleasure her body and then make her heart mine. I'd have wild, passionate sex with her, over and over, and let her know she had no choice but to choose me. I'd know before she left the cave that she'd choose me.

She was under my skin. Drawing in her scent, then touching her, seeing her naked lying on the ground had driven her into me like a nail into a board. My inner lion roared, clawing at my insides to find her again and sink first my cock, then my fangs into her. I ached for her. Yearned for her. I felt like a man who hadn't had food in months, then had been invited to a lavish banquet only to be ordered not to eat.

Growling, I pulled my clothes off and stacked them under a bush. After I ran, after I released some of the tension whirling inside me, I'd come back and get dressed. Then I'd run to the cave and meet her when she arrived. Although it was risky shifting with the girls in the woods, if I didn't give my lion freedom soon, I'd break in half. I just had to believe she'd stay safe until I came back.

The transformation hit me as it always did, fast and hard. It hurt, but I could handle the kind of pain that came with bones breaking and reforming, with fur replacing skin. Within a minute, I'd shifted into my lion body. I growled, lower, softer this time, then bounded into the forest, heading away from Mia.

Mia

I'd thought I was in shape, but now I had to wonder. After getting past the dry gulch that was really more like a dried up creek, I'd started up an incline. That wasn't so tough, but once I ran into the rock cropping, getting onto the rocks slowed me down. A lot.

Still, it was nice to be out in the open and to feel the sun on my skin. It was all wide open spaces with no walls in sight.

I took a break and leaned against the rocks. Looking out over beautiful land, I couldn't help but think I'd found my Happy Place. Green trees and a gorgeous cloud-dotted blue sky overhead was everything I'd dreamed of. The only things missing were birds singing, a bunny hopping to its hideaway, and a babbling brook. I laughed, feeling more relaxed and more at home than I'd ever felt in the overcrowded house in Biloxi. If only I could stay on the mountain forever. Then I'd finally find the peace I'd dreamed of.

Logan's face came to me, but that was asking too much of a dream. Finding the perfect place to live along with a sexy man? Only fairytales had both of those and I wasn't the kind of girl who believed in magic.

The sun was high in the sky so I wasn't too worried about time. Unless, of course, I ran into another problem with either Ruger or Logan. Preferably Logan.

No. I can't get sidelined again. Not even with him.

The memory of my mother's tormented face, my brothers' and sisters' terrified wails tore into me as though it was happening all over again. I wasn't doing the challenge just for me. I had to do it for them. The money wouldn't keep them safe if my father found them, but it would damn sure give them a better chance of staying free of him.

My Aunt Brenda would do all she could, but she was a single woman living on a small paycheck. There was no way she could support my mom and all her kids. Now that my mom had left our home, she wouldn't even have the small bit of money she made from taking in laundry. She couldn't risk contacting those women. Not when my father might find out. She'd have to find some way to support her family. But how? I could only pray my aunt would help her find a job and a new place to live. At least until I could help out.

Still, I couldn't help but wonder. What if I could make a real choice? What if it were possible to choose the man over the money? If I could, would I? If any man was worth throwing away a fortune, it was Logan. I sighed, knowing I shouldn't give him another thought. But thinking about him couldn't hurt, could it? As long as I kept the right goal in mind, I was good to go.

Damn, but he was sexy as hell with a body no woman could ever resist. Not unless she didn't like men. Maybe not even then. He was all raw sensuality and lust rolled into one. But there was something about him. Something I couldn't put my finger on. It was more than how he looked.

I'd never been one of those girls who went gaga over good-looking guys. And especially not the bad boy types like Logan. If and when I wanted to open up my heart to a man, he'd be a solid kind of guy, one I could trust.

Yet every second I spent around Logan made me hungry in a way that had nothing to do with the fact that I hadn't eaten anything in hours. The craving I had for him was deeper, stronger than a physical kind of thing. It didn't make sense, but I wanted him on a gut level kind of way. Like I belonged with him. How fucked up was that? I barely knew him and I was already hooked.

The sun beat down on my back as I bent forward using my hands to grab hold of rock after rock. My hands had cuts on them from the sharp edges, but I could handle a little pain. God knows I'd already gone through worse.

The hill wasn't straight up like one of those fake rock walls people in gyms liked to climb. It was more like the fifteen-degree incline I'd once tried on a treadmill. But the way the rocks were jumbled together, as though a child had thrown their toy blocks in a pile, made it a difficult climb.

"If I'd known what I was getting into, I would've practiced. I suck at this." Yeah, like I could've paid to go to one of those gyms.

"Looks like you're doing fine to me."

My hand slipped off the rock I'd just grabbed, but I managed to hang on. Squinting, I peered up at Ruger. My stomach did a sickening flip-flop. Panic, much like the way I'd felt in the closet, grabbed hold of me. My limbs stiffened and my pulse raced. I gritted my teeth, determined not to let him see how afraid I was. "Get out of my way."

He chuckled, then squatted and offered his hand. "I'm not really in your way. Want some help?"

"No." I gave him the meanest look I could, then put my attention back on getting over the last few rocks. If I could have, I would've gone around him, but the only way to the top and the flat ground above me was through him. "Like you said, I'm doing fine."

I was almost at the top. Too close to him for comfort. I wouldn't have put it past him to peel my fingers off and send me falling backward. Instead of getting away from me, he stayed where he was, his forearms resting on his knees, and acted like we were having a conversation about how fresh the fruit was at the local market.

"Naw, sugar, don't be that way. I came to apologize."

"I don't give a crap why you're here. Stay the hell away from me." I glared at him again. Maybe all my time with my father had steeled me against what he'd tried to do, but I was getting more angry than afraid. I glanced down and wondered if it was worth trying to go back down the hill, then finding a way around the rock outcropping and on to the cave. But I wasn't sure I'd make it down, much less be able to find another route. I had to keep going.

Grabbing hold of the last rock, I pulled myself onto the flat landing in front of more forest and the rest of the walk. Ruger took hold of my arm, as though he was trying to help steady me, but I jerked away and put several feet between us. My quickened pulse pounded in my ears and my breath hitched in my throat.

"I told you to stay the hell away from me."

"Look, Mia, I'm sorry for what I tried to do earlier." He let out a long, hard breath. "I don't know what got me all wound up." He smiled without any trace of real warmth in it. "Okay, that's a lie. You got me all wound up. Can you blame me for wanting you?"

I stepped back, careful to keep him at a safe distance. "Is that what you'd call it? Wanting me? Like some hero in a fucking romance novel? That's bullshit."

He grimaced. "Aw, don't be so harsh. I'm only a man."

"Like I told you before. Go fuck yourself."

The huge breath he took made it seem like he was misunderstood. "Look, sugar, I know I screwed up. What I tried to do…" He dragged in anther tortured breath. "I just came at it in the wrong way."

Either he actually believes his own shit or he's the best damn liar I've ever met.

But I'd lived with lies too long to buy into his. "Again. I don't give a damn. Just get the fuck away from me."

Or what? I'd call the cops? Yell for help? I hadn't seen Logan since he'd helped me get away from Ruger. Where was he anyway? His not checking up on me hurt a little. Maybe even a lot.

"Mia, when you finish the challenge and you choose Logan, then we're going to be seeing each other a lot. You'll become one of us. I figured I needed to clear the air between us."

"Don't worry about it. I won't be around long enough for it to be a problem. I'm taking the money."

I would've sworn he almost smiled. So much for his being a great liar. He was as full of shit as a horse stall after feeding time.

"I'm sorry to hear that. Not only for Logan's sake, but for the rest of us. You'd make a damn good Kings of Beasts member."

"Your loss, I guess."

"Good one." His smile grew wider, making me want to slap it right off his face. "Look, Mia, now that we're friends—"

The man had a set of balls on him the size of the mountain we were standing on. "Are you delusional? We are not friends."

"Well, I hope that changes real soon." He stuck his hand in his pocket and brought a piece of paper similar to the one the map was drawn on. "Take this."

I shook my head. "No thanks. And keep back."

"Go on. Take it. It's not going to bite you." He smirked. "And I won't bite you, either."

Like I believed him. "What is it?"

"It's a map like the one you're using to get to Logan's cave."

He wasn't making any sense. "I still have his map. I don't

need another one."

"This one's better. It'll lead you to my lean-to. It's not much, but it's closer and more comfortable than a cave. I have food and water there."

I laughed. How could I not? "You have got to be out of your mind. Why would you think I'd go to your place?"

His eyes changed, going from the same blue-silver of Logan's eyes to more of a metallic hue. "Because you know we've got something between us. You felt it as much as I did. Why else would you have wanted to suck my cock?"

I know it was wrong. Wrong and stupid, but I couldn't help it. The man wasn't using even a small part of his brain. I laughed again. That wiped away his grin as much as my slap would've. In return, I got a black look that would've wilted flowers. But it was worth it.

"I was on my knees ready to chomp down on your stick of a dick and bite the damn thing off. If Logan hadn't come along, you'd be wailing on the ground and trying to reattach the little bugger."

Fury, mean and ugly, darkened his expression even more. He clenched his hands and gritted his teeth. For a moment, I was truly and honestly scared. My laughter died.

"Just take it."

"No. I don't want it."

Tension rippled in the air surrounding us and tightened my throat. I should've kept things civil between us all while asserting myself and making it clear I'd put up a fight if I had to. That's what I should've done. But as usual, I'd let my big mouth flap and had pissed him off but good.

"I said take it." His gaze dropped to my chest, moving up and down with every quick breath I took.

"No. I won't." If he wanted to hurt me, he could. He was bigger, stronger and probably a lot faster. But I'd stand my ground no matter what. What else could I do? I wasn't about to submit to him. I wouldn't even pretend this time.

He closed his eyes, the struggle to control himself evident in the muscles twitching in his jaw. Yet, by the time he'd opened them again, he'd returned to the Ruger who'd apologized to me.

"Okay. No problem." He bent over, then placed it under a small rock. "I'll just leave it here in case you change your mind."

"I won't." No way would I give him false hope. Not one damn little bit.

He smiled and lifted his hands into the air like he was under arrest. "I really hope you do. We could be so good together."

"Again. Not happening."

He put one hand over his heart. "You're breaking me apart. You know that, don't you?"

"Go screw yourself."

Keeping my eye on him, I started to back step toward the trees behind me. Then I'd make my way higher until I ran into the rocks separating the forest I'd gone through from the rest of the woods. According to the map, I wouldn't have to climb the second set of rocks. Instead, I'd follow a path around them and run straight into the cave. But first, I had to get away from Ruger.

"Mia, if you'll just—"

I held up my hand, cutting him off. "I don't have to do anything. If you're really sorry about what you did, then you'll leave me alone." I narrowed my eyes. "So? Are you being sincere or not?"

"I am. I promise you, I am. But it's okay. I can't blame you for not believing me. And I know when I've met my match."

I didn't think there was anything I hated more than his grin. How could any grin have so little warmth in it? "Good."

He turned, then started down the same rock climb I'd just labored over. Unlike me, however, he had no problem with them. I leaned over the edge and saw that he'd made it down to the bottom. No one could've gone as fast without rappelling. So how the hell had he done it? He waved and jogged toward the trees. Away from me.

I stood there a few minutes, watching, making sure he was really gone. Once I was sure he wasn't going to turn around and come back, I tugged the map out from under the rock and studied it. He was right. I was closer to his lean-to than to the cave. But as far as I was concerned, it could've been right next to me and I wouldn't have looked inside, not even for the prospect of food and water. The jerk might've poisoned them.

Setting my gaze on the spot where he'd disappeared, I took the paper with both hands and tore it into several small pieces. I kept my gaze locked there as I let the paper float over the side of the rocks.

"Go to hell, Ruger."

Turning on my heel, I took off, moving as quickly as I could safely go.

I didn't trust Ruger as far as I could throw him. He'd already treated me like shit and no amount of apologies would change that.

What had he meant about "becoming one of us?" What were the Kings of Beasts? A cult? A motorcycle club? Or something in between? If I had my way, I'd never find out.

What really bothered me was how Logan could be a friend to a guy like Ruger. They were polar opposites. Or was Logan hiding a dark side?

Groaning, I looked up at the sky and pushed on. If I was going to make it before dark, I couldn't waste any more time.

A few minutes later, I sensed something behind me. I stopped and looked around, but saw nothing. Adrenaline pumped into me as I lifted my sight to the thick trees above. Was it my claustrophobia getting to me? The forest was thicker, giving me that awful closed-in feeling. Or had I really heard something? I checked all around me, but again, came up empty.

Calm down. Breathe. You're letting him get to you.

I closed my eyes to center myself.

Just breathe. That's it.

My heart beat slowed down and the fear spinning in my mind, imagining myself trapped under fallen trees, gradually eased.

Good. Now just keep on going.

I hadn't taken a step when someone grabbed me from behind. A hand over my mouth smothered the scream tearing from my lips. I grasped at his arms, trying my best to get free, but he was too strong. The more I struggled, the harder it was for me to breathe. I couldn't get on my feet. He held me, one of his massive arms running across my chest to crush me next to his hip as he dragged me along with him.

Anger mixed with panic giving me the ability to still think. Letting my body go limp, I became dead weight. When I did so, I managed to stick my arm through his legs, causing him to stumble. He turned me loose just as he hit the ground. I was ready.

Breathing in much needed air, I crawled on my hands and knees away from him, then scrambled to my feet. A cry escaped me as I heard him roar his rage and come after me. I was fast, running as hard as I could, the panic burning the air in my throat. But not fast enough. All at once, my feet were taken out from under me. He snagged the back of my shirt and yanked me against him.

"Stop fighting, you fucking cunt."

I screamed, but Ruger's hand covered my mouth, drowning out the sound. I kept screaming and clawed at his hand, but nothing I did worked. Terror seized me as he hauled me away.

Flashes of light blinked over me as he dragged me into the forest. I struggled, but nothing I did bothered him. I was a gnat flying into a stone wall. We were heading in a different direction than where I'd been headed.

Where was he taking me? To his lean-to?

I already knew the answer to the other question, the one of what he'd do once he got me there. He'd take what he wanted and then kill me.

Why is this happening to me?

My eyes looked toward the sky, seeking the blue as it peeked through the trees less and less. At one point, in my daze, water soaked my body up to my waist. If Ruger had turned me loose, I would've slid under the cool surface and never risen again. I prayed I would. It'd be better to drown than to face what he had planned for me.

And then we were back on land with him throwing my weakened body over his shoulder. I couldn't keep my eyes open as the ground passed under his feet, then rocks, then more hard-packed earth. The rough ride bounced me up and down, pushing hard against my abdomen every time I tried to draw in a breath.

First my father, then the trucker, and now Ruger. Why did men want to hurt me?

My lungs burned as they craved oxygen. My eyes watered

and my head pounded until, at last, thankfully, the world went black.

Logan

After running for several miles then doubling back to get my clothes, I'd followed the path Mia was supposed to take to the cave. Her scent was easy to follow until I hit the rock outcropping. After that, no matter how hard I tried, I couldn't find it again. Even after shifting enough to bring out my lion's more sensitive sense of smell I failed to pick it up.

Something wasn't right. I could feel it in my gut.

I hurried to the top of the rocks and onto the flat area leading into the next area of the forest. Her scent was there. But hers wasn't the only one I picked up.

Ruger.

My lion roared, ready to do battle, to stake my territory and claim my mate. He'd taken her. I knew it as surely as I knew my own name.

It took me a while to calm down. I'd never felt so afraid, so furious, so ready to kill. My lion growled, then clawed at my insides, demanding I turn it loose. But if I did, I'd be unable to think, unable to guess where he might have taken her.

When I was finally able to push back the black cloak of anger, I knelt and studied the tracks. He'd taken off in an opposite direction, but that made sense. He was toying with her. Frightening her, then leaving her alone, making her think she'd survived him yet again.

But where had she gone? How far had she made it before he'd finally stopped playing cat-and-mouse and grabbed her?

I confirmed my suspicions a few minutes later when I picked up their scents together. The scuff marks on the forest floor told me how she'd struggled against him. But she'd had no chance.

Ruger had her. If I didn't find her in time...

I thrust the terrifying thought away. I didn't want to think about what he'd do to her. He'd torture her for certain. He liked terrorizing girls. But what about the rest? He'd fuck her. But would he claim her? He had the right, but no one had ever gone against a pride brother that way. Even now, I doubted he'd want to take a mate. But what about the other possibility? Would he kill her?

All of a sudden, I was sure he would.

Why hadn't I realized this was what he'd do? Had our past, the times we'd spent as children blinded me? Had I simply refused to see that even Ruger would go that far?

Her death would be the perfect revenge. An eye for an eye. A death for a death. Killing Mia would tear out my heart. Although he knew I'd come after him, he'd have the pride on his side. As much as they'd despise him for what he'd done, they'd keep me from taking his life and forgive him for "accidentally" killing Mia while trying to claim her. I could almost hear the lie he'd tell them.

Maybe they'd end up running him out of the pride eventually, but no punishment would bring her back. I'd have to hope he'd fuck up once he was out of the pride, telling someone of our existence or shifting. Then the pride would go after him and I'd be able to tear him apart. But no price, not even his death, would be enough of a punishment.

"Mia." My hands shook with the need to put them around Ruger's neck. "I'll find you. I swear it."

I knew where his favorite places were. And I knew where his lean-to was. But I didn't think he'd take her to any of those. He'd know I'd look for her and wouldn't give up until I found her.

He had to have taken her to a place I didn't know about. But where? I knew the mountains better than I knew my mother's face. I started walking, following their tracks, as ideas came rushing at me.

Part of the time, he'd dragged her. Then her tracks had disappeared and his had made slightly deeper impressions in the ground. He'd started carrying her.

I followed the tracks until they came to a wide stream. Cursing, I went to the other side, but I couldn't find any sign of them. My chest tightened as I realized what he'd done. He must've stayed in the water to cover his trail. But which way did he go? Without tracks to follow, how would I find them?

I had no choice but to take a chance and pick a direction. Running alongside the water, I headed upstream and tried to ignore the anguish churning my stomach as so many questions battered me.

Would I get to her in time?

No matter what he did to her, no matter if I found her alive or dead, I vowed I'd take him apart.

Chapter Nine

Mia

Shit. He's coming.

I kicked and screamed as my father clutched a fistful of my hair and tugged me along with him. The bedroom door was wide open, like the mouth of a monster ready to devour me alive.

No. Let me go.

It was a useless plea, one I'd tried many times even though it had failed every time. All I could do was hold on to his arm and try to ease the agony searing through my head as his grip threatened to pull my hair out.

My father threw me on top of the bed. His expression was awful, a monster of his own striving to get out.

"It's time, Mia."

I scooted toward the head of the bed. "No."

"Yeah. It's time you become a real woman."

The groping, the invasion of fingers and tongue was changing. Now he'd use his cock to attack me. I'd known the time was close, but I'd denied it, shoving it to the back of my mind.

I watched in horror as he tore off his shirt, then pushed down the same khaki slacks he wore every day and heeled off his work boots. His cock sprang out like a snake ready to strike.

"No. Please."

He grinned, delighting in my anguish. "Good. I like it when you beg."

For that reason alone, I closed my mouth and glared at him. If I had to suffer through what would happen next, then I refused to give him the pleasure of hearing me beg.

He came at me. Although I tried to act brave, to feel brave, I still cowered as he positioned his body over me.

"You'd damn well better be a fucking virgin." He narrowed his eyes.

Could he see the truth in mine?

"If you've been slutting it up, I'll have to knock you around some. Enough to get the evil out of you. Have you? Better tell me the truth."

I wouldn't say. To lie would only delay the inevitable. Instead, I struck out, my fingernails slashing across his cheek. He reared back, hollering as bright red streaks of blood coursed across his skin. When he pulled his hand away from his cheek, it was slickened with the coppery smelling liquid.

"Why, you little bitch!"

I tried to hit him again, to dig my fingernails into him before the next blow came, but I was too slow. He held both wrists with one hand and tore my nightgown away as I twisted every way I could, fighting to get free. At last, he turned my wrists loose only to encircle my neck with both hands.

Darkness flowed in from the walls around us, coming closer and closer as his hands tightened around my neck and his thumbs pressed against my windpipe. I couldn't breathe, not only from his hands tightening their hold on my neck, but from the approaching walls. If my father didn't kill me first, I'd die once the walls crushed me.

My eyes bulged as I looked into his hate-filled ones. My strength was fading fast. Soon I wouldn't have enough energy to drag in a breath.

I shifted my gaze to the walls. They kept moving closer. And closer. And closer still.

I wouldn't survive. I knew that as surely as I knew my father wouldn't regret choking me to death. And yet it was his face I focused on. To look at the darkness of the walls creeping onto the bed, only inches away from me, was more terrifying.

I woke up with a start, a small cry escaping me as I clutched my neck and looked around. Fear, pain, and confusion swamped me. The dream had placed me in my father's house, but reality had taken me somewhere different.

Cold and wet pushed against my back and seeped into my shirt. With a start, I scooted away from the dirt wall, scrambling like a bug toward the one spot of light in the center of the floor. Although the light provided no real warmth, I felt safer to be within that small area of brightness. Only then did my mind calm down enough to understand where I was.

Oh, God, no. Please, no.

I was in a deep hole in the ground.

For several minutes, I stayed where I was, too frightened to do anything else. My trembling body wouldn't allow me to do more.

Ruger had put me in a hole in the ground, but where was he? Had he left me alone to die? To be crushed when the four dirt walls started closing in on me? Would he ever return? Or would my body lie here until either animals or Logan found it?

It wasn't nightfall yet. Although the trees had formed a thick barrier above me, I could still see patches of blue sky through it. But the only true light that wasn't driven away by the dense foliage was the one I'd gone to for sanctuary.

I couldn't think straight. Not when my mind was losing the battle to my shuddering body.

I'm not sure how long I sat there, but at last my breathing slowed down and my terrified mind started to work again. It could've been minutes. It could've been hours.

Once the trembling subsided, I gathered what courage I had and got to my feet. Judging distance wasn't easy for me, but I could tell the hole was big enough that it was several times my height and I couldn't reach from end to end. Its depth didn't matter. However deep it was, it was still too high for me to reach the top. An attempt to jump and touch the edge above me didn't help. I couldn't reach it.

Keep calm.

I don't know how many times I'd told myself to stay calm while growing up in my hell hole of a home. Sometimes it worked and sometimes it didn't. Right now it was working. At least enough for me to walk to the dirt wall and run my hands over it.

I wanted to throw up. Wanted to run back to the safety of the small patch of light. But I forced myself to stay.

"Damn it." I'd hoped it was loosely packed. If it had been, I might've been able to dig hand and footholds into it and climb my way out. I scraped off the first layer of cool, moist dirt, and quickly found the solid rock underneath. I'd need an axe to dig into the wall.

I whipped around toward the wall at my back. Had it moved? Logically, I knew it couldn't have, but logic often came in a distant second to my claustrophobia. My breaths came faster, shorter, as panic inched closer. My stomach churned, nausea sending its sweet taste into my mouth.

This wasn't happening. I hadn't survived my father to end up attacked by a crazier shit like Ruger. A crazy shit who'd dumped me into a pit.

Anger with its cleansing power swept through me. I wasn't going to let anyone like Ruger get me down. I'd been through too much already and I wasn't going to take any more. No way would I sit back and do nothing.

I hated to touch them, but I forced myself to skim my hands along each wall, hoping to find anything I could use to get out. But the other walls were just like the first one. Not a jagged rock or tree limb sticking out anywhere. Small rocks were scattered over the floor, but they didn't look hard enough to use as a digging tool.

I gasped as a shadow slid over me. Yelping, I rushed back to the beam of light.

Screw staying calm. This is fucked up.

Was the shadow from someone who might help? Or was I dinner and it an animal just waiting to chow down? Would anyone hear me if I shouted for help? Would Ruger? And yet, that was the only thing I could think to do. Taking a couple of big breaths first, I yelled as hard as I could.

"Hey! Can anyone hear me? Help! Please, help me!"

I was breathing heavily by the time I'd finished. But the world around me remained as silent as before.

I tried again. "Help! Please, someone! I'm in a big hole. Please, I can't get out!" Again, nothing but the sound of a few birds noisily chirping their anger at me.

A tear slid down my cheek. I was failing the challenge. Failing myself. But worst of all, I was failing my family.

If only Logan was around to help me again. But I couldn't count on him to come to my rescue.

"Please! Someone help me!"

I kept calling out, but soon my shouting was accented with sobs. I didn't want to cry. I hated to cry, but my exhaustion had taken over, leaving me with no resistance to my emotions. I'm not sure how long I called for help, but after a while, even my tears gave up.

At last, I sank to the ground, too weak to stay on my feet. One last try and I'd have nothing left to give.

"Please. Someone help me." My voice had grown raspy. My throat sore. Had I been shouting that long?

The sound of someone—or something—coming closer gave me renewed energy. I got to my feet and circled around, looking at every side of the hole. When a young girl peeked over the edge, I almost fainted with relief.

"Oh, thank you, thank you." She hadn't done anything to help me, but answering my pleading calls was enough for now.

"How'd you wind up down there?" Her long hair fell in her face as she got on her hands and knees then leaned as far as she could over the side.

I remembered seeing her at Fang's. "A man named Ruger grabbed me and put me down here. Please, can you get me out?"

She glanced around, fear lighting in her eyes. "I'm sorry, but I can't."

"Please, you've got to help me." I dragged in a breath. "You're one of the girls doing the games, right? I remember you from the bar, but I don't remember your name."

"It's Eva." She glanced around again, her movements becoming jerky, showing her nerves. "I don't see a rope or anything to use. And I can't pull you out. I'm not strong enough." She pushed up as though to leave.

"No, please, Eva, don't go. I'm Mia. You can't just leave me here."

She bit her lower lip, then shook her head. "I'm sorry, but I can't help you. It's against the rules, remember?"

I wanted to yell at her to screw the rules, but I didn't. Pushing her wouldn't get her to help me. "No one will know. I won't tell."

"No. I'm sorry. I can't. The money…" She bit her bottom lip, and for one miracle of a moment, I thought she'd change her mind. "I'm sorry, but I can't risk losing the money. But I promise, I'll tell them where you are right after the games are over." She eased back from the edge until I couldn't see her any longer.

"Eva! No! Please, come back!"

I was thrilled to see her face as she peeked over the side again. If I couldn't get her to help me, I was doomed. "I won't tell them you helped me. I swear it. And I'll even help you make it to your destination. I'll make sure you make it through your challenge. Okay? Please?"

Again, she bit her lower lip, her indecision written in her expression. To my utter disappointment, she shook her head.

"I'm sorry. I just can't."

A sob racked me as fresh tears came. If she didn't help me, who would?

"You'll be okay for two nights. Lots of people have survived in the wilderness for a lot longer. Once the games are over, I'll tell them. I swear I will."

I wiped away a tear. "I'm not sure I can last that long. If Ruger comes back…" I couldn't bring myself to say the words out loud.

"You will. I just know it. And I promise. I'll tell someone."

Before I could say anything else, she pushed away and disappeared.

"No, please." My plea came out in a whisper. It was useless.

She was gone.

Anxiety tightened my already stiff neck. What had I just seen? Was the other wall starting to move in on me, too?

I whined and dropped onto my butt, my arms wrapped around my knees in the middle of the pool of light. I was going to die, alone and afraid, in a hole. Closing my eyes, I did the only thing I could think to do. For the first time in my life, I prayed.

Logan

My beast clawed at my guts, slicing agony into my core. Time was running out. Not only for her to make it to the cave, but for me to keep her alive.

Ruger didn't want Mia. Not as a mate. He wanted her as a means to revenge, pure and simple. As a way to get back at me for letting his brother die.

Although I'd been outside the bar when the trouble had started, I'd always accepted the blame. That was the way of the Kings of Beasts MC. Like human motorcycle gangs, we had each other's backs. It didn't matter if I was there at the start of the fight or not. I'd come into it while Vic was still alive, but afterward, he was dead.

At first, Ruger had played the part of the understanding friend, but I'd been stupid to accept what he'd said as the truth. He'd waited, biding his time until he'd found the best way to hurt me. Attacking me wasn't enough. Claiming Mia wasn't enough. But taking my mate away from me after I'd drawn in her scent and embedded it within me, giving it to the lion inside me? Torturing her, then killing her? He'd exact the perfect revenge.

She'd already gone through hell. I was sure of it. But I was also sure the worst, if it hadn't come already, was about to happen. He'd toy with his prey, then punish her with rough sex. Then, sensing me getting too close, he'd kill her.

If he could drag her body out where I could find it, he'd do so. But he wouldn't. That would blow his "accidental" death alibi all to hell. Her body would be riddled with every mark, every bite he'd given her. More brutality than a simple claiming-gone-wrong would ever show. Having me see her dead body was one thrill he wouldn't get. But it was no consolation to me.

I'd already run along both sides of the banks going upstream more than once, checking and rechecking the ground for any sign or scent of Ruger or Mia. But I'd found nothing. With every passing second, I grew more anxious. If I didn't find her, she wouldn't make it to the cave before the sun set. Not that it mattered any longer. If I didn't find her soon, Ruger would have tortured her then killed her. All to get back at me.

I stood in the water and searched the shore, but I couldn't hold back any longer. Shifting partway, I let out a roar and heard the small creatures around me as they broke through limbs and bushes to run from the awful sound. My voice would travel a long way. Some of the girls in the games would hear it as well as any of the pride that might be around. If Burke or Roberta heard me, they'd recognize the fury and fear in the sound. But I didn't care. I had to let it out or I'd change and not care who saw me.

I could track them better as a lion. Yet, as much as I wanted to shift, I couldn't. I wouldn't think as clearly as I could as a man.

My lion, however, had a different idea. It threw itself at me, railing at my determination to keep it contained.

Without warning, the world around me changed, going from the bright colors of summer into gray hues caused by the silver in my eyes overtaking the blue. My lion growled, pushing its way to the surface, but I fought back.

I started running along the bank, going downstream. Every so often I would stop, search and sniff. And as I ran, my mind raced even faster, trying to think what I'd do if I didn't find anything along the stream.

Mia. Where are you?

Mia

I kept my head bowed and my eyes closed as I prayed. Over and over I asked someone to help me. I didn't really expect anyone to be listening, but to my surprise, just saying the words, just hoping someone might hear me made me feel better than I would've believed. Whether or not any higher power actually listened didn't matter. It was a soothing chant my frayed nerves needed. The sound of my voice gave me the courage to ignore the walls closing in on me. Although praying was helpful, I'd learned from an early age that the only one I could depend on was me.

A loud thump came from in front of me, jarring me out of my trance and opening my eyes wide. At first my mind couldn't understand what my eyes were telling it.

It can't be her.

Yet reality can be pushed away for only so long.

I screamed as my gaze met Eva's blank one.

"Now look what you've made me do."

I crab-crawled backward in my hurry to get away from Eva's lifeless body. Ruger sat on the edge of the hole like a big kid sitting on the side of a swimming pool. He bit into an apple and chewed with his mouth open.

"You killed her." I wasn't saying it for his benefit, but for mine. Hearing the words out loud would force me to believe.

"Yeah, I guess you could say so." He took another big chomp out of the apple then tossed it behind him. "But you're the one to blame for her death."

"Me?" He was undeniably insane.

"Yeah, you. If you hadn't hollered so much and drawn her to the hole, she'd be most of the way to her destination. Or, at least, she would've been if she hadn't gotten lost. Stupid girl didn't know she was going the wrong way. But hell. Luke's not going to like it when he finds out you got her killed."

I wouldn't take the blame. My gut twisted into a knot of rage. "Fuck you!" I glared up at him. "You didn't have to kill her. She wasn't going to help me anyway."

He closed one eye and peered at me with the other. "That's not what I heard." He laughed and slapped his knee. "You didn't know I was listening, did you? But I was. And I heard it all. She said she'd tell someone where to find you. I couldn't let her blow all my plans to hell and back."

"Why don't *you* go to hell and never come back?" I snatched a stone beside my foot and hurled it as hard as I could.

He caught it easily, then flung it to the side. "Sugar, you need to calm down. Getting all riled up won't do you any good." He grinned his awful grin. "Besides, I want you rested up when I fuck you. I wouldn't want you to just lie there and take it. I like a girl who fights back. You know how it is, right?

A little pain, a slap or a nibble goes a long way, but when the girl really tries her hardest to get free? Now that's when the real fun begins."

"You're sick."

"Naw, sugar. Just because a man likes to torture a girl before he fucks her doesn't mean he's sick." He laughed. "You see, it's this way. You'll hang out down there in the hole for a while. Sure, you'll get hungry and tired, but I'm willing to bet you're going to get mad as hell, too. Once you get pissed off, you'll want to tear me limb from limb. Then we'll start playing."

"I'm already there. Get me out and I'll rip you apart with my bare hands."

He clapped his hands, then pointed at me. "See? There it is. You're a fighter. I knew it the second I sniffed you. But you're not mad enough yet. Not by a long shot. I want you mad enough to spit bullets."

"Fuck you."

"You will, sugar. Don't you worry."

Eva's dead eyes stared up at me, accusing me. I couldn't take watching her and turned away. Yet leaning against the wall to stay on my shaky legs felt wrong. Like I was disrespecting her somehow. But what else could I do?

"Aw, now, girl, don't get all pouty and stuff. More than likely she wouldn't have made it to the end of the challenge anyway. We did her a favor killing her now instead of making her suffer. As for Luke? Hell, he won't have any trouble finding another mate. It'll take time for him to get over her, to lose her scent, but it'll happen." He snorted derisively. "Hell, now that I think about it, we did him a favor, too. Next time he'll choose a better-looking, stronger girl."

"Shut up!" I whirled around, my heart pounding as I

noticed how much closer the walls had moved. The light from above had grown less intense and what little sky I could see had gotten darker. The sun was heading toward the horizon.

I'll never make it to the cave.

As if that was my biggest problem.

He followed the direction I was looking. "It's getting late. Too late for you to make it to Logan's cave." He got to his feet and stuffed his hands into his pocket. "Don't worry about it. You might've been meant for him, but he owes me and I'm going to get what I deserve."

Swallowing was hard, as sore as my throat was. "What does that have to do with me? I don't know either one of you."

"Looked like you were getting to know him pretty good earlier on."

My empty stomach revolted, even without anything in it to get rid of. "You were watching us?"

"Sure. Y'all put on a pretty good show, too. Until you stopped him." He winked. "Tell me, sugar, did you stop because he wasn't me?"

"You're an asshole." It wasn't much of an insult, but it was all I could think of.

"Oh, come on now. Stop playing hard to get. You and me? When I get your clothes off, we're going to go hard core all the way."

I lost it. With him standing above me, taunting me, and with the walls closing in, I didn't have any fight left in me. "Then why don't you just do it?" I slumped against the wall and imagined fingers coming out of the dirt to enclose around my neck and arms. "Come on. Fuck me. I want to get it over with."

He pressed a hand over his heart and pretended to be insulted. "Damn, girl, why'd you have to say it like that? Get it over with? How about giving a shit? I know it's not champagne and roses, but who knows? You might just like it."

"I was going to bite your dick off." Trying to mimic his wicked grin was impossible, but I gave it a try. "I won't miss out if I get a second chance."

I'd half expected him to laugh again and damned if he didn't. "There it is. I knew you still had some fire left in you."

My gaze drifted to Eva again. Then I jerked it away before my head sent a reaction to my stomach. One I wouldn't be able to control twice.

"In the meantime, I need you to keep your mouth shut."

I locked onto him and wished I had the power to tear him apart with my mind.

"We wouldn't want anyone else to get hurt. Now would we?" He clucked and shook his head at Eva. "Damn. What a waste. Too bad I didn't have time to fuck her before I broke her scrawny neck."

"What are you going to do? Leave me here to starve to death?"

"Shit no. What if someone comes along and sees you? Nope. We'll have our fun and then I'll kill you way before you starve."

"Fuck you." I put all the vehemence I could muster into the words.

"I tell you what. If you do a good job fucking me, I'll make it quick and painless. You'll be headed for heaven before you realize you're dead. A body can't ask for more."

For once, I agreed with him. My life had sucked so far. Going to heaven fast would be the best thing that had happened to me in a long time.

Except for Logan.

Where was he, anyway? Had what I thought we'd shared been nothing? Or was he as full of bullshit as every other man I'd known?

"Anyway, I've got to run. You keep quiet, you hear? If not, I'll start adding bodies on top of hers."

I shouted at him as he turned to leave. "You can't leave her here." The thought of staying in a hole at night was bad enough. But with a dead body? I shuddered, unable to believe I could make it through until morning.

"Sugar, if you know what's good for you, you'll learn this right now. Ruger can do anything he damn well pleases." He wiggled his fingers in a taunting wave and was gone.

As bad as he was, at least he was someone. Once he was gone, it seemed like the world around me had suddenly gone black. I glanced upward, seeking the sky peeking through the trees again, but couldn't find it. Not wanting to lean against the wall, yet hating the idea of getting too close to Eva, I worked my way to a distance halfway between the wall and her dead body.

Night was coming and the walls of my hole were closing in. I sat down and pulled my knees to my chest.

Logan, please help me.

Chapter Ten

Logan

I am one of the Kings of Beasts. A lion. One of the strongest animals on the planet. And yet, I felt weaker than a kitten nursing at its mother's teat.

For one of the few times I could remember, I was scared. Not for myself. Not because I might come out of the games without a mate. I was frightened for Mia.

I didn't care if she made it to the cave or not. I didn't care if she finished the challenge. I wouldn't have cared if she came out of the challenge alive and took the money over me. As long as she was alive, I'd count myself a lucky man.

My inner lion, however, didn't like the idea. He wanted his mate and he'd have his mate. Come hell, high water, or Ruger.

After getting no leads from the banks around the stream, it was time to start checking places where Ruger might be. It was a long shot. If he'd done anything to Mia, then he'd be smarter than to hide her at his usual areas. But I didn't have any other leads to try.

My feet pounded the earth. Usually I was stealth, able to sneak up on a prey without making a sound, but I didn't care who heard me. Speed was more important than keeping a low profile.

At last, I came to Ruger's lean-to. It wasn't much. Just some two-by-fours loosely thrown together. A tent would've made a better shelter. I didn't need to look inside to know Mia wasn't there. Ruger's scent was all over the place, but there was no hint of her. I groaned, then made a quick check around, looking for any other clues. And found nothing.

"Logan."

I whirled, ready to shift. Instead of Ruger, I found another pride member, Luke, striding toward me. "Yeah?"

"Are you looking for Ruger?"

"In a way." I didn't want to tell him anything. At least not yet. "Have you seen him?" I tried to sound casual, as though nothing were wrong.

"No. I was trying to pick up the trail of my mate."

We weren't supposed to help our mates, but most of us trailed along after them or even ran along beside them, unseen until they made it to their destinations. I remembered the girl he'd chosen. "Sorry. I haven't seen her."

"Huh. It's weird. I had to run to town for Burke and it took longer than I figured. Which meant catching up with her, but I never found her tracks so I went ahead to the cabin. I figured she would've shown up by now."

Like many of the pride, Luke's family owned a secluded cabin in the woods. My family had preferred a cave like the cougars living on the mountain. Some people thought the cougars were extinct, but we knew better.

If I'd known about Mia hating closed-in places, I would've chosen a different place. I tried to ignore the darkness holding me in its grip. "Did you see my girl? Black hair? Pretty?"

"Sorry, man." Luke wasn't the smartest one of our pride, but he was smart enough to realize something was off. "What's going on?"

Could I trust him to keep quiet? As a fellow Kings of Beasts, I knew he'd have my back, but his loyalties would fall to the pride first. Still, I was desperate.

"Go on, Logan. I can see you're messed up. What's going on?"

I decided to take the chance. "I think Ruger's taken my mate."

Luke's mouth dropped. "You're fucking kidding me."

"Wish I were."

"Hell, I know it's allowed and all, but no one's done that since the olden days. Fuck, that's messed up. Damn, man, I'm sorry."

"I'm not letting him get away with it."

"Which is your right. I hate to say it, but if he's got her, he's more than likely already bitten her."

I almost wished I could be sure of that. At least then he might let her live. "Maybe. But I think he's going to do something worse to her."

"Like what?"

I gave him a look he couldn't misinterpret.

"Shit. You think he might kill her? But why?"

"Because of Vic."

Luke knew what I was talking about. The entire pride had talked about Vic's death for weeks after I'd brought his body back home. No one other than Ruger had put any blame on me. I'd done it on my own.

"Damn. He's been holding back for a while."

I checked the lean-to again, more for the sake of doing something rather than seeing Luke's look of pity. Losing Mia would kill me and he knew it.

"Maybe you should tell Burke."

I straightened up, hating that I was leaning toward doing what he'd suggested. But what kind of a man, a mate, or a lion would I be if I ran for help? Besides, Burke would just shrug and say it was Ruger's right to claim her.

"I'll find her. And if he's taken her, I'll settle the score with him."

He had the fucked-up right to claim my mate. If he'd already done so, I'd be expected to obey the old way and back off. But I wouldn't. He'd pay for insulting me and for taking my mate. One way or another.

And if he'd hurt her? If he'd killed her? Nothing would stop me from tearing him apart.

"Come on, Logan. If he's done it, then it's over." He studied me, getting the gist of what I'd really meant. "Oh, shit, man. Calm down. A pride member killing another pride member? You're just asking to get exiled. Hell, I don't know. Maybe even worse. We don't know what they'll do. No lion's ever killed one of his own."

I turned on him, my inner lion taking control before I realized it was climbing toward the surface. Taking hold of his shirt, I slammed his back against a tree. Exile, death, I didn't care what they threw at me. If Ruger had hurt Mia, then he deserved whatever the hell I did to him. "She's mine and nothing will change that. And if he's done worse? Then he deserves to die."

Luke didn't fight back. Instead, he took the brunt of my anger and waited until I'd calmed down. At least, as calm as I was going to get before I found Mia.

"Logan, listen, man. You don't know Ruger took her. Not for sure."

"Yeah, I do." But I had to back down from his intense stare.

"His tracks and scent are with hers at the last place I could find a trace of her. It doesn't take a genius to figure it out."

"You have to have more proof. Don't go doing anything you'll regret later."

I nodded, agreeing, at least outwardly. But I wasn't sure I wouldn't tear Ruger apart the first chance I got.

"Find her first, then figure out if he's involved. If he didn't interfere and you do, then you could get her disqualified. And you sent packing. You don't want that to happen, right?"

I didn't tell him I'd already interfered. Instead, I did what had never come easy to me. But I had to ask. "Will you help me?"

He blinked, the only reaction to my question. Not many lions ever asked for help. "Sure. Okay. We'll look for Mia and my girl Eva together."

"Thanks." I relaxed a little. Having him by my side would help keep my head straight and I didn't want to mess that up.

"Don't mention it. It's one for all, and all for one, right?"

I shook my head and pushed him ahead of me. "That's the Three Musketeers, not the Kings of Beasts."

Mia

The sun had set. And along with it, not only my chance to win the money, but maybe to save my life. Ruger wouldn't let me live. Whatever twisted things he wanted to do to me would wind up with me being as dead as Eva.

I should close her eyes.

But I couldn't bring myself to get near her, much less touch her. I hadn't known her, but no one deserved a death like hers.

If I made it out of my prison hole, I'd make him pay if it was the last thing I did.

I closed my eyes, whispering to myself, as I searched for my Happy Place. But it wouldn't come. Maybe I was too tired. Or maybe I'd finally realized a place like that couldn't exist. Not even in my imagination. At least not for me.

Something skittered behind me. I twisted around and tried to see into the darkness. Two yellow eyes stared back at me, the small dark body pressed against the wall.

"Get. Scat." Was it a rat? Or a different animal? Without getting closer, I couldn't be sure. And getting closer was the last thing I wanted to do.

I jumped at its squeak and hurried to get to my feet. "Damn it. Get out of here." It scurried away, disappearing into the darkness of the other wall.

My breathing grew shallow, my body tensing up as I measured the distance between me and the walls. Had they moved? Having the open sky above me helped a little, but it wasn't enough. Nothing over my head would keep the walls from crushing me.

"Please, Logan. Where are you?"

Had he given up? Was he waiting at the cave? Either way, I was shit out of luck. He might not look for me until tomorrow. Or maybe not at all.

I was hungry and cold. Nausea, a common companion to my rising panic, sickened me, making it harder to concentrate. I couldn't count on Logan's help. Some way, somehow, I had to get myself out of the hole.

A growl came from above, drawing my attention to the edge of the pit. Some kind of animal was nearby. Judging from its deep growl, it was a big one.

Another growl sent me rushing to the wall. At least the walls moving in on me was a fear I was familiar with. I peered into the growing darkness and saw it.

Oh, no, please, no.

A lion stood at the edge of the pit.

Terror strangled me, keeping me silent. Had one of the Kings of Beasts' lions escaped?

Either that or I'd gone out of my mind. Or I was having a nightmare.

I prayed it was a nightmare. I wasn't in the woods at all. I was back home, still locked in the closet.

Wake up.

The third growl, however, made me all too aware that I wasn't asleep or caught in a nightmare. I was trapped in a hole in the ground with a real life African lion standing at the edge.

It shook its mane, then roared again. I stayed close to the wall—was that a hand I just felt against my neck?—and hoped the shadows would hide me. Its tail swished back and forth, its ears pointed in my direction.

Oh, God. Please, someone help me.

I don't know how I knew, but I did. It was about to attack.

When it leapt, I didn't make a sound. Instead, I closed my eyes and waited for death to come. I didn't want to see it as it struck out, slashing its powerful claws through my neck. I only waited to feel the gush of my blood flowing over my body and pain burning through me. All I could wish for was a quick death and a release from my prison.

I heard the lion hit the dirt floor with a thud and felt the vibrations ripple through the ground. Holding my breath, I opened my eyes, ready to find its sharp fangs and glowing silver eyes inches from my face.

Silver eyes.

I wasn't sure why the color of its eyes struck a chord with me. I tried to remember, but that part of my mind had checked out.

The lion paced around Eva's body as though examining it for wounds. It shook its head, snarled, then put its nose to her leg and pushed. Rigor mortis had already started to set in. Had I been there that long? Time no longer meant anything to me.

My head swam with fear and anticipation. Soon it would attack me, ripping its claws through me, then dragging my dead body over to Eva's.

It shook his full mane again, then turned those silvery eyes my way. I clapped a hand over my mouth, stifling a sob, as it padded toward me.

Shit. Shit. Shit.

Logan, please help me.

I closed my eyes again. What was it waiting for? It was almost as though the lion was taunting me, enjoying my fear.

Just like my father had done. Just like Ruger had done.

And that just pissed me off.

A warm blast of foul-smelling breath pushed the hair away from my face. Fear battled with anger inside me, but I was determined to have anger win. Opening my eyes, I found myself looking into the face of a predator.

For a moment, we just stared at each other, its silver gaze meeting mine. And then it roared again, the sound so loud I wanted to cup my hands over my ears. Instead, I trembled and fisted my hands together. If I was going to die, then I'd do it fighting to stay alive.

"Fuck off, asshole."

I pulled back my arm then let loose.

My fist connected with its muzzle.

I wasn't sure which one of us was more surprised. Its eyes narrowed and its lips lifted into a snarl.

Oh, fuck.

Just as I prepared to feel the agony of its fangs sinking into my throat, it spun around, its tail whipping over my breasts as it padded back to the dead body.

The dead body. It wasn't Eva any longer. It couldn't be. Only by thinking of it as a dead body and not a person I'd seen living and breathing, could I withstand the horror that came next.

The lion put its paw on top of her pelvis, then bent over and tore a chunk of her out of her stomach. I turned toward the wall and upchucked. The sounds of it eating, slurps and chews, echoed in the pit and churned my stomach, bringing yet another round of dry heaving. By the time it had finished chewing, I was too weak to stay on my feet any longer. I sat back against the wall, no longer concerned if hands would sneak out of the dirt and grab me. No longer worried about dying.

I was ready to welcome death.

But I wouldn't get off so easy.

The lion's rumble of a growl floated on the air. It licked his lips, then took hold of an arm and turned to stare at me with those strangely beautiful eyes. Hunkering down, it hurled himself upward, taking the body along with it. The lion landed gracefully, then shook the dead body like a dog playing with a chew toy. Flinging the body away, it turned to face me.

A whimper escaped me, but it was driven away at the sound of another growl. I would've sworn it grinned at me. A grin as sick and evil as Ruger's.

I couldn't take any more. Exhausted, bewildered, I put my

knees to my chest and my head on my forearms. Sobs racked my body.

Logan

Luke and I wouldn't have admitted it to each other, but we were both worried. More than worried. I'd never experienced real fear before but now I knew what it felt like.

We kept going during the night. Although real lions were nocturnal animals, we didn't like traveling at night. Maybe it was the human part of us that wasn't fond of the dark. I didn't know. The only thing I could think was that I had to find Mia. If Ruger had her, she'd already gone through more than anyone should ever have to experience.

"Eva!" Luke had resorted to calling for her, no longer caring if he got her disqualified and himself exiled.

I kept silent. What good would it do? If Mia or Eva was in trouble and could answer, then they'd hear Luke's call and shout back. If they couldn't, then yelling their names wouldn't help. I still held out hope that Mia had gotten lost. If so, then I'd take her to the cave then lie and tell everyone she'd made it before nightfall. I wouldn't be the one to get her disqualified from earning the money.

I had to find her. Although it wasn't impossible to find another mate, I knew I'd never want anyone other than Mia.

Mia

Something hard pressed against my body. I swiped at my arm as tiny stings raced over it. I didn't want to wake up. Instead, I closed my eyes tighter and wished myself back to sleep.

But my wish didn't come true.

I opened my eyes and screamed. Scrambling on my hands and knees, I made it to the farthest side of the hole then pushed myself to a standing position. A rat sat up on his hind legs, its beady, soulless eyes staring at me as I brushed the ants off my arm.

"Go away, you motherfucker."

"Aw, sugar, he just wants to play."

I screamed again as Ruger jumped into the hole and stalked toward me. He made a show of looking around for Eva's body. "What happened? Did your house guest up and leave? How rude."

"Stay the hell away from me."

He grinned, obviously enjoying my fear. I tried to put on a brave front, but couldn't. I was too tired, too hungry, and too thirsty. Every inch of my body ached.

"I bet you could use a little water about now, huh?" He held out the thermos. "Want it?"

My pride fought against my dry mouth. "Fuck you."

"Sugar, you need to stop asking me to fuck you. I will, don't you worry about it." He held the thermos closer to me. "The way I like it is this. I like anticipation. You know. A little flirting, a little touch-and-grab. I'm not one of those guys who doesn't like foreplay. In fact, you could say foreplay is my thing.

Rough foreplay, of course."

I got pissed off again. Anger was my new best friend. "Oh, sure. You're the real *romance the girl* kind of guy, right?"

He held his arm straight out, putting the water bottle within my reach. "There you go. Yeah. I'm a romantic. It's just instead of giving you roses and champagne, I gave you your own home away from home." He spread both arms wide as though we were standing in the middle of a penthouse suite.

I swallowed, thinking how wonderful the liquid would feel going down my throat. It made me sick to do it, but I had to have water. I reached out, but he jerked his arm back, keeping me from getting it. Like I shouldn't have expected him to do exactly that.

"Give it to me."

"Sure, sugar. But first things first." His lust-filled gaze slid down my body. "Take your clothes off."

"What?" Did he seriously think I'd strip for him?

"You heard me. Get naked." He shook the thermos. "You want the water, don't you? Then you're going to have to do what I tell you to do."

"Go to hell."

"No thanks. I've already been there and back." He shrugged. "Makes no difference to me. One way or another, I'm going to see you naked." He chuckled. "It's just like the games. You've got two choices. Strip or I tear your clothes off you and shred them."

I wanted the water badly, but I hated giving into him. Yet if I didn't, I knew he'd make good on his threat.

"Why are you doing this to me?" I should've asked long before, but I'd been too frightened to think straight.

His smile died. "The reason doesn't matter. Now take it off.

You're getting me riled up and not in a good way."

Demanding anything from him wouldn't work. Instead, I lost a little of my dignity by asking. But I had to know. "Please, tell me. At least give me a reason."

For a moment, I thought I saw another side of him. A softer, kinder side that had been hurt more than it had been able to handle.

"Logan owes me."

"For what? Did he have an affair with your girlfriend? What could he have done to make you this... angry?" I'd started to say *psycho*, but managed to hold it back.

"Naw, worse. He killed my brother."

"He killed your brother?" I didn't know Logan well, but my gut told me he wouldn't hurt anyone without a good reason. "I don't believe you."

"He didn't pull the trigger, but he should've been there to stop it. Instead, he left my brother alone to defend himself." He laughed, but it soon changed into a scowl. "No one comes back from a bullet to the brain. Not even one of us."

Not knowing the whole story, I couldn't argue in defense of Logan. Besides, it wouldn't have done any good. Ruger was out for revenge. "But what does that have to do with me?"

The softness, the heartache I'd seen for a brief moment was gone. "You're his mate. Or at least, you were supposed to be. He took from me and now I'm taking from him."

I shook my head. Maybe I could reason with him. "But I'm not his. I wasn't going to pick him. It's the money I want, not Logan."

My heart whispered back, challenging the lie.

"And I would've loved to see you reject him. But I can't count on you going through with it. No, sugar. I want to see his face when I tell him how hard I fucked you." He chuckled again. "Before you had a nasty accident."

"Accident?" He was going to kill me. Even having assumed he would earlier didn't help me handle it now. "You don't have to kill me. Just let me go and I won't tell anyone what happened."

A wicked gleam shone in his eyes. "And if I let you live and claim you? What then?"

He was playing me. Giving me false hope so he could snatch it away just as he'd done with the water bottle. I had no doubt he'd kill me. Still, I had to try. "But you can't. It's my choice and I'd never choose you."

He was getting a kick out of my attempts to sway him. "Just watch me. By tomorrow night, I'll have fucked your brains out. It'll kill him, knowing what I did to you." His gaze slid over me. "Hell, if you're good enough, I just might let you live. It might even be worth taking you as my mate. Wouldn't that just chap his butt?"

His malicious expression returned. "You and me? We're going to have a good time together." He pointed at me, accusing me. "Hey, not bad. You're a smart one. I'll give you that. You got me talking instead of tearing off your clothes. Even got me thinking about keeping you alive. Hell, even about taking a fucking mate. But you can't fool me for long. Now get to it."

He growled and it reminded me of the lion. I shivered and hugged myself. "No. You won't make me do it. You're better than that." It was another lie, but one my heart didn't mind me telling.

"Sugar, you couldn't be more wrong." He stepped toward me, his intent clear.

If I wanted to keep my clothes intact, I had to do what he said. "Don't come any closer. I'll do it on my own."

Crossing his arms, he rested his weight on one leg and waited like a man standing at a bus stop.

My anger wasn't helping me any longer. In fact, it took me back to my house and my father. And all the times he'd whispered in my ear, telling me how one day he'd see me naked. How one day, he'd fuck me and make me a real woman.

I took off my shoes, taking my time. I prayed he'd change his mind.

"You're going too slow. Jeans."

Maybe if I got it over with, he'd leave. Maybe if I gave him what he wanted, I could still talk him into letting me go. Staying wasn't an option. Not with the walls continuing to move a fraction of an inch closer every time I checked. "Will you let me out of the hole? Please. I can't stand being in closed-up places."

"Claustrophobic, huh?" He motioned for me to keep taking it off, then set the bottle on the ground at his feet.

"Yes."

"Too damn bad. But at least you can see above you."

Explaining how I felt wouldn't work. Instead, I undid my jeans and tugged them over my hips to puddle at my ankles. I clasped my hands in front of me, hiding what little my panties covered.

"Damn, sugar, speed it up. Take off your shirt."

I tugged off my T-shirt, then put my arms at my sides. The way he looked at me, as though I was nothing more than a piece of meat, a whore he could fuck, made me feel dirty. But I vowed I wouldn't let him break me. My father had tried, but I'd won against him and I'd win against Ruger.

"Girl, you are smokin'. I'm going to love tapping your ass."

I stayed quiet and let my glare say it all. He could take my clothes and make me do as he liked, but he'd never touch the real me. The part of me I kept safely inside.

He came toward me, walking around me like the lion had circled the dead body. I gritted my teeth and waited for the inevitable. When he did touch me, grazing his fingers along my butt cheek, I didn't even flinch.

Do whatever you like, asshole. I'll win in the end.

"Bra. Now."

I went cold, stuffing down my screams, deadening my emotions. If I didn't feel anything, he couldn't hurt me. My father had taught me how to go cold.

I remained as still as a statue when he reached around from behind and cupped my breasts. He squeezed, hard, and I bit back a whimper.

"Fuck, but you've got great tits. Nice and big."

Cold. I'm cold. Solid ice.

He pinched my nipples as he slid his tongue along my shoulder. The rise in his jeans pressed against my lower back.

"Yeah. You and me? We're going to have a lot of fun. Take the last bit off." He backed up. "Bend over, girl. Show me your ass."

I thumbed my panties over my hips and let them join my jeans. Putting my hands on my knees, I bent over. I hated that I hadn't expected it, but I couldn't help but jump when he spanked me.

"Fucking your ass is going to be great."

"Just do it and get it over with." I'd reached a breaking point. He wanted to toy with me, to torment me, but I'd put a stop to it. Even if it meant getting fucked.

Another slap came, stinging into my skin. "Don't tell me what to do. I'll fuck you when I'm damn good and ready." He pulled me straight then enveloped me with his arms. One hand fondled my breast while he slid the other between my legs.

Don't cry. Don't give him the satisfaction.

My father had loved it when I'd cried. Later, I learned to deny him that pleasure. As much, maybe more, than they wanted sex, Ruger and my father wanted my humiliation. Torment was their greatest joy. A joy I wouldn't give them.

I closed my mind to it just as I'd done with my father. If I didn't think about it, it couldn't hurt me.

At last, my mind jumped to my Happy Place. But this time, Logan was there.

Ruger's hands were all over me. He moaned and told me the nasty things he'd do to me.

But I wasn't there. I was gone. Safe in another world with Logan. Logan smiled at me, telling me he'd be with me soon.

Pain seared through me as he slapped my thigh, earning a quick jerk from me. His cock, freed from his jeans, shoved against my ass, pushing its way toward my anus.

Logan held me and told me how beautiful I was. His arms surrounded me, keeping me safe. I wanted to believe him. I had to believe him. If I didn't, I'd be lost.

All at once, Ruger backed away from me. It was a jolt as my mind was forced back to the here and now, back to the hole.

"Shit."

I didn't know what had stopped him. Had Logan finally found me?

Ruger, fury on his face, turned to me and grabbed me by the throat. "Someone's out there."

I sucked in air and looked toward the edge of the pit. My

heart thundered against my chest. Would they see Eva's body? Would they look in the pit?

"Keep your mouth shut. If you don't, someone's going to die."

I froze, realizing what he meant. He'd kill whoever heard me scream.

Putting his mouth to my ear, he whispered, "I'll be back tomorrow to fuck you up right, girl. If you're good enough, I might just keep you for a while."

He threw me down and when I looked up, he was gone. But how? How could anyone, even a man as tall as he was, jump out of the deep hole?

I tugged my clothes on, then scrambled for the water he'd left behind. Clutching it to my chest like a rat with a piece of cheese, I scurried to the center of my prison.

Where was he? Had he left for good? Was it safe to scream for help?

In the next moment, my questions were wiped away. In their place came complete terror. Ruger had hold of a tarp and was pulling it over the pit, blocking out the coming sunrise.

I ran to the wall and reached for him. "Please, no. Don't cover me up. Please."

He ignored me, bringing the darkness and plunging me into hell.

Chapter Eleven

Logan

"Logan, slow down. We need to rest."

"Not until we find them."

Luke struggled to keep up as we hurried over an outcropping of rocks. We'd already gone over them once, but I didn't know what else to try. Believing Ruger hadn't had the time to take her very far, we'd concentrated on a two-mile area expanding outward in a circle using the place where I'd last picked up her scent as the center. Her scent was long gone now, erased by the wind and the paw prints of passing animals.

The morning sun was coming up. I should've spent the night at my cave getting to know her. Instead, I'd spent the night running, desperately hoping to find her.

Luke grabbed my arm and I whipped around, teeth changing to fangs. The shift hit me hard with my lion pushing to get free, pushing to get out and find its mate. The more worried I became, the harder it was to keep my lion from taking over.

"Easy, man." He backed off, his hands held up in a defensive posture. "I want to find Eva as much as you want to find Mia. But if they're in trouble, we're not going to be much use to them half-dead."

I'd brought up the idea a couple of times before and I

brought it up again. "We should shift. We could find them better as lions."

"And then what? Show them what we are? You know we can't do that. It's against the rules."

"I don't give a damn about the rules. Finding her is more important."

"And what if one of the other girls sees us? Two lions running around a mountain in North Carolina? That'll be hard to explain."

"Again. I. Don't. Care." I took off, unwilling to let any more time pass. Every minute could be her last. My stomach was in knots from hunger and thirst, but mostly from worry. "Damn it. She's near. I can feel it. We must've missed something."

Luke stayed on my heels for another quarter of a mile before taking my arm again. He was already backing up when I whirled to confront him a second time. "I swear if you grab me again…" I held back from hitting him, but just barely.

"Listen to me."

I snarled, my chest heaving with the effort to restrain my shift. "What?"

"I think we need to expand our search area. Or change the center of it."

He had a point. "Yeah. Okay." And yet, as soon as I'd agreed, it didn't feel right. I could sense her presence close by. "No. She's here." I searched around me, praying I'd pick up on anything that would lead me to her.

"Maybe we overlooked something by going so fast."

I nodded, becoming more and more convinced that she was just out of reach. Even with our lions' sensitive senses, we could've missed a clue. How could Ruger hide when I knew the mountain as well as he did? "It's possible."

"Then we'll give it another pass before we start spreading out. After we take a breather." He sat down on one of the rocks, lowered his head between his legs, and moaned. "Damn, I knew you were fast, but I never knew you were that fast."

"Which means you need to get on your feet and get moving." I was already searching again.

"Fuck, Logan. Wait up."

But I couldn't. My instincts told me Mia was in trouble and time was something she didn't have.

Mia

Hell was everywhere around me. I scrunched my body together, my knees drawn to my chest, my hands on the back of my head. I tried not to see into the darkness of the pit, but I couldn't not look, either.

Here they come.

The walls had started inching closer from the moment Ruger had pulled the tarp over the hole. I couldn't see them, but I could hear them. Mud, dirt and twigs oozed their way toward me. They crept toward me, but doing it slowly enough to make me wish they'd move faster and end my torment.

Unlike the closet at home, I couldn't see any slashes of light. It was pitch black, but it wasn't empty. I whimpered and moaned, making sounds I wouldn't have recognized as coming from me. I pleaded with Logan to find me. I even pleaded for Ruger to come back. Anything was better than facing the darkness alone.

A squeal escaped me as something scampered over my feet.

Shuffling them, I tried to pull myself into an even tighter ball. Sobs ran tears down my cheeks, but I didn't dare wipe them away. I had to keep my hands on top of my head and my arms shielding my face. They wouldn't protect me, but at least, once the walls touched my arms, I'd know to prepare for the worse. To prepare to have my head crushed.

Please, Logan. I need you.

Go to the Happy Place.

I closed my eyes and concentrated on breathing. I'd go to my Happy Place where I'd see Logan for the last time. Without wanting to, without even realizing it, he'd come to mean more to me than I'd have thought possible.

My mind latched on to him. Maybe by thinking about Logan, I'd be able to ignore the panic seizing me.

I didn't really know him, and yet we had a connection. It was a physical one, but it was more, too. Love at first sight? I'd never believed in it, but had I found it anyway? Would I ever find out if we really were meant to be together?

Logan. Please.

The image of him, so tall, so sexy, came to me. He was smiling, telling me it would be all right. I wanted to believe him, ached to believe him. And I tried. But just as I was starting to believe, I heard the slushy crawl of the walls as they crept another inch toward me.

Logan. Think about Logan.

If I was going to die, if I was going to be crushed to death, then I wanted to die thinking about him.

Mia

Logan lifted his eyebrows, the blue-silver of his eyes giving way to more silver highlights. I moaned and took hold of his hands flattened against my pelvis. I couldn't see the rest of his face. Not when it was hidden by my mons. When he finally lifted his head from between my legs, my juices were spread around his mouth.

"You taste so fucking good."

"Yeah?" My voice shook as the remaining shudders from the previous orgasm worked their way out of me.

"Yeah."

"And I fuck even better."

"You sure as hell do."

His movements were graceful and sleek like a cat as he drew his body over mine. He was gorgeous, buff and primed, ready for action. I opened for him, aching to feel his huge cock inside me again.

He took my nipple into his mouth then feathered kisses along my skin and up to my ear. I arched and locked my heels behind him, yanking his body toward me.

His chuckle warmed my ear. "Are you trying to tell me something, baby?"

"Hell, yeah. Fuck me, damn it."

"Yes, ma'am."

It was his hair I yanked this time, making him look at me. "Don't ever call me ma'am. I'm not an old married lady."

He nibbled at my jaw, then tunneled his fingers through my hair. "Nope. You're an old mated lady."

I feigned shock. "Who are you calling old?"

He rolled me over, putting me on top of him, and spearing me with his cock. The man knew how to win an argument.

"Baby, you'll never be old to me."

He worked his hips like a machine driving bolts into metal. I leaned forward, offering my breasts to him and he took them, relishing them with a satisfied groan. Gripping my ass, he helped me rock to his rhythm.

The sun shone above us adding warmth to our heated bodies as we made love in the middle of a grassy field. Nothing could surround me there, caging me within its walls. I was free with no worries or fears.

Up and down he moved, bumping me, jiggling my breasts. His pecs were mountains with two small rocks on them. The muscles in his arms flexed as he slid his hands over my body, finding all his favorite places to explore.

His eyes, his strange, amazing eyes held the one thing I'd looked for. The one thing no amount of money could ever buy. The one thing that would never make me feel trapped.

His eyes held love.

I began circling my hips and saw the smile form on his lips. "Do you like that?"

"You bet I do."

A pinch there, a twist of the nipple, and he had another orgasm rising to the surface. Elation filled his face, matching my own feeling as he thrust into me, harder than ever.

We moved together as though we'd known each other all our lives. He was my mate, my man. And I was his woman.

The climax hit me hard, forcing a cry from my lips. Sitting up, he wrapped his arms around me, melding our two bodies together as our releases took over. His growl-groan rumbled against my breasts until, at last, I had no strength to stay upright. Satisfied, I closed my eyes and let him lower me to my back.

I sighed a very happy sigh. "Oh, my God."

"Yeah. My thought exactly."

"Can we do it again?"

"Sure, sugar. We can do it right now."

Sugar?

I came awake to find Ruger fondling my breasts.

"No!" Shoving him off me, I rolled away.

"Where you going?"

My fingers dug into the ground as I pushed myself up. Yet instead of digging into loose dirt, my hand closed around a rock. It wasn't large, but it was big enough. At least, I hoped so.

"Time to make you mine." Ruger seemed to grow larger, his T-shirt straining under the muscles in his arms.

I moved away from him, keeping my hand behind my back. The chances of my being able to hurt him were slim to none, but I had to try. To give in would mean more than surrendering my body. I'd be surrendering my mind as well.

He came closer. His eyes lost their silver-blue color and turned to a gun metal gray. His lips pulled back into a snarl that wasn't quite human.

Terror spun wild inside me, but I held on, fighting as I'd always had to fight. "I'll never be yours."

"Yeah, you will. At least for a while. You can count on it. I'm going to fuck you six ways from Sunday. On your knees, on your back, and tied up. You're going to fight and scratch, but in the end, you're going to whimper and ask me to let you live. Then, when I'm through with you, I'm going to sink my fangs into your soft, supple skin and rip your throat out. I'm going to watch the life die in your eyes." He chuckled, so low it sounded like a growl. "I'm going to miss the fighting and fucking part of it. Maybe if you're good and obey your new master, I might let you live a few days longer."

Fangs? What was he talking about? And yet, the way he curled his lips, showing the tips of sharp, razor-like teeth, had me expecting to see fangs. I pressed against the wall as hard as I could.

"Logan will find me."

"Naw, he won't. Nobody knows about this place. Hell, even I didn't until I stumbled on it a couple of months back. The mountains are funny that way. Just when you think you know every inch of them, they surprise you. This place was right here, in front of my face, all these years and I'd never seen it. Still wouldn't have if I hadn't gotten so caught up in chasing a rabbit that I barreled right through it and came out into this clearing. Scratched me to hell, but it was worth it. As soon as I saw it, I knew it'd be the perfect place to carry out my plan."

"And Eva? How'd she find it?" I didn't want to think about poor Eva. But keeping him talking was the safest thing to do. Anything to delay the inevitable.

He shrugged. "There's another way, one that goes around the thicket. But unless you're looking for it, you'd probably go right by it. It was just dumb luck that she wandered in here."

"He'll keep looking. I know he will." Hopefully, he didn't hear the uncertainty in my voice.

"Enough of your bullshit. It's time for some fun."

"Stay away from me." I lifted my hand over my head, showing him what I held. Like my pitiful weapon would scare him off.

His eyes blazed silver hatred. In the next moment, he was on me.

I had no time to react. No time to even attempt to strike out. Crying out, I tried to hang on to the rock, but the strength of his hand around my wrist hurt too much. I dropped the rock and squirmed away, then started to run to the other side of the pit.

I didn't get very far. He caught me, shoved me to the ground and pushed me onto my stomach. "No. Leave me alone."

"Not a chance, bitch." He flipped me over, tearing my shirt and bra away. His hungry gaze settled on my breasts. "Yeah, that's what I want to see. Fucking hot, sugar."

He was on top of me, his hands pulling at me, his hands fondling me. He put his mouth to mine, his fingers forcing my jaws apart, and held me there. I wanted to bite down on his tongue, but his grip was too strong. I fought him every way I could, but it was useless.

Straddling me, he sat up, keeping my wrists pinned to the ground. I looked into his face, but it wasn't Ruger's face I saw. It was my father's.

I screamed, more in rage than in fear, and kicked my legs, trying to buck him off. He laughed, just as my father had done. I couldn't take it any longer. If I died trying, I wouldn't let another man grope me.

Just as with my father, I had to gain control. I had to outwit him. Only then could I survive.

"Ruger." I stopped struggling, my chest heaving with my pants. "I give in."

He looked surprise. "Already? Damn. Come on, sugar. You've got more fight in you than that. Hell, even that skinny bitch Eva put up more of a fight."

Had he forced Eva to do horrific things before he'd killed her? If I lived long enough to see him pay, I'd consider myself lucky.

But I didn't want to give him the satisfaction of fighting him. At least not yet. Until I could take my one last chance, I wouldn't struggle. "You've known all along, haven't you?"

He frowned, obviously not understanding what I meant. "Sure." But his tone wasn't confident.

Giving him a seductive look was one of the hardest things I'd ever done. "I was hoping you had. But a girl's got a right to play hard to get, right?"

He grew sly, taking my bait. "You want me instead of Logan."

I smiled, giving him another sexy look. "Shit, yeah. But I knew from the start you'd like it better if you took me away from him." I flicked my tongue over my lips. "Give me a kiss. Then show me I picked the right man."

His grip on me loosened as he grabbed hold of my hair, hurting me, and tugged my face to his. Crushing his mouth to mine, he shoved his tongue into my mouth. I kissed him back, trying to pretend he was Logan. It took everything I had not to throw up.

My hand slid lower, down to the waistline of his jeans. Understanding my intention, he broke the kiss, sat back and helped me unzip them.

"Give me your cock, Ruger."

At his hesitation, I added, "What's the matter? You don't really think I'd bite it off, do you?"

He thought about it and I did my best to act hurt that he'd really think I'd cause him pain. "Please. I want to swallow your cum. Give it to me and I promise, I'll fuck you like you've never been fucked before. I'm going to love being fucked by a real man."

A real man. Just like my father had said.

That did the trick. He leaned over me, putting his cock close to my face.

I closed my eyes, gathered my nerve, then opened them. No matter what came next, I'd have the pleasure of knowing I'd hurt him in the worst possible way.

But I couldn't do it. It was just too much. I remembered the way Logan had gaped at me, horrified as I knelt before Ruger. If nothing else, I wouldn't disrespect the man I loved by taking Ruger's cock into my mouth. I'd rather die.

"Come on, bitch. What are you waiting for?"

"Nothing."

Something. Anything.

Please, someone help me.

Logan, where are you?

I couldn't take any more of his torture. Not and stay sane. When I saw him close his eyes, I knew it was time to do the only thing I could do.

Saying a silent good-bye to Logan, I grabbed Ruger's balls and drove my fingernails into the soft flesh as hard and as fast as I could.

Ruger shouted, the angry sound morphing into howls of pain as he struck me in the head. I rolled onto my side. My head swam, but at least I was free of him.

For the moment.

His shouting deafened me, terrifying me into action. I got onto my feet and stumbled toward the nearest wall. When I turned to confront him, I froze, my gaze starting at the blood covering his crotch, then lifting to his face.

This can't be real

"You fucking whore! I'm going to tear you apart!"

Ruger started tearing off his clothes. Long, sharp teeth slid over a mouth that was no longer human. Instead, it grew longer, stretching the chin and jaw. His ears became more rounded. He lifted his arms and flexed his hands. Curved claws replaced fingernails. His eyes glittered, the silver brilliant against the dark golden fur sliding over his skin. His arms twisted into odd angles and the fur continued to travel, slipping over his body like a waterfall over a cliff.

He was changing. But changing into what?

Soon enough, it became clear.

Ruger was transforming into a lion. I screamed as he crouched, then hurled his body at me.

Logan

Her scream tore me apart, inside and out. I slammed to a stop, took one look at Luke, then started running toward the sound.

Mia.

Another scream rent the air and I twisted toward the right. Although my sensitive hearing could pick up sounds from far away, I knew she was near. I'd been right. My instincts had told me she was close and she was.

We'd already checked this part of the mountain. I didn't understand how we could've missed her, but we had. I kept moving, then realized I hadn't heard her scream again. Was she injured? Dead? Or had Ruger silenced her?

Luke took my side. "Come on," he murmured.

He thought it was Eva, but I knew better. The sound had traveled through me. The girl who'd screamed was Mia, but I didn't tell Luke. First we'd find Mia, and if we got lucky, we'd find Eva, too.

It was too damn quiet. If I didn't hear her again, I might not be able to find her.

Please, Mia.

As if on cue, another scream came, but this time the scream was a name.

"Logan!"

Luke grabbed my arm and pointed to the left. "Over there."

He'd pointed at a thick grove of trees with a tumble of vines running through them. Getting through the vines would be hard, and then the trees on the other side might be too dense to move easily. I'd gone past the grove a thousand times, but had never thought to go into them.

"In there." I sniffed the air, hoping to pick up her scent. I didn't.

"But how?"

"I don't know, but I'm going to find out."

Luke followed me to the vine-covered trees and started yanking the twisted plant away. I grabbed a thick rope and put all my weight into tearing it away.

"There has to be another way past these." I'd grown up in the mountains and knew them well, but I'd never noticed the mass of tangled vines and foliage. Or maybe I had, and through the years, they'd become invisible to me, like landmarks passed so often that they'd faded into the background.

I stepped away from the jumbled mass as Luke kept working. If I could get around them, then I could reach the other side faster. At the rate we were going, we wouldn't get through for at least an hour. And an hour would be too long.

Keeping the wall of vines to one side of me, I began moving around it, holding on to them to keep me going in the right direction. There was no trail so I had to guess and hope I didn't get mixed up. Once I thought I was making headway, then the path I'd taken would disappear behind more bushes. I'd made an arc around half of the thick bushes when I saw the small opening into a tunnel formed by branches meeting overhead. More branches had once covered it, but they'd been broken and shoved aside by either a large animal… or Ruger.

"Luke. Here." I whispered, suddenly aware that if I could hear Mia, then Ruger could hear me.

Luke followed me into the opening. It led into a tunnel that wound through the jumbled vines and trees. Although the passage couldn't have been very long, it felt like it took a lifetime to get through as we worked our way along the uneven path.

Mia. Scream again. Call my name.

But this time, my silent plea wasn't answered. I pushed on, urgency propelling me faster than was safe to go.

Panic took hold of me, quickening my breath and dragging down my heart. If we didn't find the end soon, I doubted we ever would. I wasn't even sure there was another opening on the other side of the thicket. But I didn't have anything else I could hold on to. If this didn't work, I would have failed Mia.

"Logan, we have to turn around and find another way," whispered Luke.

"No. Not yet. Just a little farther." I kept going, my hands against the vines, guiding me on.

Suddenly, just as I turned another corner, light filtered into the tunnel and I knew I was near the end. I wanted to shout for Mia when I caught the sound of a struggle. Mia's cries were softer, but determined, as though she fought for her life. I picked up speed, charging toward the opening only a few feet away from me.

"No." Luke pushed me out of the tunnel, knocking me to my feet, and rushed past me.

By the time I'd gotten up, he was already bent over the body of a young girl. Her body was mangled, bloodied and half-eaten. The trail of how'd she'd been dragged to the spot had lion tracks around it. Fear strangled me.

Please, don't let it be Mia.

And yet, it couldn't be. I could still hear her cries.

She's still alive.

Rushing past Luke, I ran into the small clearing. Sunlight came through a few openings in the trees above me, but I could see the huge hole in the ground in front of me clearly. I skidded to a stop just in time to keep from falling into it.

Fury whipped through me. Ruger, partially transformed, stood over Mia. She kicked and struck out, but her attack was useless against the shifter.

"You're going to pay, bitch."

Ruger had his back to me, but I could tell by his garbled words that his fangs were out and ready to sink into her. My lion pounced, roaring, clawing its way to the surface. As Ruger bent over her and held her down with one hand, his claws digging into her skin, I turned my lion loose.

Ruger heard my snarl as I started shifting in mid-air, tearing my clothes from my body as the change rushed over me. By the time he twisted around, it was too late. I knocked him away from her, throwing his body against the other side of the pit. I finished shifting and planted my paws into the ground, ready to do battle for the woman I loved.

Mia

I was in a living nightmare. Ruger had changed into a half man, half animal. Saliva dripped from his long fangs as he pulled his lips into a snarl.

I was going to die a horrible and painful death.

Then, all of a sudden, Logan was there, standing at the top of the pit. His gaze met mine then slid to Ruger. He snarled, then jumped into the air, his clothes tearing away from his body as his body changed. He landed behind Ruger, growling. With one quick strike, he tossed Ruger aside like a child throwing a rag doll away.

I pushed myself into a sitting position and hugged my knees to me, my body and my mind rebelling at the sight. Even if I could have gotten out of the hole, I doubt I would've had the strength to run.

Both men kept changing. Fur replaced skin as their bodies shifted, changing from one thing to the other. Before my mind could accept what I was seeing, two lions, their thick manes surrounding their heads, crouched in front of me.

The second lion—the one who had been Logan—turned his head toward me and met my gaze with his silver one. Then he turned toward Ruger. His roar was deafening and I clamped my hands over my ears.

Two men. Two lions. I stared, not truly believing, but knowing it was real.

They came together, throwing their bodies at each other like beastly gladiators. Their roars blasted the air. I could feel the thunder of their paws as they pounded the earth. Claws and fangs bit and raked at each other, splattering blood against the walls.

I couldn't stand to watch, and yet I couldn't turn away. The lion that was Logan slashed out, cutting a gaping wound in Ruger's stomach. Ruger snarled his anger then dug his paws into Logan and took him to the ground. Dark red covered their golden fur and the coppery smell of blood filled my nostrils.

I had to help Logan, but how? All I had were the small

stones scattered on the ground. But using them was better than doing nothing. Picking up the largest stone I could find, I paced back and forth, jumping out of the way whenever their massive bodies got close to me.

I had to make the shot good. If nothing else, I could distract Ruger long enough for Logan to strike a killing blow.

They spun around, neither one of them willing to turn loose of the other. I lifted my arm and got ready.

When the moment came, I hurled the rock, grunting as I put every bit of power I had into the throw. At the last moment, they whirled around again, then broke apart, putting Logan in my direct line of fire. The stone struck him dead center in the forehead. It didn't even break the skin, but it was enough to take his attention away from Ruger.

I screamed as Ruger took advantage of my mistake and threw his body against Logan. He went down on his back, kicking out his hind legs and fighting to get on his feet. But Ruger stayed on top and held him down.

I couldn't lose Logan. Not after everything I'd gone through.

Frantically, I searched for something, anything to use as a weapon. Throwing another stone was all I could think to do. At least when I threw the next one, I'd make damn sure I was close enough to hit the right lion.

Lion.

My brain protested the word.

At last I found a large rock half buried in the corner of the wall, hidden by the shadows. I couldn't throw it, but I could pick it up with two hands and slam it against Ruger's head. It was heavier than I'd thought, but I managed to dig out the third of it that was buried in the wall, then hefted it over my head.

Staggering toward Ruger, I got ready to bring it down as hard as I could.

Another roar, one that hadn't come from either Ruger or Logan, startled me. Looking up, I saw yet another lion spring off the edge of the pit and land on Ruger's back. I stumbled back, dropping the rock, as I threw my body out of the way.

Ruger's furious roars mixed with the other lion's. Lifting onto his back legs, Ruger fell backward, taking the darker-colored lion with him. They landed with a thud, but were back on their paws in no time.

Logan leapt up, going past me as he bounded toward them. His fur brushed my skin as he sped past me.

Logan and the third lion stood side by side, facing Ruger. They'd cornered him. He paced the small space in front of them, showing his fangs and growling his anger. I waited, expecting Logan and the third lion to pounce on Ruger and finish him off.

Instead, Logan started changing, his body blurring as fur disappeared and skin came back. I heard the chilling sound of bones breaking as they bent and reformed into human limbs. In only a minute or so, Logan the man had returned. Moments later, Ruger changed back into his human body. Blood covered both men and flesh hung from wounds.

Was the third lion a man, too?

"Why'd you do this?"

Ruger scowled at Logan. "You know damn well why." He growled, cupping his bloody crotch. "That fucking cunt dug her claws into my balls."

"Did you do this because of Vic? Fuck, man, I told you. My being inside the bar wouldn't have made any difference. He started the fight and the man ended it. I tried to help him, but I was too late."

Ruger's face twisted, contorting into a mask of pain and anger. "You should've never left him alone. He was my brother and your friend. Hell, he was as much your brother as he was mine. Your family was my family. Fuck you, Logan. You should've died fighting with him. Hell, you should've taken the bullet for him."

"I went outside for five lousy minutes. How was I to know he'd hit on the guy's girlfriend?" Logan shook his head, denying Ruger and sending drops of blood and sweat into the air. "I got into the fight as soon as I could, but they knocked me out. Damn it, Ruger. Don't you think I wish he was still here? Don't you think I'd give my life to have him back?"

The pain in Logan's face tore at me. He'd lost a friend and had paid a huge price for it. And he was still paying.

"You should've done more." Ruger's shout was filled with agony. "You should've died. Not Vic."

Whatever had gone on between the men had taken more of a price than one man's death. It was hard to believe, but I felt almost as sorry for Ruger as I did for Logan.

The anger left Logan's body, relaxing his muscles, but the pain was still there. It was on his face, reflecting the real agony buried deeper inside him. "I swear. If I could take his place, I would. But I can't."

"No, you can't." Ruger's eyes gleamed. "But you can still die."

Ruger came at Logan, changing into a lion as he ran.

Chapter Twelve

Mia

I shouted to warn Logan, but he was already shifting and ducking out of the way. Logan, however, wasn't his target. Instead, Ruger twisted in mid-air and struck out, his massive paw slicing through the air. The other lion tried to dodge the attack, but didn't get out of the way in time. Blood spurted from the wound in his chest as Ruger's claws tore a gaping gash into him. The lion roared, then fell back, stumbling as he dropped to the ground.

Fully changed, Logan leapt at Ruger, meeting him head-on as Ruger turned from his first victim, ready to claim another. Fangs and claws tore into each other as they fought more violently than before.

There was nothing I could do.

The two massive creatures battled, rolling over, end over end, then coming up on their feet again. The other lion let out a moan as it struggled to its feet, then lunged forward, drawing Ruger's attention. When he did, Logan was ready.

Logan opened his huge mouth, his fangs glinting a moment before he sank them into Ruger's neck, spreading blood over his Kings of Beast MC tattoo. Ruger fought to get free, but his wild thrashing only opened up the wound more. He roared, the sound morphing into a strangled moan as he tried to get his claws into any part of Logan. But Logan had him down on his side, his body on top of his, holding him in place.

Blood was everywhere. My body was splattered with large blotches of red.

Was any of this real? Or had the walls finally closed in on me, caging my mind in its terrible hold?

Ruger's efforts were growing less and less. Logan had a death grip on him and wouldn't let go. His mighty jaws clamped down on Ruger's neck, tearing away parts of the tattoo. He dug his fangs deeper into fur and skin until Ruger's head hung from his body. After one feeble attempt to claw at Logan, Ruger went still. His blank eyes, reminding me of Eva's, found mine. And yet, unlike with Eva, I felt nothing but relief. Logan shook Ruger's limp body, then growled and backed off.

I stared, shocked and fascinated as all three men shifted back into their human forms. Logan bent over Ruger and closed his lifeless eyes.

"Luke, are you all right?"

How could he think he was all right? The man lay on the ground, bloodied with a long raw gash across his chest. His breathing was heavy, his panting becoming short blasts of harshly expelled air.

"Yeah. I'll be fine." He fingered the wound. "It's starting to heal."

He was right. As though I hadn't already witnessed enough unbelievable sights, the wound started closing in, working the skin back together. "Holy shit."

Logan came to me, but stopped short of touching me. "I thought I'd lost you." He gathered my torn shirt and handed it to me.

My mind raced with questions tumbling end over end. I was

alone in a pit with two—three—men who could change into lions. "This is fuckin' real. You—" My gaze jumped to Ruger, then to the other man before landing on Logan. I dragged in a hard breath. "You're all lions. The Kings of Beasts. That's why you're called that."

"Yeah. We are. I'm sorry you had to find out this way. Are you all right?"

He stepped forward, growing closer, and, although I wanted nothing more than to be in his arms again, I took a step back.

"Mia, I know this is hard to handle, but first you have to know that you're safe. We'd never hurt you."

"What are you?"

"We're shifters. People who can change into animals."

"I've lost my mind. You're talking like a crazy person and I'm beginning to believe you."

"No, baby, you're not crazy. What you've seen is real."

I wanted to laugh and cry at the same time. "You're shifters? Like werewolves." The laugh won out, but it sounded more like a cough. "Like on T.V. or in the movies." I still couldn't get my mind around it. How could people like Logan exist and no one know?

"But how?"

"How am I a shifter?" He shrugged. "I don't know. How are you a human? I just am."

"This is too much." My head swam and I felt weak. "Shit. That was men I saw."

"What men? Where?"

"Outside Fang's. When I was still on the road. Before I went into the woods."

He closed his eyes for a moment. When he opened them, they'd grown blue-silver again. "If you're talking about the two lions fighting, then yeah. It was Ruger and me."

"Oh, my God."

He reached out for me, but again, I stayed away. I really had gone insane. Wanting to be held and yet fearing to let him take me into his arms.

"Mia, let me hold you. If I don't, I think I'll break in half."

With the shock wearing off and the fight over with, I suddenly grew aware that I was still in the hole. Although Logan would do his best to protect me, I had to get out before the walls started closing in again. Pacing, I went back and forth in front of him, heading to a wall, then moving away from it like a moving target in a carnival shooting booth.

"I have to get out of here. The walls—" I paused to check again. Had the walls moved closer? "Please. Get me out."

"Easy, baby, easy. It's okay. I'll get you out."

Logan didn't touch me. Instead, he opened his arms and let me decide to come to him. I hesitated, wondering if the part of him that was a lion might break free.

"It's all right, baby. I'd never hurt you. As a man or as an animal."

Two more hard breaths helped settle me. After all I'd been through, he was what I needed. He was what I wanted most of all.

And I trusted him. If I had nothing else in this world, I had my trust in him. Falling against him was one of the best feelings I'd ever had. It didn't matter that he had more blood on him than I did. He wrapped his arms around me, securing me safely against him.

"Luke."

"Yeah, Logan. I'll take care of him."

Without any effort, Luke took hold of Ruger's body and

tossed it out of the pit. He jumped out, then leaned over and offered his hand to me. Once again, I hesitated. Part of me didn't want to take the hand that had touched Ruger's dead body. Yet, although he wasn't Logan, if Logan trusted him, then I would, too. Logan took me under my arms to lift me up, and I clasped Luke's hand. He pulled me out of the hole without any effort. I backed away as Logan jumped out.

His movements were graceful, fluid, like a cat springing upward onto a perch. Relief swamped me, weakening my knees as he drew me into his arms again. I couldn't have stayed in the hole one more minute. Feeling even weaker, I leaned against Logan, letting him support me.

He gestured to the other man who'd gathered clothing from the ground and was tugging on a shirt. "This is Luke. He's—" he stopped. "He was supposed to be Eva's mate."

I nodded, then averted my gaze away from the half-naked man.

"Ruger killed her, didn't he? Tell me."

The agony in Luke's tone tightened my chest. He'd wanted her, maybe even loved her, and now she was gone. "Yes. She found me in the hole. He killed her to keep her from telling Logan or anyone else where I was."

Luke's strangled groan sliced through me. "She must've gotten lost on the way to my lake house. Otherwise, she wouldn't have been anywhere near here."

"I'm sorry. If she hadn't found me, she might still be alive. She was..." I tried to face him, searching for something to say. But what? That she was nice? But I hadn't really known her.

His jaw clenched, but he kept his head held high. "It's not your fault. Only Ruger's to blame."

I didn't want to see his pain any longer and sought Logan's

bright gaze instead. "I still can't believe it. You change into lions." Maybe if I said the words enough times, I'd start to believe.

"That's right." He was patient with me, understanding that I needed time to let it sink in.

"And you can change any time you want to? So that's why you call me your mate?" I gazed up at him, wonder slowly replacing the sorrow and pain numbing me. "Because I'm the girl you want?"

"Yes. I want you. I have from the first moment I saw you. You're my mate, but you can call yourself anything you want. It's the same thing as being a wife." He caressed my cheek. "But you're a woman. Not a girl. Not any longer."

"And there are more of you?" One question led into another. Would there ever be enough time to ask all of them?

"Aside from the women, the men you saw at Fang's were all shifters. And Burke's mate, Roberta, too. They're all part of our pride. The Claiming Games is how we find our mates. Once we have, and if the girl chooses the man, then we make them one of us."

I jerked back. "*Make* me one of you? How? As a woman?" I leaned away. "Oh, shit. You're going to turn me into a lion, aren't you?"

"A lioness, yes. Or at least, I was." He glanced at Luke, who stood solemnly over Ruger's dead body. "If you'd chosen me."

"She doesn't have a choice now."

Flecks of silver sparked to life again. "Yes, she does. No one has to know what happened."

Logan turned me loose, then faced off with Luke. I was afraid they'd shift and go at each other. "Please. Don't fight."

"We aren't fighting. But Logan knows as well as I do that if a girl sees a lion shift before she's made it back to Fang's, then she's forced to join us. That's our law."

Forced to join them? How could they make me stay?

"And Ruger had a right to claim her?" Logan snarled, sounding all too animal-like. "That's an old fucked-up law. No one's ever taken advantage of it, man, and you know it. The pride won't stand for it."

"I know and I'm with you, but until the law is changed—"

"Until it's changed? Fuck, no. Are you saying I shouldn't have interfered? I should've stood by and let him kill her? Is that what you would've done if you'd had the chance to save Eva?"

"He had a right to claim her, but not to kill her." Luke planted his feet apart. "We should've taken him back to face the others. He would've paid for killing Eva."

"That's bullshit and you know it. He never would've let us take him back."

"Still, he had the right to claim her." Luke's voice faltered as though his conviction was fading.

"But that's not what he was going to do. You know that. He took her, tortured her and—" He paused, glanced my way, asking the question without having to say the awful words. I shook my head.

"He was going to kill her to get back at me."

"He's right." I was fighting for my freedom and for Logan. "He was going to kill me. If you two hadn't found me, I'd be dead right now." I hated using his loss to make my point, but I had to get through to Luke. "I'd be dead just like Eva. He deserved to die."

Logan strode toward him, power emanating from his hard body. "Look, I've already broken the rules. One more won't matter. But I won't let them force her to join the pride. Not when I won't be there to mate her."

"What? Why wouldn't you be there?" Had he decided he didn't want me? "I don't understand."

The muscle in his jaw flinched. "Like Luke said. We're not allowed to show our lion side to our mates before she's made her choice and picked the man. If she takes the money instead, then she leaves and never finds out what we are. But you already know. That means the pride can't let you go. We have to protect the secrecy of our existence."

"So they'll make me a prisoner? How? Will they put me in a cage?" Cages had bars I could see through, but they were still closed, confined spaces. Places where I couldn't leave whenever I wanted to. I'd rather die than live inside a cage. "You can't let them do that. I won't let them do it."

"I know what you're saying, but there's no way you can stop them. They'll keep you with us by changing you into one of us whether you want them to or not. Once you're changed, you won't want to leave. You'll need to have the pride around you."

"They're going to change me into a lion?" The idea was too incredible to comprehend. "If that's what they're going to do, then wouldn't you be the one to change me? I'm supposed to be your mate, right? Why would you leave?"

"I can't stay. I killed Ruger. They'll exile me for interfering, for helping you. I'm not sure what they'll do since no lion has ever killed one of his pride."

"But they aren't the law. We could go to the police or a lawyer. There's got to be someone who can help us."

"The pride is our law. They can and will do whatever they decide is right."

The look in his eyes told me what I feared the most. "Are you saying they'll kill you?"

"Like I said, this has never happened. I don't know what they'll do, but I can guess how it's going to go down. They'll exile me for sure. As for killing Ruger? I don't know." Desperation put a sharp edge on his short laugh. "I'm just beating them to the punch and deciding my own fate."

"But it was self-defense. You saved me. Doesn't that count for anything? He was trying to hurt you. Me. All of us. And he killed Eva. This is full of shit. He deserved to die and I'm not sorry you killed him." The thought of losing Logan was hard enough. But to think his own people would execute him? That was unbearable.

He cupped my cheek and I leaned into the feel of his palm against my skin. I couldn't live without him. How could he live without me?

"Luke will tell them how Ruger killed Eva." He took me by the arms, forcing me to look at him. "Listen, Mia. You need the money and you're going to get it. Luke can put you back on the path to my cave. He'll check on you and make sure you make it. Then, once you return to Fang's, you tell them you stayed there both nights, but I never showed up. Stick to the story so you can claim the money."

I couldn't go through with it. Even if I thought I could lie in a convincing way, I didn't want the money now. I wanted the man. I wanted Logan. I'd find another way to help my family. But he was determined. "You're really going to leave, aren't you?"

"It's the only way."

"No, it's not. I'm going with you. Luke can tell them that Ruger killed me, too."

He backed up, putting more than space between us. "I won't have you living a life on the run. They'll come after me.

And if they find us, they'll make us pay one way or another."

"They can't be that cruel. If we tell them everything, they've got to understand."

He was back at me, taking my arms and shaking me. "You're the one who has to understand. They aren't cruel, but they are lions. Don't you get it, Mia? We take pride in keeping our family strong, in following the rules we've put into place. They'll do whatever they have to do to keep the pride safe from the outside world. Even it means killing an innocent person like you."

"But I love you." There. I'd said it. Flat out without any doubt.

His eyes widened and I saw joy there before he covered up his reaction and tried to find the words to lie. In the end, he couldn't deny me. "I love you, too. But it doesn't change anything."

"There's another way." Luke had grown quiet until then, leaving us to work things out.

"How?" I'd welcome any solution that kept me with the man I loved.

"I'll tell them that Ruger killed Eva. Then, when I found her body, I went crazy and killed him. You take Mia to the cave and let her finish the challenge. She can claim the money or you, whichever one she wants." He shifted his gaze toward Eva's body. "At least one of us should end up with our mate."

I let out a small whimper and tried to find the words to thank him. What he was offering to do was too much. But I was selfish and I ached to tell Logan to do as Luke said. Not that it mattered to Logan. From the look on his face, he'd never go along with it. He had too much honor and dignity to let his friend take the blame.

"No, Luke. That's not how it's going to go down. I won't let you sacrifice yourself for me."

Luke shrugged. "I would've killed him if you hadn't taken him out first."

"Maybe, but I won't let another man shoulder my responsibility."

Frustration and anger came to a boiling point. Hadn't I been through enough? Didn't we deserve to be together? And if Luke was willing to take the blame, then why shouldn't we let him? "Do what he says. I don't care about the money. All I want is to be with you."

"No. I killed him and I'll take my punishment and leave. If they want me dead, then they can come after me and kill me. My leaving will give you time to finish the games and claim the money before they find out what happened. Follow the plan and you'll buy me time to get away."

"No, Logan. I can't. I don't want to be without you."

"Mia, think of your family. Think about your mom."

"I can't let you leave." I clung to him, not caring if I sounded pitiful. "Please, stay with me. My mom would want me to choose you. She told me so. I'll figure out another way to help them."

His throat moved as he worked to get the words out. "I'm sorry, baby. I can't. This is the only way." He turned away from me. "Luke, will you do it?"

Luke nodded. "Yeah. Ruger killed Eva trying to force himself on her, then you killed Ruger. I found their bodies and you told me what happened. Mia had nothing to do with any of it."

His kiss was a good-bye I didn't want, but I couldn't push him away. The urgency, the need for more stunned me.

Please, stay with me, Logan. I need you. I want you.

I put everything into my kiss, hoping it would convince him.

Instead of my kiss changing his mind, he turned me loose.

"No. Please don't go."

His face was cold, expressionless as the silver overtook the blue in his eyes. "Luke, get her to the cave." He turned on his heel and stalked away, not even bothering to gather the remnants of his clothing.

Logan

By morning, I'd put very little distance between me and Fang's, often circling back without even realizing it. I was stupid not to use the time to get as far away as I could, but leaving Mia behind was killing me. She was a magnet drawing me back to her. Being dead would feel better than this.

And yet, as I walked along the highway, I knew I'd had no choice. If Mia had followed the plan, she'd have gone to the cave, stayed the night, then made her way back down to Fang's to claim the money.

She might not have slept in the cave, but as long as she'd stayed close by, she could've dashed inside if someone came around. She would've been okay, especially with Luke looking in on her. I just hoped no one had come to check the cave the first night. It was unlikely, though. Burke and Roberta sometimes checked, but for the most part, the pride counted on the males telling them whether or not the girl had made it. Making sure the girls had the stamina to get through to the end of the games proved she could handle becoming one of us. If she didn't complete the challenge, then she was out.

I groaned, catching myself going back toward Fang's again. If I showed up there, I'd risk not only my life but hers. Luke would keep her safe and back up her story. Once he told the others how I'd killed Ruger, they'd decide if my self-imposed exile was punishment enough. If they wanted me dead, they'd come looking for me.

My future was unimportant. All that mattered was that Mia made it out alive and claimed the money she needed for her family.

But what if she hadn't made it back? What if they'd found out she didn't do the challenge? Should I go back and convince them that she'd suffered enough at Ruger's hands? She'd survived his torment. Didn't that show she was more than strong enough to become a member of the pride?

Suddenly, all the questions became too much. I had to know that she was all right. I'd hide in the woods outside Fang's and watch until she left. Then I'd grab my ride and get the hell out of there for good.

Mia

"I hurt all over."

Luke walked beside me as we headed back down the mountain. "You should've slept inside the cave last night. At least the bugs wouldn't have bothered you as much."

I wasn't going to tell him why. As soon as I'd seen the cave, I'd known there was no way I'd step foot inside it. Even if I didn't have a problem with closed-up spaces, I wouldn't have. Not with the prospect of bats, bugs, snakes, and who knew what else living inside the dark recesses of the cave.

Luke had been nice about it, though. He'd built a roaring fire then had made a bed for me out of leaves and pine needles. He'd even brought me a little water and food. And another shirt to wear. It wasn't like home, but it beat the hell out of a dark hole in the ground.

I'm not sure how much sleep I'd gotten, but it wasn't enough. Dreams of Logan had mixed with nightmares of Ruger and my father. Yet every time I jolted awake, crying out for Logan, it had been Luke who had been there.

Although he was suffering, grieving for Eva, he tried to hide it. He hadn't known Eva—at least as far as I knew—but I could see that his heart was broken. My own heart felt like it always had. Locked inside a cage.

Still, there was a difference. Before meeting Logan, I'd been the one to keep my heart enclosed, safe from anyone hurting it. Now, I'd keep it locked inside, waiting for him to come back and claim it. Until then, it would be safe.

Luke stepped out of the woods and onto the back parking lot of Fang's. The place looked empty. Only two motorcycles remained. One was Logan's and I assumed the other one was Luke's.

"We're late."

I groaned, having heard the same complaint all day. Luke had almost had to push me to get going, but my heart just wasn't in it. I shrugged. "It doesn't matter anyway. I don't deserve the money because I didn't do the challenge."

"Logan trusted me to get you here to claim your money. I should've thrown you over my shoulder and carried you."

"Which is another reason why I don't deserve the cash." I couldn't take it any longer. If I couldn't have Logan, then what the hell was I doing there? "Look. I just want to get out of here. Can you go inside and get my backpack?"

"Get it yourself."

I spun around, my stomach falling.

Burke stood at the back door. "You're late."

I cursed under my breath, but from the way his eyebrows shot up, he'd heard me. But how long had he been listening? I didn't bother arguing that he'd never said when we were supposed to return to Fang's. What did it matter now?

"I know. I've already been told a hundred times today. And like I've told Luke a hundred times, it doesn't matter. I didn't make it to the cave. I didn't complete the challenge so I don't deserve the money."

"Or the man?"

"I never wanted Logan. It's the money I came for." It wasn't a lie, but it wasn't the truth, either. I hadn't come to find love, but in the end, I'd found it anyway. And because I had, I'd do whatever I could to keep Logan safe.

"Why'd you fail?"

I closed my eyes, then set my sights on Burke, giving him an answer he'd understand. "I was too weak. I never made it to Logan's cave because I got lost."

"That's why we do The Claiming Games. To weed out the weak ones." Burke's gaze shot to Luke. "He didn't come back and neither did your mate."

Luke's pain was palpable. "Eva's dead. Ruger killed her."

Burke crossed his arms and leaned against the building. He was so calm, as though he heard about someone dying every day. No big deal. "Tell me about it."

"Ruger tried to force her to have sex the rough way. You know how he liked it. He finally went too far, screwed up, and killed her. Logan saw what he was doing and tried to get Ruger off her." A long, low growl rumbled in his throat. "Yeah, he interfered. But if Logan hadn't killed him, I would've. We need to change that fucking law. No male should be allowed to claim another's."

Burke waved away Luke's argument. "Never mind about that right now. Why the hell would he help her? She was your mate."

He shrugged. "You know how Logan is. He's the hero type. Or maybe it was more about the rift between those two guys than anything to do with Eva. How the hell should I know? I didn't come across them until it was all over. That's when he asked me to check on Mia and see if she made it back."

I ignored the hard, accusatory look Luke gave me. He had no choice but to go along with my lie.

"Instead, I found her lost and wandering around the woods."

Burke's eyes narrowed. "So Logan killed one of our own for a woman that wasn't even his?"

I swallowed back the fear stiffening my spine. Burke wasn't buying Luke's story. Which meant he wouldn't believe mine.

"You know how those two were. Ruger tried to cover it up, but we all knew he blamed Logan for Vic's death. After he killed Eva, he turned against Logan. Logan had no choice. He killed him in self-defense."

Would having killed Ruger in self-defense make a difference? Could we have tried to make Burke and the rest understand? Maybe they would've let him stay. I ached to know, but asking would reveal that I knew what they were. If that happened, I'd be forced to become one of them—without Logan as my mate.

"Why didn't he come back and explain it to us?"

Luke shifted from one foot to the other. "Why would he? He still broke the rules and he knew the consequences. He interfered and he killed Ruger. It doesn't matter why and he knew it."

Burke studied us even harder. "He should've shown up and faced us. Instead, he took the coward's way out." He let out a low groan that sounded more like a growl. "There's no room in our ranks for cowards."

If only I could tell him. Logan was no coward. He'd stood up to Ruger to save me. He should've been given a reward instead of being exiled.

"Whatever. It's over with and he's gone. I've had enough trouble for today. Luke, you can tell everything to the others tomorrow."

"Yeah, fine. But I need to go back and get the bodies."

"What for?"

I gaped at Burke. He'd let their bodies rot in the woods? Ruger deserved that and more, but Eva didn't.

"I'm going to get their bodies." Luke's voice was cold and unrelenting.

Burke didn't bother arguing. "Whatever. As long as I don't have to deal with them, do what you want."

I wiped away a tear. I could've had a life with Logan, could've found a new family with the pride, but all that was gone. Gone because of one man's need for revenge.

"Aw, shit, bitch. What the hell are you crying about? I thought you didn't care about Logan. You came for the money, right?"

I had to get my shit together and play it cool. "I don't care about him. I'm just worn out, that's all. I cry when I'm tired."

"Uh-huh."

Luke shot me a warning glance. "She needs to get her

backpack." He gave a slight shake of his head, intended only for Burke. "She's good. There's no need for her to hang around."

Nonetheless, Burke's suspicion zeroed in on me. "Then we're done here."

I shrugged, shoving down the urge to tear up. "I just want to go home." If only I could figure out where home was. With my aunt and my family? I doubted it. I'd go to them, and do what I could to help, but I wouldn't stay long. It was time for me to be on my own.

He grunted. "Guess I had you and Logan sized up wrong. I thought you'd be one of the pairs to make it. Still, why do I get the feeling that you two are holding back on me? Logan's not here, but his ride is."

I shrugged again and averted my gaze. Keeping quiet was safer.

"He left on foot. You know, the old way."

Burke still wasn't satisfied with Luke's explanation by a long shot, but he didn't push it and I wasn't about to volunteer any information. After what had to be only a few short moments, but felt like a lifetime, he shouted into the bar.

"Roberta, get Mia Traver's backpack. She failed and she's leaving."

A moment later, Roberta came outside and held out my backpack. "I'm surprised. I thought you'd make it."

It was humiliating, but I'd go through anything to keep our story from unraveling. "Me, too." I glared at Burke, at once hating him and wishing I could become one of his pride members. "Can I go now?"

"Yeah. Go. Get the hell out of here."

Turning to Luke, I sent him a silent thank you I hoped he'd pick up on. Then I slung my backpack over my shoulder and started walking.

Chapter Thirteen

Logan

I'd experienced heartache before, but nothing had ever hit me as hard as leaving Mia behind. Although I knew it was the right thing to do, the only way to keep her safe, it was killing me. The only thing that made me feel better was knowing she'd go on and make a life without me.

Shit.

I hunched behind the bushes and watched the three of them outside Fang's. Luke and Mia stood side by side while Burke leaned against the building. I shifted part-way, trying to hear what they were saying, but still couldn't pick up anything.

At first, I worried that Burke didn't believe them. He looked relaxed, as though they were telling him about the weather instead of Ruger's and Eva's deaths. But I knew him too well. He was suspicious.

Come on, Luke. Make it sound good.

Having Luke make my explanation was bad enough. As a lion, I should've come back to Fang's and admitted that I'd interfered in the games. That I'd killed one of our own. But I couldn't. Not without letting them know that Mia had seen us in our animal forms. I'd have been exiled, if not worse, and she would've faced a life as a secondary pride member. No male would've ever mated her and the women wouldn't have treated her as an equal.

I should've gone away. I should've kept going, but I'd had to come back. I had to make sure Mia was going to be okay. Once she left Fang's and Cripple Creek, then I could leave forever.

They continued talking, taking way too long. It should've been a simple thing. Mia would've told Burke she'd done the challenge and that should've been all it took. Instead, they stayed, not going inside the bar, but not leaving, either.

But she'd come back late. If Burke wanted to, he could deny her the money just for that. No exact time had been set for them to get back to Fang's, but we knew from experience that, if the girls were going to make it back at all, they'd get there in the afternoon. Mia, for whatever reason, had shown up after everyone else had already claimed the man or the money.

My lion couldn't stand the uncertainty any better than I could. Claws sprang out as my fangs erupted, replacing human teeth. I bent over, putting my head to the ground so I wouldn't see them any longer. I fought with the animal inside me harder than I ever had before.

Don't give in. If you do, Mia's the one who will pay.

I stayed bent over, hating that I couldn't watch her. After today, after these last few moments, I'd never see her again. But her safety was more important than my pain of losing her.

When I finally lifted my head, they were gone.

New pain, deep in my chest, wrenched through me as I scanned the parking lot, then slipped out from behind the bushes. I made a quick dash to my motorcycle, then hopped on the back. Just before the games had started, I'd stashed some money in the pack resting behind my back. Had I suspected it would end this way? Yet how could I have known?

As soon as I got away from the mountains, I'd sell the bike and get a different one. Using cash, ditching my phone, and getting another ride would help conceal my tracks in case the pride decided to come after me.

I doubted they would. I'd killed a fellow pride member, but I'd done it in self-defense. If Luke could convince them of that, then I doubted they'd bother with me. I'd already taken the consequence of exile.

After putting my ride into second gear, I held in the clutch and pushed it toward the road. When I was far enough from Fang's not to be heard, I released the clutch and hit the starter. Revving the engine, I pointed the bike up the mountain.

I wouldn't go through Cripple Creek. Someone might spot me. Instead, I'd take a different route, then come back around and get on the highway.

Riding the road had always given me a rush that nothing else could. But now all I felt was emptiness. I'd lost the girl who was going to be my mate, the girl I loved, and the only home I'd ever known.

Mia

It didn't take me long to snag a ride with a trucker. I borrowed his phone to call my Aunt Brenda and talk to my mom. So far, my father hadn't tried to contact them or shown up on my aunt's doorstep. Knowing my aunt, she'd have no problem calling the cops then pulling out her Glock to get him the hell off her property.

My Aunt Brenda had balls.

If only she'd been able to convince my mom to leave my

dad sooner. But Mom had been too embarrassed to admit the truth to her sister. I hope she'd finally opened up to Aunt Brenda and told her everything.

"We're here."

I jerked my mind back to the here and now as Donny Wallis, the trucker I'd hitched a ride with, pulled into the Stop and Grab truck stop. After all I'd been through, I didn't look forward to seeing Lee Ann again. And I sure as hell wouldn't tell her that men really could change into lions.

Donny was already sliding out of the cab. "You coming?"

I was starving and as dry as a drunk the morning after a binge. "Yeah."

He gave me one of those looks my mother used to give me. One that dove into my soul, searching for an answer she wasn't sure she wanted to hear.

"Hey, don't take this the wrong way, but you look like you've gone through hell. If you want to take some time and clean up, I'll order you a burger and fries. My treat."

Donny was a good guy. I was thankful he'd been the one to pick me up off the side of the highway.

"So you're saying I stink?"

He didn't want to insult me, but he couldn't deny it. "Yeah. Sorry, but you're pretty ripe. Why'd you think I had the windows down?"

I laughed and slid out of the passenger side. "Then I'll take you up on it. How far did you say you were going?"

"Gotta get to Atlanta to deliver this load. You're welcome to stick with me all the way." He smiled his good-humored, slanted smile. "As long as you get cleaned up and don't smell like road kill any more."

Road kill. I'm sure I smelled like death. At least I'd taken the time to hide behind some bushes and change out of my blood-splattered clothes before hitching. "It's a done deal. Consider me clean."

As soon as we walked into the diner, Lee Ann saw us and lifted her hand. Her hand in the air to greet us didn't stay up for long, though. Instead, it dropped to her side as she took in my appearance.

Donny led the way to the counter with everyone watching as we passed by. I saw one lady lean away from me and put her napkin over her nose.

"What happened to you?" Lee Ann held up her hands. "Girl, you've got to get washed up before you can sit at my counter." She did another sweep over me, checking me out again. "Washed up or hosed down."

"Got any towels I could use? I've got a clean pair of clothes in my bag." It was my last change of clothing.

She reached under the counter and brought out four large white and very clean towels, reminding me of Maggie May doing the same thing. "When you're through with them, take them outside and put them on top of my car. I'll take them home and wash them. It's an old red Honda." Her brow furrowed, concern on her face. "Are you sure you're all right? You look kind of banged up."

Kind of? I had bruises all over my body, dirt on my arms and face, and my hair was a mess of tangles.

"I'm fine." I took the towels, half expecting the rest of the diners to break into cheers. "Thanks. Back in a bit. Donny's going to order for me."

Donny slid onto the stool. "Take your time. I need to give a call home to my wife first and study the menu some. Whenever I'm on the road, I like to try new food."

So Donny was a foodie. I never would've guessed. "Whenever you're ready, go ahead and order me anything. I'm not picky, especially when it's free." I wouldn't have turned down a few pain killers, either, as I trudged down the hall toward the unisex restroom.

Once I got a good look at myself in the mirror over the pedestal sink, I could understand why everyone had stayed clear of me. I looked like I'd been ridden hard and put up wet.

Sighing, I laid the towels out across the toilet lid and got to work. Fifteen minutes later, I looked more like my old self. Better yet, I felt more like myself.

At least on the outside. Another part of me, the part that had caged my heart for so many years trying to protect it, held an emptiness I was sure I'd never be able to fill. I'd thought I'd locked my heart away, but before I knew it, Logan had unlocked the cage, reached in and taken my heart along with him. As though it had always been meant to be his.

I stared at my reflection. What would it have been like to be his mate? To be his wife? If things had been different, would I have learned how to live on the mountain with him?

I had so many questions and no answers.

He hadn't understood my claustrophobia, but not many people did. Still, he hadn't made me feel bad about it or treat me like I was weird. The fact that I'd told him about it said a lot. That I trusted him. That I loved him. That I wanted to share everything about me with him.

I closed my eyes and imagined my Happy Place. I could see myself lying beside him in the open field, no walls to cage us, and only the blue sky above us. We'd be free to do as we liked, free to ride on his motorcycle and keep going until we felt like stopping. I had a feeling I might never be free from the curse of claustrophobia, but he would've made sure my life was as open as it could be.

Now I'd never get the chance to find out.

Would I have changed for him? The idea of becoming a lioness was appealing. I'd always valued my stronger side, the side of me that had kept me going even when locked inside a closet, then trapped in a pit. As a lioness, I would've been even stronger. Maybe even strong enough to keep the walls from ever closing in on me again.

I checked the walls of the bathroom, made sure they weren't moving closer, and made quick work of cleaning up. Instead of getting the money I'd needed, I'd fallen in love and then lost the man, too.

"Life sucks."

But whining about it wouldn't help.

I gathered my dirty clothes and the now-filthy towels, then slung my backpack over my shoulder. Walking down the hallway toward the back of the building brought back memories of the time I'd taken a similar path and had wound up shoved against a wall, having sex with a man whose name I didn't know. Now I knew he'd already taken my heart the first moment he'd kissed me. I just hadn't realized it until it was too late.

I pushed the back door open with my shoulder, then made my way over to the beat-up red Honda next to the building. After putting the towels over the hood of the car, I dug into my backpack, pulled out the clothes I'd worn on the challenge and sent them flying into the nearby Dumpster. Even if I could get the blood out of them, I didn't want to keep them. They reminded me of too many bad things. I threw the clothes I'd just taken off into the Dumpster, too. I'd have to find new clothes soon.

And it was over. Every last thing reminding me of my time on the mountain was gone.

But I'd never forget Logan. The best I could do was hope I'd learn to live with the awful sense of loss eating at me.

By the time I'd made it back inside the diner, Lee Ann already had a hamburger, fries, and a huge chocolate milkshake waiting for me. "Wow. That's a lot of food."

Donny reached for my plate. "Hey, if you don't want it—"

I slapped his hand good-naturedly. "Keep your paws off my food, man."

"Down, girl." He grinned and took a big bite of his pot pie.

The food was delicious. Whether that was because I'd had only bread and water at the cave or because it was actually tasty, I wasn't sure. I tried not to act like a pig by shoving it down my throat.

"Are you going to want seconds? Still on the house, if you do."

I shook my head since my mouth was full. But when I looked up at her, I saw her gaze skip past me and into the parking lot.

Without her saying anything, I knew. I could sense him and her widened eyes only confirmed my feeling. My ears seemed full, like when I'd had too much waxy build-up in them. My breathing became harder. I put the burger down, swallowed, then pushed on the counter to swivel the stool around.

And there he was. Sitting on his motorcycle just like the first time I'd seen him.

I didn't think. Instead, I was off the stool and running for the front door. I shoved the door wide and didn't slow my pace until he lifted his head and saw me. My own joy was reflected in his face.

And then his smile died as he lifted his hand and brought me to a stop. "No, Mia."

"No what? No, you're not happy to see me? No, you don't want me to get any closer? Because I saw your face and I know the answers to those questions. You're just as happy to see me as I am to see you. You want me close. Real close."

He shook his head, then swung his leg back over the bike. "We've already made our decision." He scowled, morphing the scowl into a frown. "Did you get the money?"

"No. I was late."

His sexy blue-silver eyes narrowed at me. "Naw. Luke would've talked them into giving you the money anyway. Especially since you didn't get a chance to choose me over the money. What really happened?"

"I told Burke the truth."

"Fuck. Why?"

"No, wait. I told them the truth about not making it to the cave. I failed and I owned up to it."

"Damn it, Mia. You needed that money to help your family. Trust me. The Kings of Beasts can afford it with no problem. You should've stuck to the plan."

"I couldn't lie and I couldn't take money I didn't earn. After everything we'd gone through, I just didn't have it in me." I took a step closer.

"Damn it. You earned it more than any of the others did." He let out a hard breath. "Did Luke tell him about Ruger?"

"Yes. And Eva, too. And that you killed Ruger trying to save her."

"Doesn't matter why. I killed him. So I'm exiled." He hung his head, then lifted it and thrust out his chin. "It's the way it should be. The way is has to be."

"Logan."

"No, Mia. We can't."

"No, Logan, listen." I didn't pay any attention to his raised hand this time. Who did he think he was to order me around? I was his mate, a lioness in the making. "There's no reason we can't be together. I didn't take their money and I didn't tell them that I knew what they are. You're exiled. Why would they give us another thought?"

He wanted to agree with me, but he held back. I could see it in his eyes, in the way he'd started to speak, not once, but twice, then stopped. Why did he have to be so damn stubborn? And so damn sexy, too?

"We don't know what they're going to do. I hope they'll forget about me. But if they don't, it won't be safe. We can't be together. I can't risk putting you in danger again."

"For a lion, you're a fucking scaredy-cat."

He blinked, then laughed. "Maybe I am."

"Then maybe you should grow a pair."

Irritation flashed in his eyes. Silver flecks mixed with the blue.

"Maybe you should've told me from the first. If I'd known you were such a coward, I would've cut you free before the games started."

"Mia, don't push me."

That was exactly what I wanted to do. "Go on, Logan. Admit it. You're more afraid for yourself than you are for me."

A low growl rolled out from deep inside his chest. "I'm warning you."

"See? Even they can tell you're spineless." I pointed at the group of people who'd gathered to watch us. Outside, two truckers stood several yards away from us, obviously enjoying the show. Donny was nearing the door, ready to come and help me, but I shook my head, keeping him where he was.

"Mia." Logan's face changed, taking on a stone-cold look that, if I didn't know he'd never hurt me, would've sent me hightailing it out of there. His eyes danced with silver.

I straightened to my full height and threw my shoulders back. "If you really love me like you say you do, then you'll take me with you." I hadn't expected to, but suddenly, I had to know. "Unless it's my problem. Is that it? You can't handle a little claustrophobia?"

"Of course I can. I can because it's part of who you are."

I almost sighed like some stupid girl watching a romantic comedy. But seriously, could he have said anything sweeter?

"All that doesn't matter. And what about your mom?"

"I'll figure out another way to help her. We'll figure it out together."

He shook his head, still being bullheaded. "No. It's not fair to you. I won't let you—"

I whipped out a finger, silencing him. "No. Shut up. What I do with my life, where I go, and who I go with isn't your decision to make. It's mine and only mine. I'm not having another man tell me what to do or try and lock me up, whether it's in a closet or in a big fucking hole."

He was on his feet and striding toward me. I didn't have time to think. I just stepped back, cowed by his advance. But I wouldn't let him stop me from having my say.

"You don't think they're coming after you. I don't think they're coming after you. So why not take a chance? I don't want to live without you. If they come after us, if they hurt you and me both, then that's okay. At least what little life I'll have lived would've been with you."

He towered over me, so close that if I'd thrust out my breasts, I would've touched them to his stomach. It took every bit of strength I had not to back down.

"Are you finished?"

I bit the inside of my lower lip and nodded. "Yeah."

"Good. Now it's my turn."

"Okay, but you're not going to talk me out of—"

Logan grabbed me and crushed his mouth against mine. Shock quickly gave way to sheer delight as I wrapped my hands around his neck and held on. He was insistent, taking his tongue and surging it into my mouth. He wrapped his hands around me to grip both butt cheeks and slam my body against his.

I kissed him back with as much heat as he gave me. My body melted into his, the yearning I'd held in check since leaving the mountain breaking free. I was his to command and his to take as his prisoner. He already had my heart and could keep it locked inside a cage of his choosing for as long as he wanted. As long as he gave me his heart to cage.

And he did. I knew it with every fiber of my being. He was my man and I was his woman. We'd gone through hell to get there, and if we had to put ourselves in danger to stay together, then we'd do it.

He nibbled at my lips, then grinned as the sound of laughter and applause broke out around us. Long before I was ready to end the kiss, he pushed me back and gripped me by the arms.

"Do you give up?" I grinned at him.

He lifted his hands. "Yeah. You're one tough bitch."

"Damn straight I am." I let the bitch part slide.

"This isn't going to be easy, you know."

"No, Logan. It won't be. Nothing good ever is. But it's worth it. We're worth it."

He kissed me again, this time quickly before he tilted his head to the side. I glanced at the large window and saw the people gathered there. Donny smiled at me and Lee Ann did a thumbs up.

"I was thinking I'd head to Colorado. Gotta have mountains around me."

"I can do mountains. As long as I can get out in the open, I don't care if we're in the middle of a forest or out in the desert."

"Do you want to—" His gaze darted to the nearby truckers. "Change?"

"Yeah. I think I do. Give me some time to think about it."

"I'm still not sure this is a good idea, but—"

"Logan, we've already decided. Now get on your bike and wait for me. I've got to get my backpack."

"Okay. But hurry up. All these people are making me nervous."

"Will do." I pecked him on the lips, then hurried to the diner.

Lee Ann met me at the door and handed over my backpack. "Are you sure about this?"

"You bet. He's the last ride I'll ever have to hitch." I turned to go, then faced her again. "Donny, thanks for the ride and, Lee Ann, thanks for the food."

"No problem," answered Donny.

I couldn't move fast enough. Hooking my backpack to the rear of his bike, I slung my leg over and scooted up close. "You know we're supposed to wear helmets, right? It's the rules of the road."

"Depends on where you are, but I don't care. I can't stand

fucking helmets." I felt his chuckle rumble through his back. "Besides, rules are made to be broken."

"And if we get pulled over?"

He craned his neck around and grinned at me. "Then I guess you'll have to flirt your way out of a ticket."

I scooted closer, putting my crotch against his firm, tight ass as best I could. "Uh-uh. We're stopping at the first place we see and buying a couple of helmets. I'm not spending the night in jail because you don't want to mess up your hair."

He started the bike then called over his shoulder. "Damn it. You're already trying to pussy-whip me."

"Is it working?"

"Yeah. It is."

He looked at me, the heat in his gaze making my nerve endings stand on end. As soon as we could, I'd have him pull off to a secluded spot and fuck his brains out.

"Ride, Logan. Ride."

Continue reading to enjoy an excerpt from
The Captured Heart...

The Captured Heart

Book One of The Claiming Games

A chance to win money. A chance to find love. But only one can be claimed.

Dear Ms. Pierce,

This is your opportunity to fulfill all your dreams.

Do you yearn to capture a man's heart and have him capture yours? Do you dare to find a man who will treat you to your deepest desires, awaken your heart, and claim you for his own? Are you strong enough to find an extraordinary man?

If so, read on…

Erin Pierce and her two closest girlfriends seek adventure and love. After each receives an invitation to enter The Claiming Games, they travel to Fang's Bar and Grill, ready to take on the challenge of a lifetime. When they arrive, they're greeted by the amazing, sexy men of The Kings of Beasts MC. But these men have a dark side. They're bad boys with fangs and claws.

If Erin survives the games, she has a choice to make. Claim $250,000 in prize money or the man of her dreams. But Erin doesn't believe in dreams coming true. She has a terrible secret, one she believes will send a man running, destroying any chance at love.

When Erin meets Colter Quaid, she has no idea that his secret is just as shocking as her own. Can they forget their terrible pasts? Or will Erin survive the challenge only to lose her future?

Enter The Claiming Games and find out.

Enjoy an excerpt from *The Captured Heart*.

"Erin Pierce, are you a virgin?"

If I hadn't already been sitting, I would've ended up on the floor.

What the hell, man? Who asks questions like that?

Even as unnerved as I was, I had to take a stand. Channeling my surprise and my irritation together, I spoke in my go-to-hell voice. "That's none of your business." I'd half expected him to get angry and had stiffened even more, waiting for him to tell me that I was the one going to hell. Or hit me. Or tell me to get out.

"Aw, now, that's no way to act."

His weird blue-silver eyes drew me in yet again. The intense sensation they gave me made me clench my teeth to keep from moaning.

Burke, the men at CeeCees', the hunk? They all had the

same blue-silver eyes. But how?

"Don't worry." He brushed the hair away from my shoulder. "I'll find out soon enough."

I drew in a hard-won breath. Had he just said he was going to fuck me? That he'd be the one to take my virginity if it was still intact? I wanted to fire back, letting him know in no uncertain terms that, although I wasn't a virgin, I wasn't an easy lay. Did he think he could take whatever he wanted, including me?

When I'd finally gained enough courage to tell him, I froze at the sinful look in those blue-silver depths and I knew. Yes. He was a man who took what he wanted, whenever he wanted, and however he wanted. It wouldn't matter what I said.

He put his face close to my hair. I could feel his breath on my ear.

Oh, shit. Did he just sniff me?

What kind of man sniffed a girl? My gaze met Nina's as she watched, her mouth parted as though she'd started to speak, then had lost her voice.

I frowned and tried to identify the sound close to my ear. But what it sounded like was impossible. At least coming from a man. I would've sworn the delicious, sexy man had just purred.

Okay. I'm losing it big-time.

But if I was losing it, I was losing it in a very good way. My body tingled and he hadn't even touched me. Would he kiss me? Would I let him? The truth came to me as clear as anything ever had. I'd let this man do more than just touch me. More than just kiss me. If he'd wanted, he could've taken me outside and done whatever the hell he wanted to me. Sexually speaking, that is.

Mike had turned me on, but the way I felt with the gorgeous hunk of male in front of me was different. Way different. Where Mike had made me feel pretty, he made me feel sexy. Where Mike had gotten me moist between the legs, he made me flood with my juices. His very being tugged at me as though pulling something carnal and instinctively...*right*...out of me. There was no other word for it. I *craved* him. Like a good bottle of wine or a giant bar of my favorite chocolate. I shivered when I wasn't cold and ached when I wasn't in pain. All because of him.

I wanted him so much that I was no longer worried about what might happen. As long as he stayed close to me, I knew I'd be safe. At least, safe from the others. But safe from him? Not a chance.

Oh, hell, yeah.

How could any man, even someone like him, make me feel this way?

He straightened up and jerked his head at his friend who still hovered over Mia. Then, before I had a chance to react, they were gone, striding back to the side of the room. The men who'd surrounded Maddy shook their heads and moved to the next table to check out the other girls. More men surrounded us, each taking their time to study us like we were theirs for the taking. We'd tense with each new inspection, then let out a breath when they finally moved away.

The entire experience was both irritating and exhilarating.

Until, that is, a familiar voice took the pleasant feeling away, leaving only the irritation.

"Hey, girl."

I grimaced as Hector grabbed hold of the arms of my chair and put his face close to mine. Why did he have to get so fucking close?

I crossed my arms and glared at him. "Please get away from me."

"Not until I get a good whiff of you." And he did. A long and disgustingly slow sniff. "Yep. Just as sweet smelling as I remember."

Asking him to leave wasn't working, so I tried a different approach. "Look, Hector, I'm sure you're a nice guy." I gave him a good once-over. "Underneath it all. But I'm not interested. Please leave me alone."

"Hector, get your ass back to the wall."

If anyone had told me I'd love hearing Burke's voice, I would've said they were crazy. But right then, he sounded like an angel.

Hector straightened up. "Talk to you soon, girl."

Not wanting to give him any reason to stay, I remained quiet and looked away. Then let out a hard breath once he was gone. When I looked up again, the amazing hunk was watching me, but he didn't look happy.

"What the hell was all that for?" Maddy made a face, then wiped off the expression just as Burke looked her way.

I almost laughed and was more thankful than ever to have brought Maddy and Nina along. "I have no idea. Did you feel like we were on the sale block? I felt like I had a sign painted across my forehead saying I was fifty percent off. All sales final." And yet it hadn't offended me. It had, in fact, made me feel sexy as hell. As though I was the only woman in the world who mattered. "I think the dark-haired one could tell what color my panties are." I followed his every move, trying not to be obvious, yet unable to stop.

"I know, right? That was pretty amazing. Don't look now, but he's staring at you again." Nina turned her head and pretended to watch the girls at the next table.

Yeah, I knew.

Buy *The Captured Heart* from Amazon
http://tinyurl.com/l5hrg7d

About the Author

Bestselling author Beverly Rae lives in Georgia along with her husband and her "fur" babies. She began writing early, first with poems, then with song lyrics. Later, after she'd found her own real romance hero, she penned her first book and kept on writing.

Beverly's books range from the contemporary to the paranormal. Some are hotter than others. Some are darker than others. Some of them have a touch of humor. But they're all written from her heart, with a belief in a happy ending.

To learn more about Beverly Rae and her books, please visit www.beverlyrae.com.

Send an email to Beverly at info@beverlyrae.com or follow her on…

Facebook at:
https://www.facebook.com/beverly.rae

Twitter at:
www.twitter.com/Beverly_Rae

More books by Beverly Rae –
The Captured Heart (The Claiming Games 1)
Cannon Pack series
Wild Things series

Coming soon –
The Chained Heart (The Claiming Games 3)
Touch Me
Fooled Twice boxed set